How to Breathe Underwater

STORIES

Julie Orringer

PENGUIN BOOKS

PENGUIN BOOKS

Published by the Penguin Group
Penguin Books Ltd, 80 Strand, London WC2R 0RL, England
Penguin Group (USA) Inc., 375 Hudson Street, New York, New York 10014, USA
Penguin Group (Canada), 10 Alcorn Avenue, Toronto, Ontario, Canada M4V 3B2
(a division of Pearson Penguin Canada Inc.)
Penguin Ireland, 25 St Stephen's Green, Dublin 2, Ireland
(a division of Penguin Books Ltd)
Penguin Group (Australia), 250 Camberwell Road, Camberwell, Victoria 3124, Australia
(a division of Pearson Australia Group Pty Ltd)
Penguin Books India Pvt Ltd, 11 Community Centre, Panchsheel Park, New Delhi – 110 017, India
Penguin Group (NZ), cnr Airborne and Rosedale Roads, Albany, Auckland 1310, New Zealand
(a division of Pearson New Zealand Ltd)
Penguin Books (South Africa) (Pty) Ltd, 24 Sturdee Avenue, Rosebank 2196, South Africa

Penguin Books Ltd, Registered Offices: 80 Strand, London WC2R 0RL, England

www.penguin.com

First published in the United States of America by Alfred A. Knopf 2003
First published in Great Britain by Viking 2004
Published in Penguin Books 2005
5

Copyright © Julie Orringer, 2003
All rights reserved

The moral right of the author has been asserted

Grateful acknowledgement is made to the following magazines, where these stories first
appeared: *The Yale Review*, "What We Save" and "The Isabel Fish"; *The Paris Review*, "When
She Is Old and I Am Famous" and "Note to Sixth-Grade Self"; *Ploughshares*, "Pilgrims"; and
Zoetrope: All-Story, "The Smoothest Way Is Full of Stones." "When She Is Old and I Am
Famous" also appeared in the 2001 *Pushcart Prize Anthology*. "Pilgrims" also appeared in *Best
New American Voices 2001*, edited by Charles Baxter; in *New Stories from the South: The Year's
Best, 2002*; and in the 2003 *Pushcart Prize Anthology*.

Printed in England by Clays Ltd, St Ives plc

For Ryan,

and for my family

Contents

How to Breathe Underwater

Pilgrims

It was Thanksgiving Day and hot, because this was New Orleans; they were driving uptown to have dinner with strangers. Ella pushed at her loose tooth with the tip of her tongue and fanned her legs with the hem of her velvet dress. On the seat beside her, Benjamin fidgeted with his shirt buttons. He had worn his Pilgrim costume, brown shorts and a white shirt and yellow paper buckles taped to his shoes. In the front seat their father drove without a word, while their mother dozed against the window glass. She wore a blue dress and a strand of jade beads and a knit cotton hat beneath which she was bald.

Three months earlier, Ella's father had explained what chemotherapy was and how it would make her mother better. He had even taken Ella to the hospital once when her mother had a treatment. She remembered it like a filmstrip from school, a series of connected images she wished she didn't have to watch: her mother with an IV needle in her arm, the steady drip from the bag of orange liquid, her father speaking softly to himself as he paced the room, her mother shaking so hard she had to be tied down.

At night Ella and her brother tapped a secret code against the wall that separated their rooms: one knock, I'm afraid;

two knocks, Don't worry; three knocks, Are you still awake? four, Come quick. And then there was the Emergency Signal, a stream of knocks that kept on coming, which meant her brother could hear their mother and father crying in their bedroom. If it went on for more than a minute, Ella would give four knocks and her brother would run to her room and crawl under the covers.

There were changes in the house, healing rituals that required Ella's mother to go outside and embrace trees or lie face-down on the grass. Sometimes she did a kind of Asian dance that looked like karate. She ate bean paste and Japanese vegetables, or sticky brown rice wrapped in seaweed. And now they were going to have dinner with people they had never met, people who ate seaweed and brown rice every day of their lives.

They drove through the Garden District, where Spanish moss hung like beards from the trees. Once during Mardi Gras, Ella had ridden a trolley here with her brother and grandmother, down to the French Quarter, where they'd eaten beignets at Café du Monde. She wished she were sitting in one of those wrought-iron chairs and shaking powdered sugar onto a beignet. How much better than to be surrounded by strangers, eating food that tasted like the bottom of the sea.

They turned onto a side street, and her father studied the directions. "It should be at the end of this block," he said.

Ella's mother shifted in her seat. "Where are we?" she asked, her voice dreamy with painkillers.

"Almost there," said Ella's father.

They pulled to the curb in front of a white house with sagging porches and a trampled lawn. Vines covered the walls and moss grew thick and green between the roof slates. Under the porte-cochere stood a beat-up Honda and a Volkswagen with mismatched side panels. A faded bigwheel lay on its side on the walk.

"Come on," their father said, and gave them a tired smile.

4

"Time for fun." He got out of the car and opened the doors for Ella and Ben and their mother, sweeping his arm chauffeur-like as they climbed out.

Beside the front door was a tarnished doorbell in the shape of a lion's head. "Push it," her father said. Ella pushed. A sound like church bells echoed inside the house.

Then the door swung open and there was Mister Kaplan, a tall man with wiry orange hair and big dry-looking teeth. He shook hands with Ella's parents, so long and vigorously it seemed to Ella he might as well say *Congratulations*.

"And you must be Ben and Ella," he said, bending down.

Ella gave a mute nod. Her brother kicked at the doorjamb.

"Well, come on in," he said. "I have a tree castle out back."

Benjamin's face came up, twisted with skepticism. "A what?"

"The kids are back there. They'll show you."

"What an interesting foyer," their mother said. She bent down to look at the brass animals on the floor, a turtle and a jackal and a llama. Next to the animals stood a blue vase full of rusty metal flowers. A crystal chandelier dangled from the ceiling, its arms hung with dozens of God's-eyes and tiny plastic babies from Mardi Gras king cakes. On a low wooden shelf against the wall, pair after pair of canvas sandals and sneakers and Birkenstocks were piled in a heap. A crayoned sign above it said SHOES OFF NOW!

Ella looked down at her feet. She was wearing her new patent-leather Mary Janes.

"Your socks are nice too," her father said, and touched her shoulder. He stepped out of his own brown loafers and set them on top of the pile. Then he knelt before Ella's mother and removed her pumps. "Shoes off," he said to Ella and Ben.

"Even me?" Ben said. He looked down at his paper buckles.

Their father took off Ben's shoes and removed the paper buckles, tape intact. Then he pressed one buckle onto each of Ben's socks. "There," he said.

Ben looked as if he might cry.

"Everyone's in the kitchen," Mister Kaplan said. "We're all cooking."

"Marvelous," said Ella's mother. "We love to cook."

They followed him down a cavern of a hall, its walls decorated with sepia-toned photographs of children and parents, all of them staring stone-faced from their gilt frames. They passed a sweep of stairs and a room with nothing in it but straw mats and pictures of blue Indian goddesses sitting on beds of cloud.

"What's that room?" Benjamin asked.

"Meditation room," Mister Kaplan said, as if it were as commonplace as a den.

The kitchen smelled of roasting squash and baked apples and spices. There was an old brick oven and a stove with so many burners it looked as if it had been stolen from a restaurant. At the kitchen table, men and women with long hair and loose clothes sliced vegetables or stirred things into bowls. Some of them wore knitted hats like her mother, their skin dull-gray, their eyes purple-shaded underneath. To Ella it seemed they could be relatives of her mother's, shameful cousins recently discovered.

A tall woman with a green scarf around her waist came over and embraced Ella's mother, then bent down to hug Ella and Benjamin. She smelled of smoky perfume. Her wide eyes skewed in different directions, as if she were watching two movies projected into opposite corners of the room. Ella did not know how to look at her.

"We're so happy you decided to come," the woman said. "I'm Delilah, Eddy's sister."

"Who's Eddy?" said Ben.

"Mister Kaplan," their father said.

"We use our real names here," Delilah said. "No one is a mister."

She led their parents over to the long table and put utensils into their hands. Their mother was to mix oats into a pastry crust, and their father to chop carrots, something Ella had never seen him do. He looked around in panic, then hunched over and began cutting a carrot into clumsy pieces. He kept glancing at the man to his left, a bearded man with a shaved head, as if to make sure he was doing it right.

Delilah gave Ella and Benjamin hard cookies that tasted like burnt rice. It seemed Ella would have to chew forever. Her loose tooth waggled in its socket.

"The kids are all out back," Delilah said. "There's plenty of time to play before dinner."

"What kids?" Benjamin asked.

"You'll see," said Delilah. She tilted her head at Ella, one of her eyes moving over Ella's velvet dress. "Here's a little trick I learned when I was a girl," she said. In one swift movement she took the back hem of the dress, brought it up between Ella's knees, and tucked it into the sash. "Now you're wearing shorts," she said.

Ella didn't feel like she was wearing shorts. As soon as Delilah turned away, she pulled her skirt out of her sash and let it fall around her legs.

The wooden deck outside was cluttered with Tinkertoys and clay flowerpots and Little Golden Books. Ella heard children screaming and laughing nearby. As she and Benjamin moved to the edge of the deck, there was a rustle in the bushes and a skinny boy leaped out and pointed a suction-cup arrow at them. He stood there breathing hard, his hair full of leaves, his chest bare. "You're on duty," he said.

"Me?" Benjamin said.

"Yes, you. Both of you." The boy motioned them off the porch with his arrow and took them around the side of the house. There, built into the side of a sprawling oak, was the biggest, most sophisticated tree house Ella had ever seen. There were tiny rooms of sagging plywood, and rope ladders hanging down from doors, and a telescope and a fireman's pole and a red net full of leaves. From one wide platform—almost as high as the top of the house—it seemed you could jump down onto a huge trampoline. Even higher was a kind of crow's nest, a little circular platform built around the trunk. A red-painted sign on the railing read DAGNER! Ella could hear the other children screaming but she couldn't see them. A collie dog barked crazily, staring up at the tree.

"Take off your socks! That's an order," the skinny boy said.

Benjamin glanced at Ella. Ella shrugged. It seemed ridiculous to walk around outside in socks. She bent and peeled off her anklets. Benjamin carefully removed his Pilgrim buckles and put them in his pocket, then sat down and took off his socks. The skinny boy grabbed the socks from their hands and tucked them into the waistband of his shorts.

The mud was thick and cold between Ella's toes, and pecan shells bit her feet as the boy herded them toward the tree house. He prodded Ella toward a ladder of prickly-looking rope. When she stepped onto the first rung, the ladder swung toward the tree and her toes banged against the trunk. The skinny boy laughed.

"Go on," he said. "Hurry up. And no whining."

The rope burned her hands and feet as she ascended. The ladder seemed to go on forever. Ben followed below, making the rope buck and sway as they climbed. At the top there was a small square opening, and Ella thrust both her arms inside and pulled herself into a dark coop. As she stood, her head knocked against something dangling from the ceiling on a length of string. It was a bird's skull, no bigger than a walnut. Dozens of others hung from the ceiling around her. Benjamin huddled at her side.

"Sick," he said.

"Don't look," Ella said.

The suction-cup arrow came up through the hole in the floor.

"Keep going," said the boy. "You're not there yet."

"Go where?" Ella said.

"Through the wall."

Ella brushed the skulls out of her way and leveled her

shoulder against one of the walls. It creaked open like a door. Outside, a tree limb as thick as her torso extended up to another plywood box, this one much larger than the first. Ella dropped to her knees and crawled upward. Benjamin followed.

Apparently this was the hostage room. Four kids stood in the semidarkness, wide-eyed and still as sculptures, each bound at the ankles and wrists with vine handcuffs. Two of the kids, a boy and a girl, were so skinny that Ella could see the outlines of bones in their arms and legs. Their hair was patchy and ragged, their eyes black and almond-shaped. In the corner, a white-haired boy in purple overalls whimpered softly to himself. And at the center of the room a girl Benjamin's age stood tied to the tree trunk with brown string. She had the same wild gray eyes and leafy hair as the boy with the arrow.

"It's mine, it's *my* tree house," she said as Ella stared at her.

"Is Mister Kaplan your dad?" Benjamin said.

"My dat-*tee*," the girl corrected him.

"Where's your mom?"

"She died," said the girl, and looked him fiercely in the eye.

Benjamin sucked in his breath and glanced at Ella.

Ella wanted to hit this girl. She bent down close to the girl's face, making her eyes small and mean. "If this is so your tree house," Ella said, "then how come you're tied up?"

"It's *jail*," the girl spat. "In jail you get tied up."

"We could untie you," said Benjamin. He tugged at one of her bonds.

The girl opened her mouth and let out a scream so shrill Ella's eardrums buzzed. Once, as her father had pulled into the driveway at night, he had trapped a rabbit by the leg beneath the wheel of his car; the rabbit had made a sound like that. Benjamin dropped the string and moved against Ella, and the children with ragged hair laughed and jumped on the platform until it crackled and groaned. The boy in purple overalls cried in his corner.

9

Benjamin put his lips to Ella's ear. "I don't understand it here," he whispered.

There was a scuffle at the door, and the skinny boy stepped into the hostage room. "All right," he said. "Who gets killed?"

"Kill those kids, Peter," the girl said, pointing at Benjamin and Ella.

"Us?" Benjamin said.

"Who do you think?" said the boy.

He poked them in the back with his suction-cup arrow and moved them toward the tree trunk, where rough boards formed a ladder to the next level. Ella and Benjamin climbed until they had reached a narrow platform, and then Peter pushed them to the edge. Ella looked down at the trampoline. It was a longer drop than the high dive at the public pool. She looked over her shoulder and Peter glared at her. Down below the collie barked and barked, his black nose pointed up at them.

Benjamin took Ella's hand and closed his eyes. Then Peter shoved them from behind, and they stumbled forward into space.

There was a moment of terrifying emptiness, nothing but air beneath Ella's feet. She could hear the collie's bark getting closer as she fell. She slammed into the trampoline knees first, then flew, shrieking, back up into the air. When she hit the trampoline a second time, Benjamin's head knocked against her chin. He stood up rubbing his head, and Ella tasted salt in her mouth. Her loose tooth had slipped its roots. She spat it into her palm and studied its jagged edge.

"Move," Peter called from above. The boy in purple overalls was just climbing up onto the platform. Peter pulled him forward until his toes curled over the edge.

"I lost my tooth!" Ella yelled.

"Get off!"

Benjamin scrambled off the trampoline. Ella crawled to the edge, the tooth gleaming and red-rimmed between her fingers, and then the trampoline lurched with the weight of the boy in purple overalls. The tooth flew from her hand and into the bushes, too small to make a sound when it hit.

When she burst into the house crying, blood streaming from her mouth, the longhaired men and women dropped their mixing spoons and went to her. She twisted away from them, looking frantically for her mother and father, but they were nowhere to be seen. There was no way to explain that she wasn't hurt, that she was upset because her tooth was gone and because everything about that house made her want to run away and hide. The adults, their faces creased with worry, pulled her to the sink and held her mouth open. The woman with skewed eyes, Delilah, pressed a tissue against the space where her tooth had been. Ella could smell onions and apples on her hands.

"The time was right," she said. "The new tooth's already coming in."

"Whose is she?" one of the men asked.

Delilah told him the names of Ella's parents. It was strange to hear those familiar words, *Ann* and *Gary,* in the mouths of these longhaired strangers.

"Your mother is upstairs," Delilah said, her eyes swiveling toward some distant hidden room. "She felt a little swimmy-headed. Your dad just took her some special tea. Maybe we should let her rest, hmm?"

Ella slipped out from beneath Delilah's hand and ran to the hall, remembering the stairway she'd seen earlier. There it was before her, a curve of glossy steps leading to nowhere she knew. Her mother's cough drifted down from one of the bedroom doors. Ella put a foot onto the first stair, feeling the eyes of the adults on her back. No one said anything to stop her. After a moment, she began to climb.

In the upstairs hallway, toys and kids' shoes were strewn across the floor, and crumpled pants and shirts and dresses lay in a musty-smelling heap. Two naked Barbies sprawled in a frying pan. A record player sat in the middle of the hall, its vacant turntable spinning. Ella stepped over the cord and went into the first room, a small room with a sleeping bag on the bare mattress ticking. In a cage on the nightstand, a white rat scrabbled at a cardboard tube. A finger-painted sign above the bed said CLARIES ROOM. Her mother's cough rose again from down the hall, and she turned and ran toward the sound.

In a room whose blue walls and curtains made everything look as if it were underwater, her mother lay pale and coughing on a bed piled high with pillows. Her father sat on the edge of the bed, his hands raised in the air, thumbs hooked together and palms spread wide. For a moment Ella had no idea what he was doing. Then she saw the shadow of her father's hands against the wall, in the light of a blue-shaded lamp. A shock of relief went through her.

"Tweet-tweet," Ella said.

"Right," her father said. "A birdy."

Ella's mother turned toward her and smiled, more awake, more like her real self than earlier. "Do another one, Gary."

Ella's father twisted his hands into a new shape in the air.

"A dog?" Ella guessed.

"A fish!" said her mother.

"No," he said, and adjusted his hands. "It's a horsie, see?"

"A horsie?" said Ella's mother. "With fins?"

That made Ella laugh a little.

"Hey," her mother said. "Come here, you. Smile again."

Ella did as she was told.

"You lost your tooth!"

"It's gone," Ella said. She climbed onto the bed to explain, but as she flopped down on the mattress her mother's face contracted with pain.

"Please don't bounce," her mother said. She touched the place where her surgery had been.

Ella's father gave her a stern look and lifted her off the

bed. "Your mom's sleepy. You should run back downstairs now."

"She's always sleepy," Ella said, looking down at her muddy feet. She thought of her tooth lying out in the weeds, and how she'd have nothing to put under her pillow for the tooth fairy.

Her mother began to cry.

Ella's father went to the window and stared down into the yard, his breath fogging the glass. "Go ahead, Ella," he said. "We just need a few minutes."

"My tooth," Ella said. She knew she should leave, but couldn't.

"It'll grow back bigger and stronger," her father said.

She could see he didn't understand what had happened. If only her mother would stop crying she could explain everything. In the blue light her mother looked cold and far away, pressed under the weight of tons of water.

"I'll be down soon," her mother said, sniffling. "Go out and play."

Ella opened her mouth to form some protest, but no words came out.

"Go on, now," her father said.

"It fell in a bush!" she wailed, then turned and ran downstairs.

The other children had come in by then. Her brother stood in line at the downstairs bathroom to wash before dinner, comparing fingernail dirt with the boy in purple overalls. Hands deep in the pockets of her velvet dress, Ella wandered through the echoing hall into a room lined from floor to ceiling with books. Many of the titles were in other languages, some even written in different alphabets. She recognized *D'Aulaires' Book of Greek Myths* and *The Riverside Shakespeare* and *Grimm's Fairy Tales*. Scattered around on small tables and decorative stands were tiny human figurines with animal heads: horse-man, giraffe-man, panther-man. On one

13

table sat an Egyptian beetle made of milky green stone, and beside him a real beetle, shiny as metal, who flew at Ella's face when she reached to touch his shell. She batted him away with the back of her hand.

And then, just above where the beetle had fallen, Ella saw a shelf without any books at all. It was low, the height of her knees, with a frayed blue scarf pinned against its back wall. Burnt-down candles stood on either side of a black lacquer box, and on top of this box stood a glass filled with red water.

Ella reached for the glass, and someone behind her screamed.

She turned around. Clarie stood in the doorway, dress unbuttoned at one shoulder, face smeared with mud.

"Don't touch that," she said.

Ella took a step back. "I wasn't going to."

Clarie's eyes seemed to ignite as she bent down and took the glass in both hands. She held it near a lamp, so the light shone through it and cast a wavering red oval upon the wall.

"It's my mother," she said.

For dinner there was a roasted dome of something that looked like meat but wasn't. It was springy and steaming, and when Mister Kaplan cut it open Ella could see that it was stuffed with rice and yams. Benjamin tried to hide under the table, but their father pulled him up by the arms and set him in his place. He prodded his wedge of roast until it slid onto the tablecloth. Then he began to cry quietly.

"The kids aren't vegetarian," their father said, in apology to the men and women at the table. He picked up the slice of roast with his fingers and put it back on Ben's plate. The other men and women held their forks motionless above their own plates, looking at Ella's mother and father with pity.

"Look, Ben," said Delilah. "It's called seitan. Wheat gluten. The other kids love it."

The boy and girl with almond-shaped eyes and ragged hair

stopped in mid-chew. The girl looked at Benjamin and narrowed her eyes.

"I don't eat gluten," Benjamin said.

"Come on, now," their father said. "It's great."

Ella's mother pressed her fingers against her temples. She hadn't touched her own dinner. Ella, sitting beside her, took a bite of wheat gluten. It was almost like meat, firm and savory, and the stuffing was flavored with forest-smelling spices. As she glanced around the table she thought of the picture of the First Thanksgiving on the bulletin board at school: the smiling Pilgrims eating turkey and squash, the stern-faced Native Americans looking as if they knew the worst was yet to come. Who among them that night were the Native Americans? Who were the Pilgrims? The dark old house was like a wilderness around them, the wind sighing through its rooms.

"I jumped on the trampoline," said the boy with ragged hair, pulling on the sleeve of the woman next to him. "That boy did a flip." He pointed at Peter, who was smashing rice against his plate with his thumb. "He tied his sister to the tree."

Mister Kaplan set down his fork. He looked sideways at Peter, his mouth pressed into a stern line. "I told you never to do that again," he said. He sounded angry, but his voice was quiet, almost a whisper.

"She made me!" Peter said, and plunged a spoon into his baked squash.

Mister Kaplan's eyes went glossy and faraway. He stared off at the blank wall above Ella's mother's head, drifting away from the noise and chatter of the dinner table. Next to him Delilah shuttled her mismatched eyes back and forth.

Ella's mother straightened in her chair. "Ed," she called softly.

Mister Kaplan blinked hard and looked at her.

"Tell us about your Tai Chi class."

"What?" he said.

"Your Tai Chi class."

"You know, I don't really want to talk right now." He pushed back his chair and went into the kitchen. There was the sound of water and then the clink of dishes in the sink. Delilah shook her head. The other adults looked down at their plates. Ella's mother wiped the corners of her mouth with her napkin and crossed her arms over her chest.

"Does anyone want more rice?" Ella's father asked.

"I think we're all thinking about Lena," said the man with the shaved head.

"I know I am," said Delilah.

"Infinity to infinity," said the man. "Dust into star."

The men and women looked at each other, their eyes carrying some message Ella couldn't understand. They clasped each other's hands and bent their heads. "Infinity to infinity," they repeated. "Dust into star."

"Matter into energy," said the man. "Identity into oneness."

"Matter into energy," everyone said. Ella glanced at her father, whose jaw was set hard, unmoving. Her mother's lips formed the words, but no sound came out. Ella thought of the usual Thanksgivings at her Uncle Bon's, where everyone talked and laughed at the table and they ate turkey and dressing and sweet potatoes with marshmallows melted on top. She closed her eyes and held her breath, filling her chest with a tightness that felt like magic power. If she tried hard enough could she transport them all, her mother and father, Benjamin and herself, to that other time? She held her breath until it seemed she would explode, then let it out in a rush. She opened her eyes. Nothing had changed. Peter kicked the table leg, and the collie, crouched beside Clarie's chair, whimpered his unease. Ella could see Clarie's hand on his collar, her knuckles bloodless as stones.

Mister Kaplan returned with a platter of baked apples. He cleared his throat, and everyone turned to look at him. "Guess what we forgot," he said. "I spent nearly an hour peeling these things." He held the platter aloft, waiting.

"Who wants some nice baked apples?" he said. "Baked apples. I peeled them."

No one said a word.

After dinner the adults drifted into the room with the straw mats and Indian goddesses. Ella understood that the children were not invited, but she lingered in the doorway to see what would happen. Mister Kaplan bent over a tiny brass dish and held a match to a black cone. A wisp of smoke curled toward the ceiling, and after a moment Ella smelled a dusty, flowery scent. Her mother and father and the rest of the adults sat cross-legged on the floor, not touching each other. A low hum began to fill the room like something with weight and substance. Ella saw her father raise an eyebrow at her mother, as if to ask if these people were serious. But her mother's shoulders were bent in meditation, her mouth open with the drone of the mantra, and Ella's father sighed and let his head fall forward.

Someone pinched Ella's shoulder and she turned around. Peter stood behind her, his eyes small and cold. "Come on," he said. "You're supposed to help clean up."

In the kitchen the children stacked dirty dishes on the counter and ran water in the sink. The boy and girl with almond eyes climbed up onto a wide wooden stepstool and began to scrub dishes. Peter scraped all the scraps into an aluminum pan and gave it to Clarie, who set it on the floor near the dog's water dish. The collie fell at the leftover food with sounds that made Ella sick to her stomach. Clarie stood next to him and stroked his tail.

Then Benjamin came into the kitchen carrying the glass of red water. "Somebody forgot this under the table," he said.

Again there was the dying-rabbit screech. Clarie batted her palms against the sides of her head. "No!" she shrieked. "Put it down!"

Benjamin's eyes went wide, and he set the glass on the kitchen counter. "I don't want it," he said.

The boy in purple overalls squinted at the glass. "Looks like Kool-Aid."

"She gets all crazy," said Peter. "Watch." Peter lifted the glass high into the air, and Clarie ran toward him. "You can't have it," he said.

Clarie jumped up and down in fury, her hands flapping like limp rags. Her mouth opened but no sound came out. Then she curled her fingers into claws and scratched at Peter's arms and chest until he twisted away. He ran across the kitchen and onto the deck, holding the glass in the air, and Clarie followed him, screaming.

The ragged-haired brother and sister looked at each other, arms gloved in white bubbles. In one quick movement they were off the stool, shaking suds around the kitchen. "Come on!" said the boy. "Let's go watch!"

Benjamin grabbed Ella's hand and pulled her toward the screen door. The children pushed out onto the deck and then ran toward the tree castle, where Clarie and her brother were climbing the first rope ladder. It was dark now, and floodlights on the roof of the house illuminated the entire castle, its rooms silver-gray and ghostly, its ropes and nets swaying in a rising breeze. The children gathered on the grass near the trampoline.

Peter held the glass as he climbed, the red water sloshing against its sides. "Come and get it," he crooned. He reached the first room, and they heard the wall-door scrape against the trunk as he pushed it open. Then he moved out onto the oak limb, agile as the spider monkeys Ella had seen at the zoo. He might as well have had a tail.

Clarie crawled behind him, her hands scrabbling at the bark. Peter howled at the sky as he reached the hostage room.

Benjamin moved toward Ella and pressed his head against her arm. "I want to go home," he said.

"Shh," Ella said. "We can't."

High above, Peter climbed onto the platform from which they had jumped earlier. Still holding the glass, he pulled himself up the tree trunk to the crow's nest. High up on that small railed platform, where the tree branches became thin and sparse, he stopped. Below him Clarie scrambled onto the jumping platform. She looked out across the yard as if unsure of where he had gone. "Up here," Peter said, holding the glass high.

Ella could hear Clarie grunting as she pulled herself up into the crow's nest. She stood and reached for the glass, her face a small moon in the dark. A few acorns scuttled off the crow's-nest platform.

"Give it!" she cried.

Peter stood looking at her for a moment in the dark. "You really want it?"

"Peter!"

He swept the glass through the air. The water flew out in an arc, ruby-colored against the glare of the floodlights. Clarie leaned out as if to catch it between her fingers, and with a splintering crack she broke through the railing. Her dress fluttered silently as she fell, and her white hands grasped at the air. There was a quiet instant, the soft sound of water falling on grass. Then, with a shock Ella felt in the soles of her feet, Clarie hit the ground. The girl with the ragged hair screamed.

Clarie lay beside the trampoline, still as sleep, her neck bent at an impossible angle. Ella wanted to look away, but couldn't. The other children, even Benjamin, moved to where Clarie lay and circled around, some calling her name, some just looking. Peter slid down the fireman's pole and stumbled across the lawn toward his sister. He pushed Benjamin aside. With one toe he nudged Clarie's shoulder, then knelt and rolled her over. A bare bone glistened from her wrist. The boy in purple overalls threw up on the grass.

Ella turned and ran toward the house. She banged the screen door open and skidded across the kitchen floor into the

hall. At the doorway of the meditation room she stopped,
breathing hard. The parents sat just as she had left them,
eyes closed, mouths open slightly, their sound beating like a
living thing, their thumbs and forefingers circled into perfect
O's. She could smell the heat of them rising in the room and
mingling with the scent of the incense. Her father's chin
rested on his chest as if he had fallen asleep. Beside him her
mother looked drained of blood, her skin so white she seemed
almost holy.

"Mom," Ella whispered. "Mom."

Ella's mother turned slightly and opened her eyes. For a
moment she seemed between two worlds, her eyes unfocused
and distant. Then she blinked and looked at Ella. She shook
her head no.

"Please," Ella said, but her mother closed her eyes again.
Ella stood there for a long time watching her, but she didn't
move or speak. Finally Ella turned and went back outside.

By the time she reached the tree castle Peter had dragged
Clarie halfway across the lawn. He turned his eyes on Ella,
and she stared back at him. The sound of the mantra contin-
ued unbroken from the house. Peter hoisted Clarie again
under the arms and dragged her to the bushes, her bare feet
bumping over the grass. Then he rolled her over until she was
hidden in shadow. He pulled her dress down so it covered her
thighs, and turned her head toward the fence that bordered
the backyard.

"Get some leaves and stuff," he said. "We have to cover
her."

Ella would not move. She took Benjamin's hand, but he
pulled away from her and wandered across the lawn, pulling
up handfuls of grass. She watched the children pick up twigs,
Spanish moss, leaves, anything they could find. The boy in
purple overalls gathered cedar bark from a flower bed, and
Peter dragged fallen branches out of the underbrush near the
fence. They scattered everything they found over Clarie's
body. In five minutes they had covered her entirely.

"Go back inside," Peter said. "If anyone cries or says anything, I'll kill them."

Ella turned to go, and that was when she saw her tooth, a tiny white pebble in the weeds. She picked it up and rubbed it clean. Then she knelt beside Clarie, clearing away moss and leaves until she found Clarie's hand. She dropped the tooth into the palm and closed the fingers around it. A shiver spread through her chest, and she covered the hand again. Then she put her arm around Benjamin and they all went back inside. Drawn by the sound of the chanting, they wandered into the hall. All around them hung the yellow photographs, the stony men and women and children looking down at them with sad and knowing eyes. In an oval of black velvet one girl in a white dress held the string of a wooden duck, her lips open as if she were about to speak. Her eyes had the wildness of Clarie's eyes, her legs the same bowed curve.

At last there was a rustle from the meditation room, and the adults drifted out into the hall. They blinked at the light and rubbed their elbows and knees. Ella's mother and father linked arms and moved toward their children. Benjamin gave a hiccup. His eyes looked strange, the pupils huge, the whites flat and dry. Their mother noticed right away. "We'd better get going," she said to Ella's father. "Ben's tired."

She went into the foyer and pulled their shoes from the pile. Mister Kaplan followed, looking around in bewilderment, as if he could not believe people were leaving. He patted Benjamin on the head and asked Ella's mother if she wanted to take some leftover food. Ella's mother shook her head no. Her father thanked Mister Kaplan for his hospitality. Somewhere toward the back of the house the dog began to bark. Ella pulled Benjamin through the front door, barefoot, and her parents followed them to the car.

All the way past the rows of live oaks, past the cemetery where the little tombs stood like grounded boats, past the low flat shotgun houses with their flaking roofs, Benjamin sat rigid on the back seat and cried without a sound. Ella felt the sobs leaving his chest in waves of hot air. She closed her eyes and followed the car in her mind down the streets that led to their house, until it seemed they had driven past their house long ago and were moving on to a place where strange beds awaited them, where they would fall asleep thinking of dark forests and wake to the lives of strangers.

When She Is Old
and I Am Famous

There are grape leaves, like a crown, on her head. Grapes hang in her hair, and in her hands she holds the green vines. She dances with both arms in the air. On her smallest toe she wears a ring of pink shell.

Can someone tell her, please, to go home? This is my Italy and my story. We are in a vineyard near Florence. I have just turned twenty. She is a girl, a gangly teen, and she is a model. She is famous for almost getting killed. Last year, when she was fifteen, a photographer asked her to dance on the rail of a bridge and she fell. A metal rod beneath the water pierced her chest. Water came into the wound, close to her heart, and for three weeks she was in the hospital with an infection so furious it made her chant nonsense. All the while she got thinner and more pale, until, when she emerged, they thought she might be the best model there ever was. Her hair is wavy and long and buckeye-brown, and her blue eyes have a stunned, sad look to them. She is five feet eleven inches tall and weighs one hundred and thirteen pounds. She has told me so.

This week she is visiting from Paris, where she lives with her father, my Uncle Claude. When Claude was a young man he left college to become the darling of a great couturier, who introduced him to the sequin-and-powder world of Paris drag.

Monsieur M. paraded my uncle around in black-and-white evening gowns, high-heeled pumps, and sprayed-up diva hair-dos. I have seen pictures in his attic back in Fernald, Indiana, my uncle leaning over some balustrade in a cloud of pink chiffon, silk roses at his waist. One time he appeared in a couture photo spread in *Vogue.* All this went on for years, until I was five, when a postcard came asking us to pick him up at the Chicago airport. He came off the plane holding a squirming baby. Neither my mother nor I knew anything about his having a child, or even a female lover. Yet there she was, my infant cousin, and here she is now, in the vineyard, doing her grape-leaf dance for my friends and me.

Aïda. That is her terrible name. Ai-ee-duh: two cries of pain and one of stupidity. The vines tighten around her body as she spins, and Joseph snaps photographs. She knows he will like it, the way the leaves cling, the way the grapes stain her white dress. We are trespassing here in a vintner's vines, spilling the juice of his expensive grapes, and if he sees us he will surely shoot us. What an end to my tall little cousin. Between the purple stains on her chest, a darker stain spreads. Have I mentioned yet that I am fat?

Isn't it funny, how I've learned to say it? I am fat. I am not skin or muscle or gristle or bone. What I am, the part of my body that I most am, is fat. Continuous, white, lighter than water, a source of energy. No one can hold all of me at once. Does this constitute a crime? I know how to carry myself. Sometimes I feel almost graceful. But all around I hear the thin people's bombast: *Get Rid of Flabby Thighs Now! Avoid Holiday Weight-Gain Nightmares! Lose Those Last Five Pounds!* What is left of a woman once her last five pounds are gone?

I met Drew and Joseph in my drawing class in Florence. Joseph is a blond sculptor from Manhattan, and Drew is a thirty-six-year-old painter from Wisconsin. In drawing class we had neighboring easels, and Drew and I traded roll-eyed glances over Joe's loud Walkman. We both found ourselves drawing in techno-rhythm. When we finally complained, Joe told us he'd started wearing it because Drew and I talked too much. I wish that were true. I hardly talk to anyone, even after three months in Florence.

One evening as the three of us walked home from class we passed a billboard showing Cousin Aïda in a gray silk gown, and when I told them she was my cousin they both laughed, as if I had made some sort of clever feminist comment. I insisted that I was telling the truth. That was a mistake. They sat me down at a café and made me talk about her for half an hour. Joseph wondered whether she planned to complete her schooling or follow her career, and Drew had to know whether she suffered from eating disorders and skewed self-esteem. It would have been easier if they'd just stood in front of the billboard and drooled. At least I would have been able to anticipate their mute stupor when they actually met her.

Aïda rolls her shoulders and lets her hair fall forward, hiding her face in shadow. They can't take their eyes off her. Uncle Claude would scold her for removing her sun hat. I have picked it up and am wearing it now. It is gold straw and fits perfectly. What else of hers could I put on? Not even her gloves.

"Now stand perfectly still," Joseph says, extending his thumb and index finger as if to frame Aïda. He snaps a few pictures, then lets the camera drop. He looks as if he would like to throw a net over her. He will show these pictures to his friends back home, telling them how he slept with her between the grapevines. This will be a lie, I hope. "Dance again," he says, "this time slower."

She rotates her hips like a Balinese dancer. "Like this?"

"That's it," he says. "Nice and slow." Surreptitiously he adjusts his shorts.

When Drew looks at my cousin I imagine him taking notes for future paintings. In Wisconsin he works as a professional muralist, and here he is the best drawing student in our class, good even at representing the foot when it faces forward. I am hopeless at drawing the foot at any angle. My models all look like they are sliding off the page. I've seen photographs of Drew's murals, twenty-foot-high paintings on the sides of elementary schools and parking structures, and his figures look as though they could step out of the wall and crush your car. He does paintings of just the feet. I can tell he's studying Aïda's pink toes right now. Later he will draw her, at night in his room, while his upstairs neighbor practices violin until the crack of dawn. "If she didn't live there I'd have to hire her to live there," he tells me. She may keep him up all night, but at least she makes him paint well.

There are certain things I can never abide: lack of food, lack of sleep, and Aïda. But she is here in Italy on my free week because our parents thought it would be fun for us. "Aïda doesn't get much rest," my mother told me. "She needs time away from that business in France."

I told my mother that Aïda made me nervous. "Her name has an umlaut, for crying out loud."

"She's your cousin," my mother said.

"She's been on the covers of twelve magazines."

"Well, Mira"—and here her voice became sweet, almost reverent—"you are a future Michelangelo."

There's no question about my mother's faith in me. She has always believed I will succeed, never once taking into account my failure to represent the human figure. She says I have a *style*. That may be true, but it does not make me the next anybody. Sometimes I freeze in front of the canvas, full of the knowledge that if I keep painting, sooner or later I will fail her.

My cousin always knew how important she was, even when she was little. Over at her house in Indiana I had to watch her eat ice-cream bars while I picked at my Sunmaid raisins. I tried to be nice because my mother had said, "Be nice." I told her she had a pretty name, that I knew she was named after a character from a Verdi opera, which my mom and I had listened to all the way from Chicago to central

Indiana. Aïda licked the chocolate from around her lips, then folded the silver wrapper.

"I'm not named after the *character*," she said. "I'm named after the *entire opera*."

The little bitch is a prodigy, a skinny Venus, a genius. She knows how to shake it. She will never be at a loss for work or money. She is a human dollar sign. Prada has made millions on her. And still her eyes remain clear and she gets enough sleep at night.

Joseph has run out of film. "You have beautiful teeth," he says hopelessly.

She grins for him.

Drew looks at me and shakes his head, and I am thankful.

When she's tired of the dance, Aïda untwines the vines from her body and lets them fall to the ground. She squashes a plump grape between her toes, looking into the distance. Then, as though compelled by some sign in the sky, she climbs to the top of a ridge and looks down into the valley. Joseph and Drew follow to see what she sees, and I have no choice but to follow as well. Where the vines end, the land slopes down into a bowl of dry grass. Near its center, surrounded by overgrown hedges and flower beds, the vintner's house rises, a sprawling two-story villa with a crumbling tile roof. Aïda inhales and turns toward the three of us, her eyes steady. "That's where my mother lives," she announces.

It is such an astounding lie, I cannot even bring myself to respond. Aïda's mother was the caterer at a party Uncle Claude attended during his "wild years"; my own mother related the story to me long ago, as a cautionary tale. When Aïda was eight weeks old her mother left her with Claude, and that was that. But Aïda's tone is earnest and forthright, and both Joseph and Drew look up, confused.

"I thought you lived with your dad in Paris," Joseph says.

He shoots a hard glance at me, as if I've been concealing her whereabouts all this time.

"She does," I say.

Aïda shrugs. "My mother's family owns this whole place."

"Really?" Joseph says.

"My mom and I aren't very close," Aïda says, and sits down. She ties a piece of grass into a knot, then tosses it down the hill. "Actually, the last time I saw her I was three." She draws her legs up and hugs her knees, and her shoulders rise and fall as she sighs. "It's not the kind of thing you do in Italy, tote around your bastard kid. It would have been a *vergogna* to the *famiglia,* as they say." Aïda looks down at the stone house in the valley.

Joseph and Drew exchange a glance, seeming to decide how to handle this moment. I find myself wordless. It's true that Aïda's mother didn't want to raise her. I don't doubt that it would have been a disgrace to her Catholic family. What baffles me is how Aïda can present this story as truth when she knows *I* know it's bullshit. What does she expect will happen? Does she think I'll pretend to believe her?

Aïda stands and dusts her hands against her dress, then begins to make her way down the slope. Joe gives us a baffled grin, shakes his head as if ashamed of himself, and follows her.

"Where the hell do you think you're going?" I call to Aïda.

She turns, and the wind lifts her hair like a pennant. Her chin is set hard. "I'm going to get something from her," she says. "I'm not going back to France without a memento."

"Let's stop this now, Aïda," I say. "You're not related to anyone who lives in that house." In fact, it didn't look as if anyone lived there at all. The garden was a snarl of overgrown bushes and the windows looked blank, like sightless eyes.

"Go home," she says. "Joe will come with me. And don't pretend you're worried. If I didn't come back, you'd be glad."

She turns away and I watch her descend toward the villa, my tongue dry in my mouth.

These past few days Aïda has been camping on my bedroom floor. Asleep she looks like a collapsed easel, something hard and angular lying where it shouldn't. Yesterday morning I opened one eye to see her fingering the contents of a blue tin box, my private cache of condoms. When I sat up and pushed the mosquito netting aside, she shoved the box back under the bed.

"What are you doing?" I asked.

"Nothing."

"It's none of my business," I said. "But if you meet a guy—"

She gave an abbreviated *ha!* as if the air had been punched out of her. Then she got up and began to look for something in her suitcase. Very quietly, she said, "Of course, you're the expert."

"What's that supposed to mean?" I said.

She turned around and smiled with just her lips.

"Listen, shitweed, I may not be the next *Vogue* cover girl, but that doesn't mean I sleep alone every night."

"Whatever you say." She shook out a teeny dress and held it against herself.

"For God's sake," I said. "Do you have to be primo bitch of the whole universe?"

She tilted her head, coy and intimate. "You know what I think, Mira? I think you're a vibrator cowgirl. I think you're riding the mechanical bull."

I had nothing to say. But something flew at her and I knew I had thrown it. She ducked. A glass candlestick broke against the wall.

"Fucking psycho!" she shouted. "Are you trying to kill me?"

"Get a hotel room," I said. "You're not staying here."

"Fine with me. I'll sleep in a ditch and you can sleep alone."

Her tone was plain and hard, eggshell white, but for a split second her lower lip quivered. It occurred to me for the first time that she might feel shunted off, that she might see me as a kind of baby-sitter she had to abide while her father had a break from her. Quickly I tried to replay in my mind all the names she had called me, that day and throughout our kid years, so I could shut out any thoughts that would make me feel sorry for her. "Get out of my room," I said. She picked her way across the glass and went into the bathroom. Door click, faucet-knob squeak, and then her scream, because in my apartment there is no hot water to be had, ever, by anyone.

Drew and I shuffle sideways down a rocky hill toward the dried-up garden. Fifty yards below, my cousin sidles along the wall of the house. I cannot imagine how she plans to enter this fortress or what she will say if someone sees her. There's a rustle in a bank of hedges, and we see Joseph creeping along, his camera bag banging against his leg. He disappoints me. Back in New York he works in a fashion photographer's darkroom, and he speaks of commercial photography as if it were the worst imaginable use for good chemicals and photo paper. For three months he's photographed nothing in Florence but water and cobblestones. Today he follows Aïda as if she were leading him on a leash.

Aïda freezes, flattening herself against the house wall. It seems she's heard something, although there's still no one in the garden. After a moment she moves toward a bank of curtained French doors and tries a handle. The door opens, and she disappears inside. Joseph freezes. He waits until she beckons with her hand; then he slides in and closes the door behind them. They're gone. And I am not about to go any farther. The sun is furious and the vines too low to provide any shelter. A bag containing lunch for four people hangs heavy on my back. I am the only one who has not brought any drawing tools. It was somehow understood that I would carry the food.

"We might as well wait here," Drew says. "Hopefully they'll be out soon."

"I hope." The bag slides off my shoulders and falls into the dust.

Drew reaches for the lunch. "I would have carried this for you," he says. His eyes rest for a moment on mine, but I know he is only trying to be polite.

There was a time when I was the one who got the attention, when my body was the one everyone admired. In junior high, where puberty was a kind of contest, you wanted to be the one with the tits out to here. I had my bra when I was nine, the first in our grade. That made me famous among my classmates. My mother, a busty woman herself, told me she was proud to see me growing up. I believed my breasts were a gift from God, and even let a few kids have an "accidental" rub at them. It wasn't until high school, when the novelty wore off and they grew to a D-cup, that I started to see things as they really were. Bathing suits did not fit right. I spilled out of the tops of sundresses. I looked ridiculous when running or jumping. Forget cheerleading. I began smashing those breasts down with sports bras, day and night.

It doesn't matter what the Baroque masters thought. The big breasts, the lush bodies, those are museum pieces now, and who cares if they stand for fertility and plenty, wealth and gluttony, or the fullest bloom of youth? Rubens's nudes made of cumulus clouds, Titian's milky half-dressed beauties overflowing their garments, Lorenzo Lotto's big intelligent-eyed Madonnas—they have their place, and it is on a wall. No one remembers that a tiny breast used to mean desolation and deserts and famine.

Take Aïda on the billboard in Florence, wearing a gray Escada gown held up by two thin strands of rhinestones.

Where the dress dips low at the side, there is a shadow, like a closed and painted eyelid, just the edge of Aïda's tiny breast, selling this $6,000 dress. That is what you can do today with almost nothing.

The fact is, Aïda guessed right when she said I was a virgin. There were other girls at my high school, fat girls, who would go out by the train tracks at night and take off all their clothes. There were some who would give hand jobs. There were others who had sex for the first time when they were eleven. Few of these girls had dates for Homecoming, and none of them held hands at school with the boys they met by the tracks at night. At the time I would rather have died than be one of these girls, the fat ones who had sex thinking they'd be liked.

But sometimes I think about how it might have been for those girls, who touched and were touched and lived afterward with complicated varieties of shame. When I look at my drawings of men and women, there's a stiffness there, a glassiness I'm afraid comes from too little risk. At times it makes me dislike myself. Perhaps it even makes me a bad artist. Should I regret the way I conducted my life all those years? Can these things be changed now that I am, in most ways, grown up? Where would I begin?

Drew lies back on his elbows and whistles "Moon River." I wish I could relax. Somewhere below, my cousin stalks an artifact of her non-mother. I picture the tall, cool rooms with their crumbling ceilings and threadbare tapestries woven in dark colors. Maybe she will burn the place down. In another few months, I imagine, she will need to do something to get herself on the evening news. Being on a billboard can't be enough for her.

I put on Aïda's sun hat and tie its white ribbons beneath my chin. Just as I'm wondering if either of us will speak to each other all afternoon, Drew asks if I've decided to submit any works for display in the Del Reggio gallery in Rome.

"*What* works?" I say. "You've seen my sliding people. Maybe I could do a little installation with a basket underneath each painting, to catch the poor figure when she falls off the page."

"You have a talent, Mira. People criticize *my* work for being too realistic."

"But I don't plan to draw them expressionistically. They just come out that way. It's artistic stupidity, Drew, not talent."

"Well, then, I guess you'd better quit now," he says, shrugging. He picks up some fallen grapes, waxy and black, and throws them into the hammock of my skirt. "How about another profession? Sheep herding? Radio announcing? Hat design?"

"There's a fine idea." The words come out clipped and without humor. A dry silence settles between us. I'm angry at myself for being nervous and at him for bringing up the exhibition. He knows his work will go into the show.

At times I think it would be terrible to have him touch me. I can imagine the disappointment he would show when I removed my dress. One hopes to find a painter who admires the old masters, like in the personal columns I've read in the *Chicago Tribune: Lusty DWM w/taste for old wine and Rubens seeks SWF with full-bodied flavor.* Would I ever dare to call?

"So what do you think of my little cousin?" I ask.

"Why?" he says. "What do you think of her?"

"She's had a hard past," I say, in an attempt at magnanimity. Because if I answered the question with honesty, I would blast Aïda to Turkmenistan. All our lives, she has understood her advantage over me and has exercised it at every turn. When I pass her billboard in town I can feel her gleeful disdain. No matter how well you paint, she seems to say, you will remain invisible next to me.

Perhaps because Drew is older I thought of him as enlightened in certain ways, but I saw how he looked at my cousin today with plain sexual appetite. I hand him a plum from our lunch bag and turn my face away from the sun, because I am hot and tired and want to be far away from here.

As we eat, we hear the foreign-sounding *ee-oo* of an Italian police siren in the distance. Dread kindles in my chest. I imagine Aïda being wrested into handcuffs by an Italian policeman, and the shamefaced look she'll give Joseph as her lie is revealed. Will I be too sorry later to say I told her so? I can almost hear my mother's phone diatribe: *You let her break into a house with some boy? And just watched the police haul her off to Italian jail?* Drew and I get to our feet. The house below is quiet and still. A boxy police car sweeps into the lane, dragging a billow of dust behind it. It roars down the hill and screeches to a stop somewhere in front of the house, where we can no longer see it. After a moment someone pounds on the front door.

Drew says, "We'd better go down."

"They'll see us."

"Suit yourself." He flicks the pit of his plum into the grape-vines and starts down the hill.

I follow him toward the front of the house, until we see the paved area where the car is parked. He is about to step onto the paving stones. Panicked, I take his arm and pull him behind a stand of junipers at the side of the driveway. There are just enough bushes to hide both of us. The shadows are deep but there are places to look through the branches, and we can see the police officer who had been pounding on the front door. The other officer sits quietly in the car, engrossed in a map.

"This is ridiculous," Drew says. "We have to go in."

"No way," I whisper. "There's enough trouble already. What's the minimum penalty for breaking and entering in this country?"

Drew shakes his head and says, "Tell me I came to Florence to stand in a bush."

The front door opens slightly, and the policeman goes inside. After a few minutes the officer with the map gets out and goes to the door, then into the house. Everything is still. A bird I can't name alights near Drew's hand and bobs on a thin branch. We stand together in the dust. The heat coming off his body has an earthy smell, like the beeswax soap nuns sell in the marketplace. If I extended my hand just a centimeter I could touch his arm.

"Uh-oh," he says softly.

And there are Aïda and Joseph being led from the house by the policemen. Aïda's hair is mussed, as if there has been a struggle, and her dress hangs crooked at the shoulder. Joseph walks without looking at her. A woman in a black dress—a housekeeper, from the looks of her—curses at them from the doorway. They're not in handcuffs, but the police aren't about to let them go, either. Just as the first policeman opens the car door, a chocolate-colored Mercedes appears at the top of the drive. The steel-haired housekeeper stiffens and points. *"La padrona di casa,"* she says.

They hold Aïda and Joseph beside the police car, waiting for the Mercedes to descend into the driveway. Its tires are quiet on the paving stones, and its darkened windows yield no glimpse of the driver. After it rolls to a stop there's a tense moment while the dust clears. Then the lady of the house climbs out. She squares herself toward the scene in front of her villa. She is tall and lean. Her hair is caught in the kind of knot the Italian women wear, heavy and sweeping and low on the neck. Beneath her ivory jacket her shoulders are businesslike. She looks as if she would be more at home in New York or Rome than out here on this grape farm. She lowers her black sunglasses. With a flick of her hand toward Aïda and Joseph, she asks who the two criminals might be.

Aïda raises her chin and looks squarely at the woman. *"La vostra dottore,"* she says.

Your doctor. The policemen roar with laughter.

The maid tells her padrona that Aïda was apprehended in the boudoir, trying on shoes. She had tried on nearly ten pairs before she was caught.

"You like my shoes?" the woman asks in English. She tilts her head, scrutinizing Aïda. "You look familiar to me."

"She's a model," Joseph says.

"Ah!" the woman says. "And you? You are a model too?" Her mouth is thin and agile.

"A photographer."

"And you were trying on shoes also in my house?"

There is a silence. Joseph looks at Aïda for some clue as to what she wants him to say or do. Aïda glances around, and I almost feel as if she is looking for me, as if she thinks I might come down and save her now. Her eyes begin to dart between the padrona and the policemen, and her mouth opens. She lets her eyes flutter closed, then collapses against a policeman in an extremely realistic faint.

"Poor girl," the woman says. "Bring her into the house."

The police look disapproving, but they comply. One of them grabs her under the shoulders and the other takes her feet. Like an imperial procession they all enter the house, and the housekeeper closes the door behind them.

"She must be sick," Drew whispers. "Does she eat?"

"In a manner of speaking."

He climbs out of our hiding place and starts down toward the house. I have to follow him. I picture being home in bed, lying on my side and looking at the blank wall, a desert of comfort, no demands or disappointment. As I navigate the large stones at the edge of the driveway, my foot catches in a crevice and I lose my balance. There's a snap, and pain shoots through my left ankle. I come down hard onto my hip.

Drew turns around. "You okay?"

I nod, sideways, from the ground. He comes back to offer me his hand. It's torture getting up. My body feels as if it weighs a thousand pounds. When I test the hurt ankle, the pain makes my eyes water. I let go of Drew's hand and limp toward the door.

"Are you going to make it?" Drew asks.

"Sure," I say, but the truth is there's something awfully wrong. The pain tightens in a band around my lower leg. Drew rings the doorbell, and in a few moments the housekeeper opens the door. Her eyes are small and stern. She draws her gray brows together and looks at Drew. In his perfect Italian, he tells her that our friends are inside, and that we would like to ask the forgiveness of the lady of the house. She throws her hands heavenward and wonders aloud what will happen next. But she holds the door open and beckons us inside.

The entry hall is cool and dark, like a wine cavern, and there's a smell of fennel and coffee and dogs. Supporting myself against the stone wall, I creep along behind Drew, past tall canvases portraying the vintner's family, long-faced men and women arrayed in brocade and velvet. The style is more Dutch than Italian, with angular light and deep reds and blues. In one portrait a seventeenth-century version of our padrona holds a lute dripping with flower garlands. She looks serene and pastoral, certainly capable of mercy. I take this for a good sign. We move past these paintings toward a large sunny room facing the back garden, whose French doors I recognize as the ones Aïda slipped through not long ago. My cousin is stretched out on a yellow chaise longue with Joseph at her side. The policemen are nowhere to be seen. I imagine them drinking espresso in the kitchen with the inevitable cook. The padrona sits next to Aïda with a glossy magazine open on her lap, exclaiming at what she sees. "Ah, yes, here you are again," she says. "God, what a gown."

It's as though royalty has come for a visit. She seems reluctant to look away from the photographs when the maid enters and announces us as friends of the signorina.

"More friends?"

"Actually, Mira's my cousin," Aïda explains. "And that's Drew. He's another student at the university."

Drew nods politely at the padrona. Then he goes to Aïda and crouches beside her chaise longue. "We saw you faint," he says. "Do you need some water?"

"She'll be fine," Joseph says, and gives Drew a narrow-eyed look.

Drew stands, raising his hands in front of him. "I asked her a simple question."

The padrona clears her throat. "Please make yourself comfortable," she says. "Maria will bring you a refreshment." She introduces herself as Pietà Cellini, the wife of the vintner. She says this proudly, although from the state of their house it seems the family wines haven't been doing so well in recent years. As she speaks she holds Aïda's hand in her own. "Isn't she remarkable, your cousin?" she asks. "So young."

"I'm awfully sorry about all this," I say. "We should be getting home."

"She's darling," says Signora Cellini. "My own daughter went to study in Rome two years ago. She's just a little older than Aïda. Mischievous, too."

"Is that so?" I say. The pain in my ankle has become almost funny. My head feels weightless and poorly attached.

"Aïda was just showing me her lovely pictures in *Elle*," our host says. "The poor girl had a shock just now, all those police. I'm afraid our housemaid was quite rude."

"She was just protecting your house," I say.

Aïda sips water from a porcelain cup. Joseph takes it from her when she's finished and sets it down on a tiny gilt table. "Feel better now?" he asks.

"You're so nice." Aïda pats his arm. "I'm sure it was just the heat."

Black flashes crowd the edges of my vision. The ankle has begun to throb. I look past them all, through the panes of the French doors and out into the garden, where an old man digs at a bed of spent roses. Dry-looking cuttings lie on the ground, and bees dive and hover around the man. He is singing a song whose words I cannot hear through the glass. I rest my forehead against my hand, wondering how I can stand to be here a moment longer. Aïda laughs, and Joseph's voice joins hers. It seems she has done this intentionally, in reparation for the thrown candlestick or the words I said to her, or even because all my life I have had a mother and she has had none. What a brilliant success I would be if I could paint the scene in this sunny room, glorious Aïda in careful disarray, the two men drawn to her, the elegant woman leaning over her with a porcelain cup. Sell it. Retire to Aruba. I can already feel the paint between my fingers, under my nails, sliding beneath my fingertips on the canvas. And then I hear the padrona's voice coming from what seems a great distance, calling not Aïda's name but my own. "Mira," she says. "Good God. What happened to your ankle?"

In defiance of all my better instincts, I look down. At first it seems I am looking at a foreign object, some huge red-and-purple swelling where my ankle used to be. It strains against the straps of my sandal as if threatening to burst. "I got hurt," I say, blinking against a contracting darkness, and then there is silent nothing.

It is nighttime. I do not recall getting back to the apartment, nor do I remember undressing or getting into bed. The room is quiet. There is a bag of crushed ice on my ankle, and an angel bending over it as if it had already died. Translucent wings rise from the angel's back, and its face is inclined over my foot. Its hair shines blue in the moonlight. It murmurs an incomprehensible prayer.

The mosquito netting fills with wind and then hangs limp again, brushing Aïda's shoulders. Her face is full of concentration. She touches the swollen arch of my foot. I can hardly feel it. You could help me if you wanted to, she might say now. You have lived longer than I have and could let me know how it is,

39

but you don't. You let me dance and giggle and look like an idiot. You like it. You wish it. Is she saying this?

"How did we get home?" I ask her. My voice sounds full of sleep.

"You're awake," she says. "You sure messed up your ankle."

"It feels like there are bricks on my chest."

"Signora Cellini gave you Tylenol with codeine. It knocked you out."

Sweet drug. My wisdom-tooth friend. One should have it around. "Where are the guys?"

"Home. We made quite a spectacle."

"You did."

"That's what I do, Cousin Mira."

"*I* don't."

"Was I the only one to faint today?" She raises her eyebrows at me.

"Well, I didn't do it on purpose."

"You'll have to go to a doctor tomorrow."

"So be it. This is your fault, you know," I tell her. I mean for it to be severe, but the last part comes out "falyuno." I am almost asleep again, and grateful for that. With my eyelids half closed I can see the wings rising from her shoulders again, and her feet might be fused into one, and who knows, she might after all be sexless and uninvolved with the commerce of this world, and I might be the Virgin Mary, receiving the impossible news.

The next morning Aïda calls a cab and we go down to the Ospedale di Santa Maria Nuova, where a dark-haired nurse named Bella examines my ankle. *"È grave,"* she tells me, shaking her head. My ankle, if I were to reproduce it on a canvas, would require plenty of aquamarine and ocher and Russian red. Bella calls for an English-speaking doctor, who handles me gently. He orders X rays and tells the technician to take plenty of pictures. In another room the doctor puts my films up on a lighted board. He shows me a hairline fracture, which looks to me like a tiny mountain range etched into my bone. He does not understand why I smile when he gives me the bad news. How can I explain to him how apt it is? Drew would recommend a self-portrait.

When I return to the waiting room wearing a fiberglass cast from toes to mid-calf, I find Aïda eating a croissant. I feel as if I will faint from hunger.

"Hi, gimp," she says. There's a smirk. I'd like to whack her with my new weapons. Instead, we head for the door and walk down Via Bufalini toward a café where I can find some breakfast. The sun is out, and the *zanzare*. Big fat ones. Unlike American mosquitoes, these actually hurt when they bite. It's the huge proboscis. At least my ankle's safe from that for a while.

The doctor has prescribed normal activity, with caution until I learn to use the crutches better. It's my first time on them—I always wanted them when I was a kid, but somehow managed to escape injury—and I think I will stay home as long as possible. Time to paint. No more vineyards. Aïda can do what she likes for the last two days of her visit.

At the café we have a marble-topped table on the sidewalk, and a kind waiter looks at me with pity. He brings things we do not order, a little plate of biscotti and tiny jam-filled cookies. Aïda twirls her hair and looks at her feet. She is quiet today and has neglected to put on the customary makeup: something to make her lips shine, a thin dark line around the eyes, a pink stain on the cheeks. She looks almost plain, like anyone else's cousin. She actually eats the free cookies and biscotti.

Our waiter sets espresso cups on the table. Aïda's growth will be stunted forever by the staggering amount of caffeine she has consumed in Florence. Of course her father doesn't allow it, back home. "Does it hurt?" she asks, pointing at the ankle.

"Not so much anymore," I say. "All that good pain medicine."

"Too bad about the cast. I really mean it. They itch something awful."

Great.

"Now, can I ask you one question, Aïda?" I say.

"One." She lifts her cup and grins at her sneakers.

"What was all that malarkey about your mother? I mean, for God's sake."

There's a long silence. Her lips move slightly as if she's about to answer, but no words come. She sets the cup down and begins to twist her hands, thin bags of bones, against each other. The knuckles crack. "I don't know," she says finally. "It was just something to say."

"It wasn't just something to say. You broke into the house. And you made Joseph go with you."

"I didn't make him do anything." She frowns. "He could have stayed behind with you."

"You sorcered him, Aïda. You knew you were doing it."

Aïda picks up her tiny spoon and stirs the espresso, her eyes becoming serious and downcast. "I did look up my actual mother once," she says.

The admission startles me. I sit up in the iron chair. "When?"

"Last year. After the accident. I imagined dying without ever knowing her, and that was too scary. I didn't tell my dad about it because, you know, he wants me to see him as *both* parents."

"But how did you find her?"

"There was a government agency. France has tons of them, they're so socialized. A man helped me locate a file, and there she was—I mean, her name and information about her. Her parents' address in Rouen. My grandparents, can you believe it?"

I imagine a white-haired lady somewhere on an apple farm, wondering to whom the high, clear voice on the phone could belong. It sounds like the voice of a ghost, a child she had who died when she was twelve. She answers the girl's questions with fear in her chest. Does a phone call from a spirit mean that one is close to death?

"They gave me her phone number and address. She was living in Aix-en-Provence. I took a bus there and stood outside her apartment building for hours, and when it rained I stood in someone's vestibule. I didn't even know which window was hers. It's just as well, I guess. She wouldn't have wanted to see me anyhow."

I don't want to believe this story. It seems designed to make me pity her. Yet there's an embarrassment in her face that suddenly makes her look very young, like a child who has admitted to a misdeed. "Are you going to try again?" I ask.

"Maybe sometime. Maybe after my career."

"That might be a long time."

"Probably not," she says, her eyes set on something in the distance. "I'll have a few good years, and I'd better make enough money to retire on. I don't know what other job I could do."

I consider this. "So what will you do with yourself afterward?"

"I don't know. Go to Morocco with my father. Have kids. Whatever people do."

I think of those pictures of my uncle in couture evening gowns, his skin milky, his waist slender as a girl's. His graceful fingers hold roses or railings or billets-doux; his hair hangs long and thick, a shiny mass down his back. He now wears turtlenecks and horn-rimmed glasses; there are veins on the backs of his hands, and his beautiful hair is gone. I wonder if such a thing can happen to Aïda. She seems eternal, the exception to a rule. Can she really be mortal? Even when she fell off the bridge and chanted fever songs I knew she would survive to see international fame. In the glossy pages of Signora Cellini's magazines and those of women all over the world, she will never, never change.

But here on the sidewalk at the café she bites a hangnail

and looks again at my foot. "We should get you home," she says. "You need some rest." I wonder if she will survive what will happen to her. I wonder if she will live to meet her mother. There are many things I would ask her if only we liked each other better.

On e afternoon, perhaps a month after Aïda's return to Paris, I buy a bottle of inexpensive Chianti and a round loaf of bread and head down to the ancient marketplace by the Arno. There, in the shadow of a high colonnade, the bronze statue of Il Porcellino guards the empty butcher stalls. It's easy to move around on the crutches now, although the cobbled streets provide a challenge. I wear long loose dresses to hide my cast.

At the center of the piazza the white-robed Moroccans have spread their silver and leather goods on immaculate sheets. They sing prices as I pass. Because I have some lire in my pocket, I buy a thin braided bracelet of leather. Perhaps I will send it to my cousin. Perhaps I will keep it for myself. Down by the river, pigeons alight on the stones and groom their feathers. I sit with my legs dangling over a stone ledge and uncork my round-bellied bottle, and the wine tastes soft and woody. It's bottled by the Cellinis. It's pretty good, certainly not bad enough to make them go broke. I drink to their health, and to the health of people everywhere, in celebration of a rather bizarre occurrence. Two days ago I sold a painting. The man who bought it laughed aloud when I said he had made a bad choice. He is an opera patron and food critic from New York, the godson of my painting professor back in the States. He attended our winter exhibition last January and happened to be visiting Rome when the Del Reggio gallery was showing our work.

It is not a painting of Aïda dancing in the grapevines, her hair full of leaves. It is not an unapologetic self-portrait, nor a glowing Tuscan landscape. It is a large sky-blue square canvas with two Chagall-style seraphim in the foreground, holding a house and a tree and a child in their cupped hands. It is called *Above the Farm*. In slightly darker blue, down below, you can make out the shadow of a tornado. Why he bought this painting, I do not know. But there's one thing I can tell you: Those angels have no feet.

Although it's interesting to think of my painting hanging in this man's soaring loft in Manhattan, it makes me sad to think I will never see it again. I always felt comforted, somehow, looking at that child standing by his house and tree, calm and resigned to residence in the air. Five hundred feet off the ground, he's still the same boy he was when he stood on the earth. I imagine myself sitting on this ledge with Aïda, when she is old and I am famous. She will look at me as if I take up too much space, and I will want to push her into the Arno. But perhaps by then we will love ourselves less fiercely. Perhaps the edges of our mutual hate will have worn away, and we will have already said the things that need to be said.

The Isabel Fish

I am the canker of my brother Sage's life. He has told me so in no uncertain terms. Tonight as we eat hamburgers in the car on the way to our first scuba class, he can't stop talking about the horrible fates that might befall me underwater. This, even though he knows how scared I am after what happened last November.

"You could blow out your eardrums," he says. "Or your lungs might implode from the pressure."

"Shut up, Sage," I say.

"Did you know that one in twelve scuba divers gets attacked by sharks?"

"Not in a pool," I say.

Sage is sixteen, plays drums, smokes unfiltered cigarettes, and drives his beat-up black Pinto to school every morning, with me practically hanging onto the rear bumper because I'm slow getting ready. I know he sees me as a problem, a younger and more stupid version of himself, and a girl, not popular, sort of plain, with my hair pulled back in a knot most days and a walk some people make fun of. He used to be cruel to me in the normal sibling sense, but now it's worse. He is far from forgetting Isabel, and who can blame him? She'd been his girlfriend for six months before the accident, and it's only been four months since. Four months is a short time in the grand scheme of things, shorter than it's taken Sage's shaved hair to grow long again, shorter than it's taken me to grow twenty-six fighting fish from eggs for my science experiment, "The Relationship Between Aggression and Hypertension in *B. Splendens*." I got the eggs one month before the accident. When I showed them to Isabel, red and clumped together in a small tank, she laughed and said she could hardly believe that bunch of caviar would become real animals. Well, guess what? They are now.

Every day I feed them and give them liquid vitamins and alter their blood pressure with drugs, and still get my homework done and make it to school just as if I were fully recovered. Which I'm not, in many ways. My parents are aware of this. As a kind of remedy, they came up with the idea of a spring-break trip to St. Maarten in the Dutch Virgin Islands. We're not a family that tends to take spring-break trips. We've never taken one, in fact. So when my father rose from his chair at the dinner table and asked Sage and me what we thought about going to St. Maarten, I took it to mean we'd reached a state of emergency.

They've been talking about the problem between Sage and me for months, our psychologist mom trying to give us counseling, our dentist dad distracting us with jokes. Now scuba lessons, in preparation for the trip. What our parents don't understand is that their son has become cruel and unusual, and he shows no sign of changing.

We stop at a red light and Sage eats a handful of fries all at once. I stare out the window. Beneath the streetlights, snowflakes swarm like moths. It's hard to remember a time when it wasn't winter. Sage crumples the greasy bag in his lap and tosses it into the back seat.

"Anyone could fuck with your tank underwater," he says. "One turn of a knob. That's all it would take."

I lower my sandwich from the eating position. The feeling I remember is being in Isabel's car with the water coming in, filling my mouth with its cold fishy taste, and me groping in the dark for my seat belt, my lungs already hot and tight, and Isabel in the seat beside me bleeding into the darkness. Sage must know what I'm thinking about, but he won't look at me or say anything more. He revs the motor hard, three times, and then the light turns green and we're off.

At the YMCA I follow Sage into the lobby, where the chlorine smell of the pool stops me cold. Sage doesn't notice. He doesn't even look back. He just disappears down the hall toward the men's locker room, leaving me standing there alone. I look at the trophies in a glass display case, silver swimmers and wrestlers and softball players, all frozen mid-sport. The lobby is full of kids and old people milling around and getting snacks from the machines. I sit down on a bench and think about my tropicals, my pet fish, the ones I don't do experiments on. It calms me to imagine them swimming in their pH-balanced environments, the clown loaches loaching around near the bottom of the freshwater tank, the pearl gouramis flirting in a stand of bamboo plant. I have a marine tank too, with three yellow tangs and two fireworks anemones and a dusky angel-fish. Tonight, for the first time, I'll begin to know what my fish have known all their lives: how to breathe underwater.

When I get calm enough I go to the women's locker room and find an empty locker. All around me, teenagers are tying back their hair and putting their naked bodies into tank suits. Someone in the next row of lockers says she heard we're not actually scuba-ing today, just learning about the equipment and doing some laps with fins to get used to the feeling. That makes me feel a little better. When I go to St. Maarten I will have my own fins, according to my father; we have already looked at examples in the window of Arbor Valley Sea and Ski, and I have admired a translucent blue pair with a matching mask. They seem like they'd be almost invisible underwater.

Looking at those fins made it easy to imagine swimming, but now that I'm here at the Y it seems crazy. Sure, in St. Maarten there are a lot of fish you can see living their lives around coral reefs if you happen to know how to scuba. That kind of thing is attractive to an ichthyophile like me. But I am also a person who almost drowned. When my dad told us about St. Maarten, with its great diving, I wanted to ask if he and my mother were crazy. Did they think I would voluntarily walk into the ocean and let it close over my head? Before I could respond, my mother said she'd found us a scuba certification class at the Y. She and my father gave Sage and me these hopeful, anxious looks. I was speechless for a moment, and then I blurted, "Scuba?"

"We think it'll be good for you," my mother said. "We think it'll help you form positive associations with water."

"You don't have to dive at all, of course," my father said. "But we hope you'll consider it."

After all their planning, how could I say no thanks? Even Sage, who for months had hated everything, seemed interested in the trip. The next day he called the Y and signed us up for scuba lessons, and the rest of the week he walked around with a strange half-smile on his face. Now I think he was already coming up with mean things to say to me, things that would make me feel as scared as I do now.

As I get into my tank suit I cannot help noticing the mistakes of my body. The magazine look nowadays is breasts but no hips; I am the opposite. Thin, still, but with hipbones like cup handles. My chest is too flat, my legs too skinny, and there is a scar running the length of my left thigh. Under the water, car metal sliced me in a neat line. I didn't even feel it. Only at the edge of the pond afterward did I look down and see the blood. One doctor sewed it badly in the emergency room, and another had to take the stitches out the next day and do it again. Meanwhile I was in a kind of trance, not wanting to believe what my parents had told me about Isabel.

Now the scar is thin and white, like a dress seam. I turn my leg back and forth, looking. A dark-haired girl in a red suit notices, then glances away.

"It's okay," I say. "It's just a scar. You can look if you want to."

She bends down and looks, and when she meets my eyes again she seems unimpressed. "I also have a scar," she says. She pulls her hair up to show me a jagged pink keloid at the back of her neck. It looks as if someone tried to cut her head off and failed.

"Wow," I say.

The girl looks about my age, but she speaks like the Romanian women who work at the bakery near our house. "My sister threw a broken glass," she says. "She was little, six years old."

"Ouch," I say. "Are you in the scuba class?"

"Yes," she says. "You?"

"Me and my brother."

I see her giving me a side-eye look, and it occurs to me that she might recognize my picture from the news or newspapers. Then I realize this is an extremely egotistical thought, given how many unfortunate things there are on the news and in newspapers over four months. She locks her locker and throws her towel over her shoulder, then adjusts the strap of her goggles. I realize there are probably only ten or fifteen minutes between me and the experience of getting underwater again. For a moment I wish my mother or father were here. Then I remember I am fourteen and lucky to be alive.

"Ready?" the girl says. And I am, I think.

But nothing has prepared me for the experience of actually seeing the pool. It seems to go on forever, lanes and lanes of water strung with red-and-white dividers. Lines of black tile stretch along the bottom, all the way to the diving part of the deep end, where the water darkens to a holy blue. Sage is nowhere to be seen. I sit down on a bench and put my head between my knees to feel better. All around, the echoes of voices bounce off the water and the high ceiling. I'm hoping Sage will come out and just sit near me, and not say anything about messing with my tank, but when I look up again I see him talking to some guys at the other end of the bleachers, as far away from me as possible.

The instructor is a college student, a girl with blond hair and muscular thighs. She wears two tank suits like they do on swim teams. My brother is obviously looking at her breasts, which surprises me because of how much I know he still misses Isabel. But I suppose certain things do not go on hold. As we learn the names of different parts of the gear, we are required to take notes in the small notebooks we bought for the class. The girl in the red suit sits beside me writing very neatly in her notebook. She writes *buoyancy control device, pressure gauge, primary regulator, mouthpiece,* with small pictures next to each word. I try to make mine as neat as hers. We learn what seems to be a basic fact but one I never knew, that scuba stands for Self-Contained Underwater Breathing Apparatus. Over on his end of the bleachers, Sage is writing fast and using a lot of pages. Later he won't be able to read what he wrote and will come crawling to me for help. In my notes I write *Too bad your handwriting sucks so much, Sage!* but then I cross it out, thinking of how Isabel saved all of Sage's notes to her, those scrawls on torn notebook paper that they found in a Japanese box under her bed.

When we have gone through the basic principles of the equipment, the instructor invites us down to select a pair of flippers. At first it looks like there won't be enough to go around. I wait until everyone has a pair, then take my own, realizing nothing will save me now from going in the water. The girl in the red suit clomps around with her toes turned out. "Like a duck," she says, and smiles at me.

We learn that the fins are supposed to fit snugly but without smashing our toes. Everyone puts them on and sits at the side of the pool to get the feel of them in the water. The instructor tells us we'll have fifteen minutes of laps and then a water polo game to increase our agility. It sounds like fun, and it should be fun, but I look at my feet waving in the water and wonder if I'm going to brick. It's one of the main reasons I didn't want to take the class, the possibility of me freaking out and Sage having to take me home while everyone else learns deep dives and repressurization. Sage probably expects me to freak out too. I watch him moving his feet back and forth in the water with great concentration. Just to spite him I decide I will not brick. Cognitive therapy, like what my mother had me do to get comfortable in the bath again: I will not drown here with all these people watching, and me a good swimmer, and with fins on my feet. At least today there will be no tank for Sage to fuck with underwater. The girl in the red suit grins at me as we splash our feet in the pool. If I brick, I tell myself, this nice Romanian kid will think I'm an idiot.

We all line up to swim laps, starting at the deep end of the pool. Why we have to start at the deep end is quickly explained: We're practicing our roll entry, where we have to crouch down with our backs facing the water, the way you go backward off the boat with all your gear on. If the water were too shallow, people might clonk their heads. Once you fall in you're supposed to orient yourself and swim down to the shallow end of the pool, kicking in the fast smooth way you do when you're wearing fins, and then get out and wait by the starting blocks.

This would be a good time to have a brother who cared if you were feeling shitty about getting into the water, but Sage is not that kind of brother. He won't stand anywhere near me. I go to the back of my group, hoping to have more time to get calm, and I think about my sea anemones because they are the calmest of the fish, though technically they are not fish at all but flowerlike polyps of the order Actiniaria. My two anemones, a purple and a pink *Pachycerianthus mana,* are similar in size but have different personalities. The pink is shy and smart and retracts its tentacles fast when something brushes by, but the purple is slower and perhaps less smart, though when it waves its arms it looks more graceful. Thinking of them makes me forget that I am about to fall backward into a pool, gallons and gallons of water, with at least thirty people watching, including my brother and the girl in the red suit, who has already done her roll entry and is now whip-kicking toward the lighter blue of the shallow end. Sage shoots me a look that says *You'd better not fuck up.* Then it's his group's turn to fall in, and he crouches at the edge and goes backward at the count of three. It's true that I could learn something from his confidence, if only he weren't always using it to smash me down.

Finally it's my turn. The instructor gives me a smile and pats my shoulder. I stand at the edge of the pool and pretend there is no water behind me at all, but instead my bed with the quilt I wrap myself in when I get depressed, and there will be no moment when the water covers me, and I will not remember the plunge in the car as we hit the surface and started going down. The instructor begins the countdown. I bend my knees. The flippers on my feet are cold and awkward. Somewhere at the other end of the pool, my brother is watching.

"Go!" cries the instructor, and I push off the edge. There is a whirling moment as the high-up natatorium ceiling flies by, and then I plunge backward into the cold shock of water and sink almost immediately. My arms and legs go numb with panic, and my mouth fills with the bleach taste of pool water. It feels like I'm going down to that place where I was before, the cold dark pond on that November night, and if I go down farther still I will reach Isabel, her hair floating mermaidlike around her. Up above there is a commotion of water, and the echo of shouting, and then the shadow of someone following me down.

In the car on the way home, Sage says nothing. He might as well be made of igneous rock. I keep thinking of the way the red-suit girl looked, scared and sorry for me, when they heaved me up onto the deck of the pool. Through the rest of the class, as everyone finished the laps and played water polo, I was in the locker room getting dry and dressed and then waiting on a wooden bench. All I could think about was how mad Sage would be on our way home. Once again I'd given him evidence of what a non-hero I am. Both of us can plainly see how I might have failed at a crucial moment, missed my chance to pull Isabel out of the car. The thing the police told him, the thing the autopsy confirmed, was that she was already unconscious and wedged into the crushed driver's side, the steering wheel pinning her ribs. It might have been possible for me to pull her out, but if I'd tried I might have drowned too. And she might not have survived anyway. Everyone says I did the right thing by swimming up and climbing out to run for help. Still I know Sage blames me, and in my heart I agree.

At home Sage goes upstairs and closes the door of his room, leaving me in the hallway to explain everything to my dad with his anxious smile, and our mother in her nightgown and socks. After I tell them, we sit down together on the couch. They wedge me in between them the way they used to when I was little. My dad puts an arm around my shoulder. My mother looks miserable, as if she's done this to me herself.

"You swam, though," my father says. "Didn't you?"

"I fell in the water and sank."

"That's a start," he says.

My mother gives him a stern look. We all know that falling

in the water and sinking is hardly an accomplishment, and my mother's not the kind of person who pretends something is what it's not.

"I don't think scuba's for me," I say. "Maybe someday, but not now."

"But think about the fish you'll get to see in St. Maarten if you do finish the class," my father says. "Otherwise it'll just be me and Sage diving, while you and your mom play tennis."

"Don't push her, Robert," my mother says. "She knows what she can do."

"I'm not. I'm just stating the facts."

"Anyway," says my mother, "what's so bad about tennis?"

"Nothing," my father says. "But it doesn't have quite the appeal, for some people, of seeing a coral reef with triggerfish and orange spiny tangs and things of that nature."

"It's up to you, Maddy," my mother says. "We're not going to make you dive if don't want to."

I tell them I'll think about it, and that seems to satisfy them. We get up and they hug me goodnight. Then my mother goes up to check on Sage, who is undoubtedly sitting in his room thinking about Isabel, and my father kisses me on the top of my head and goes into his study.

When I climb the stairs, I see a line of light at the bottom of my brother's door. From inside I can hear the rise and fall of his voice and my mother's. I stand still outside the door, listening. "It's not my responsibility," I hear my brother say, and my mother says something too quiet for me to make out. Very faintly, from the crack at the bottom of the door, come the fumes of cigarette smoke. I imagine them both in there smoking, my mom trying to blow it out the window so as not to smoke up the carpets and furniture, Sage not caring. I'm not much of a smoker. Once or twice I had puffs off Isabel's cigarettes in the garage during band-practice afternoons, but it was never as great as she made it look. Sometimes my mom would come out and smoke a thin cigarette of her own, sitting there on the car bumper and telling us about high school and old boyfriends, stories that tended to embarrass me. But Isabel laughed like my mom was another high school girl, and my mom, who always secretly seemed to distrust Sage's girlfriends, liked Isabel in return.

Finally I hear Sage tell my mom he's going to bed, and I skeet off down the hall before I am discovered. In my bedroom the fish are awake, making their rounds. The pink anemone is shut tight, and the purple one waves smoothly. The loaches are mouthing algae from the side of the freshwater tank. Beside them, my science-experiment fish seem to be sleeping in their plastic containers. Even when they're still I could watch them all night—the red-purple of their bodies, the tiny flick of their gills. The control-group fish look particularly tired, their fins not even finning. Perhaps their natural aggressions have exhausted them. I've tried to learn everything they can teach me about the chemistry of anger, what makes it ebb and flow, how it can be controlled. Twice a day I give them their special food and make behavioral observations and take their blood pressure. It's easier than you might think to take the blood pressure of a fish. Hewlett-Packard makes a sensor that can feel the force and rate of their pulse through the water. My father likes to ask me where's the little cuff, where's the little stethoscope. He thinks it's a big joke that some fighting fish seem to die of heart attacks from so much aggression, but it's no joke if you're a fighting fish.

To be professional I tried not to name my science experiment fish, but then I realized the coincidence of there being twenty-six of them, one for each letter of the alphabet, and now they all have names. Amy, Ben, Carl, Dan, and so forth. I won't, of course, use any of their names in my report; they all have scientific tags like "Control 17." The Isabel fish is in the experimental group, fed a calming drug a couple times a day. She has a blue mark at the center of her dorsal fin, a distinction I happen to know is very rare in members of her sex and species. The Sage fish is a control, reddish-brown in color, mean and small with high blood pressure. At times, when I have been particularly mad at my brother, I've been tempted to give the Sage fish little zaps with an electrode. As a scientist, though, I have refrained.

I roll up my sleeve, put an arm down in the marine tank, and tear off a leaf from one of the underwater plants. After rinsing it in a stream of distilled water, I use it to stroke the backs of the experimental fish. No one pets fish, I know, but these fish seem to enjoy it. It calms *me,* anyhow. I pity these fish, them not knowing what's going on and being in isolation except during the aggression trials. As I stroke them I think about the girl in the red bathing suit, the look she gave me as I lay coughing on the pool deck, and then later, in the locker room, how she said in her Romanian accent that she hoped I was *ollright.* That is the normal way of things, trying to make a person feel less bad about a stupid thing they've done, as opposed to Sage's way, which is to make you feel worse.

He wasn't always that way, particularly when Isabel was around. One time the two of them caught me singing "Louie Louie" in the garage when I thought I was alone. Isabel laughed, but not in a mean way. She had her electric bass there in the garage beside Sage's drum kit, and she picked it up and asked what other songs I knew and did I want to sing while she played. She was like that, taking something I considered embarrassing and trying to make it into something cool. She said I had a retro voice like girl bands in the sixties, and she convinced Sage to play the drums while she and I belted out a couple of verses of "Respect." We sounded good. Even Sage said so. Nowadays he would sooner spit in my face than let me sing with him. I keep telling myself he cannot be angry at me forever, though maybe I am wrong.

The next morning at the breakfast table, Sage does not appear. My father, eating oatmeal with honey, tells me Sage has one of his headaches and that I'll have to catch the bus to school. Sage gets random migraines that lay him out flat for days.

As I eat my Cheerios I feel bad for my brother, even though he's been mean to me for months. Being sick is something he and I have tended to do together. Last spring, when neither of us could imagine anything like the accident ever happening in our lives, we both came down with mononucleosis. We spent a week at home by ourselves, ordering videos our parents would never have let us watch and shooting Chloraseptic into each other's throats. Years before that, we had the chicken pox together. Sage made an oxygen chamber for us out of blankets and couch cushions and told me I was not allowed to leave. We stayed in there for hours, watching cartoons and sweating through our fevers, while our mother brought us soup and juice and Children's Tylenol. This was in our house in Baltimore, with one very small room for both of us. We slept in bunk beds and played with the same toys and even wore some of the same clothes.

When I finish breakfast my father asks me to take Sage some Imitrex and a glass of water. I go up to his room but he's in the bathroom, so I leave the pills and water on his desk. As I'm leaving I see Isabel's bass lying beside the bed. Her parents let Sage keep it after she died, which makes me think they must have known how much she loved him. I pick it up and touch the smooth neck and the polished black body. The name ISABEL is painted on the bass in silver paint, my brother's work, the letters long and crooked and childlike. I pull the strap over my head, feeling the weight of the bass in my shoulders. Then the bathroom door opens. Sage comes out in just pajama pants, his hair wild. When he sees me with the bass he crosses the room in three swift steps, grabs the bass by the neck, and jerks the strap from around my shoulders.

"Don't *ever* come in here," he says, his ribs pumping, his eyes glassed with hate and headache. "Get out, or I'll fucking kill you."

I go to the door. "There's some medicine on the desk."

He gives me a shove toward the hall. When he slams the door behind me, the whole wall shakes.

I go into my bathroom, close the door, and sit down on the edge of the bathtub. Though I don't have time to cry, I cry anyway. My father says goodbye to me through the bathroom door, and I say goodbye back, trying to make my voice sound normal. To my surprise, he buys it. I wait until I hear the garage door go down, and then I wash my face, say goodbye to the fish, and get my books and lunch money. I am late again. I have to run through the snow to catch the bus, and along the way my shoe comes off and I take one cold wet step. Everyone finds this hilarious, even the bus driver.

School offers me no comfort today. In History we watch a movie about the Civil War, with cheerful fife music and reenactments of people being shot to pieces. During Biology there's a fire drill. We all stand outside shivering for half an hour. In Math I find out that the two sisters I usually eat lunch with, Salma and Meena Padmanabhan, are out of school for a Hindu holiday. So at lunchtime I go down to the loading dock near Auto Shop to smoke a crushed cigarette stolen from Sage's pack. It's bent at the end and smells like raisins. I try to light it with someone's thrown-away Bic, but the lighter won't stay lit and the cigarette's too wet and stale to do anything. I sit down on a milk crate and watch the wind blow dead leaves and bits of hard dirty snow.

This afternoon there are only two other kids out smoking: Mike Milldow, a tall stringy kid in a plaid flannel shirt, and Althea London, a girl with chopped black hair and a purple eyebrow ring. Althea, a senior, used to be friends with Isabel. She's talking to Mike about some band called Manila, which she likes and he hates. "They're even worse than Hangtooth," Mike says, and Althea says, "Hangtooth rocks." She blows smoke and flicks ashes in my direction, her eyes narrow and green and ringed with black makeup.

I know she's thinking about Isabel when she looks at me, maybe wishing it had been me who died instead. Althea was one of the last people to see Isabel alive. She'd been with us earlier that night, when we sneaked into the backyard of a new house and used the hot tub. It was Ty Thibodeaux's idea, a friend of my brother's. Ty worked weekends as a hot tub installer and knew where all the tubs were, the places where people were building houses on the north side of town. Sometimes he got the tubs hooked up weeks before the owners moved in.

I would never have gone along if I hadn't been standing around in the garage with Sage and Isabel and Althea London when Ty drove up in his old Buick. He and a couple of other guys came into the garage to fool around with Sage's equipment and smoke cigarettes. There was talk about going to check out a new hot tub. Everyone was excited except me. I'd been having a great time there in the garage, and now everyone was going to leave. I turned to go inside, and that was when Isabel said, "Hey, Maddy, you can come if you want."

"No she can't," Sage said, looking up from his drums.

"Sure she can," Isabel said.

"Yeah, why not?" said Althea London, who had no reason to hate me then.

"She's just a kid," Sage said. "She can't."

"Go get your jacket, Maddy," Isabel said, and that seemed to settle it. If Sage had been driving he probably would have fought harder, but this was before the black Pinto. So I ran inside to get a suit and towel, and then we were off, me and Sage and Isabel and Althea London, all piled in Isabel's Toyota, Isabel singing along with the radio. I felt lucky and cool and older, and a little nervous. I wished Sage would stop sulking and act like it was okay for me to be there. He sat in the passenger seat with his feet up on the dashboard, scowling.

"Sit normal," Isabel said, but he refused.

We followed Ty past broken-down farms and wooded hills and a water tower lit up yellow, all the way to the new developments, where half-built houses stood on bare dirt lots. Out on one of the cul-de-sacs there was an almost-finished house, a blue two-story with white shutters and a three-car garage. They hadn't put down sod in the yard or finished pouring the concrete of the walkway, and one wall of the garage still had to have its siding put on. But around back, in the middle of a redwood deck, was a brand-new eight-person Jacuzzi. Ty unclipped the cover and hit a switch on a control panel, and the tub lit up and started bubbling. Everyone cheered. We were out in the middle of nowhere, with no one around to hear us.

I unrolled my bathing suit from the towel and looked for a place to change, but suddenly all around me people were taking their clothes off—shirts, pants, underwear, everything. I couldn't keep myself from staring at Sage as he pulled off his shirt and jeans. I hadn't seen him naked since we were kids, and suddenly there was the dark hair between his legs, and his pale penis. Isabel was naked too, her arms crossed over her chest. She looked nervous at first, but then she opened her arms and let the wind hit her and she laughed and shivered, her hair all loose and messed up, her skin going pink. She was so beautiful that for a minute I forgot to be freaked out by what was happening. I started taking off my clothes like everyone else, feeling the wind hit my skin. Then I saw Sage looking at me, waiting for me to take my shirt off, his mouth curling as if he were getting ready to say something mean. So I went down some stairs to the side of the deck and put my suit on. It was freezing down there, in no clothes, with nothing but hard ground beneath my feet.

As much as I wanted to go up and get in the hot tub, it seemed better to wait until everyone else was already in, their parts mostly submerged. I climbed a couple of stairs and watched them. Ty was in the tub, laughing and splashing

Althea London, who had one nipple pierced. Isabel got in next
to Ty, and Sage next to her. Someone passed beers around. I
was seeing the secret world of cool older people, the world
Sage slipped off into every weekend while I stayed at home
with my fish or made cookies with the sisters Padmanabhan.
I took a breath and looked up at the stars. It was November.
Orion was bending his bow in the sky above us.

"Hey, Maddy," Isabel called from the hot tub. "Where are
you?"

I climbed the stairs and headed for the Jacuzzi as if this
were the kind of thing I did all the time. Isabel moved over to
make space for me, and I got in. Our thighs pressed together
under the water, her skin slick-smooth. The water steamed
and rolled and burbled around us. Ty Thibodeaux handed me
a beer, and I sank down in the water up to my neck and
drank. The beer was bitter and bready and cold. I thought
maybe I could develop a taste for it if I tried.

There was some talk about people at school, kids I'd seen
but never spoken to. Someone had gotten a tattoo gun from his
cousin in New York; someone else had thrown up in Calculus
class from eating pot brownies. I laughed along with everyone,
as if the people they were talking about were friends of mine.
After a while, when I was feeling braver, I told a story of my
own: Last week a wiener dog had run into our gym class and
peed on a rack of basketballs before anyone could stop him.

"I heard about that," Isabel said. "I heard Miss Cortland
freaked."

"She completely freaked!" I said. Ty laughed and handed
me another beer.

Then, as if he couldn't stand that people were talking to
me and acting like I belonged there, Sage had to start telling
the story about my fifth birthday, the pool story. I tried to
make him stop, but he wouldn't. "She was drinking Sprite all
morning," he said. "Gallons of it. We only got to drink soda on
our birthdays, because of our dad saying it would rot our
teeth." People were listening, lowering their beers and lean-

ing forward so they could hear him over the bubbles. "We were on the pool deck," he went on, "and she's dancing around like she has to pee, and our mom's like, 'Maddy, do you have to go wee-wee?'"

"Shut up, Sage," I said.

"No," Sage said. "I'm just getting to the good part." He winked at Ty Thibodeaux across the rolling water. "So I look in the pool five minutes later and there's Maddy with this peaceful expression on her face. Our mom saw it too. She got everyone out of the pool in like five seconds flat. She made them go in and have cake. Everyone was like, 'Why can't we swim anymore?' Meanwhile Maddy tried to act like she hadn't done it. She still won't admit it, will you, Maddy?" He poked me in the shoulder.

"So what?" Isabel said. "Little kids pee in the pool all the time."

"I called her the Mad Pisser that whole summer," Sage said.

"That story's a lie," I said, though probably everyone knew it wasn't.

"You'd better not have too much to drink," he said, grabbing my beer away and taking a sip. "The Mad Pisser might ride again."

He wouldn't let it rest. He kept poking me in the shoulder and saying, "Think you can hold it?" with me staring into the water and wishing he'd stop, until Isabel climbed out of the tub and stood there shivering in a towel, looking out at the empty backyard. When she started putting on her clothes Sage tried to stop her, but she pulled away and zipped her sweatshirt up.

"Why do you have to be such an asshole?" she said.

"It was funny," Sage said, and looked at Ty. "Wasn't it funny?"

"I don't know, man," Ty said, as if he didn't want to take sides.

"It wasn't funny," Isabel said, pulling her jeans on.

Sage turned away and kicked a beer bottle off the deck, and I wondered whether we'd all just go home now. Part of me hoped we would. Then the next minute floodlights were flashing and a shrill alarm was screaming. The house security system had gone off. We hadn't even known there was one. Althea London had triggered it when she tried to climb in through a window to use the bathroom.

Suddenly everyone was screaming and running around, elbowing one another as we tried to get our jeans and shoes and coats on. I was so scared I couldn't even manage to put on my pants, and Isabel had to grab my hand and run us to the front of the house where her car was parked. We got in and she started the motor.

"What about Sage?" I said. In my side mirror I could see him coming around the side of the house, his shirt bunched against his crotch.

"He can find another ride," Isabel said. Then she hit the gas, and we were off.

We tore out of the cul-de-sac at what must have been sixty miles an hour, windows down, Sonic Youth blaring from the tape player. "Woo-hoo!" Isabel screamed. Her hands were shaking as she held the steering wheel, and I couldn't tell if it was because she was cold or because she was excited. I'd never seen anyone drive so fast. The night was cold and clear, the sky shot with stars, the bare trees whipping by. The vinyl car seat was like ice against my legs, and my teeth were clacking so hard I could feel it in the top of my skull. Isabel was singing along with the tape as we roared over those roads. Every now and then she'd look at me and grin.

"We can drive all the way to Chicago," she said. "I feel like driving."

I imagined the two of us walking down Michigan Avenue, parents three hundred miles away, hot dogs in our hands. "We'd be in such deep shit," I said, and laughed.

"No, we wouldn't," she said. "I have an aunt there. She's cool. We could stay with her tonight and come back tomorrow."

"Chicago," I said. "That's crazy, Isabel."

"Let's do it," she said. "Let's go right now."

We turned in at Gettyswood Townhomes, a shortcut to US 23, and all at once I knew she was serious. I felt light-headed and frightened and almost in love with her. Together we would zip out along the open highway. We wouldn't even call our parents until we got there, and God only knew what they would say. Sage would be so jealous he would spontaneously combust. Isabel laid on the gas, and as we came around the curve near the pond I felt the jolt of the curb and a sudden hollow rush in my chest and we were airborne.

The car hit the pond nose-first. The windshield crunched and everything was dark and water poured in through the open windows, so cold it erased every part of me it touched, and suddenly it was in my mouth with its pond-scum taste and I couldn't breathe. I hardly knew what was happening. In the darkness I felt for Isabel, straining against my seat belt, and my hands brushed something warm and soft, but I couldn't make my fingers hold on to anything. My lungs began to burn. I shrugged out of the seat belt and felt for the edge of the open window, pushing through, trying to kick up to where the moon wavered like a reflection of itself. I struggled through what seemed like thick black honey, broke the sur- face, breathed, swam to the edge, and crawled out onto the frozen bank. Kneeling on the wet grass I coughed out water, waiting to see Isabel come up. I screamed to her. The trees beside the pond clicked in the wind. On my left leg a widening cut ran black and hot with blood. I got up onto the numb blocks of my feet and ran toward the townhouses, toward a phone, shouting for help.

Now, four months later, Althea London sits on the edge of the loading dock, shooting me mean glances, blowing ciga- rette smoke at me like she's trying to make me cough. I'd like to remind her that she was the genius who tripped the alarm. She has no idea what it was like between Isabel and me in the car, or what happened down under the water.

I crush the wet cigarette with the toe of my shoe and jump off the edge of the loading dock, six feet down, to land hard on hands and knees on the pavement, and then I am limping toward home.

Crime and punishment. That is the pattern between my brother Sage and me. A quiet private criminal justice system is what we've created, with Sage as judge, jury, jailer, and executioner. Our system has no checks and balances, and it allows multiple punishments for the same crime. If, in a real court, I'd been proven guilty of killing Isabel, I would have gotten my punishment and been left to live with it. In the world of Sage and me, however, I must pay and pay—even though Sage is guilty in some ways himself.

God only knows how he killed them, whether he fed them poison or put ice cubes in their water or something even worse, but when I get home from school I find eleven of my fighting fish dead, the Sage fish and the Isabel fish among them. They float on top of the water in their plastic containers, still and cold. My fish, the animals I raised from eggs. Their fins are limp, their mouths open, their little round eyes looking at nothing. Five experimental-group fish and six control-group ones. If he were smart he would have killed all the experimental ones, making me think I was somehow at fault. But I know whose stupid fault this is, from beginning to end.

Though I know it won't help, I throw the dead fish into the aggression-trial tank and administer a few electric shocks. Nothing. It's just as well. If they did wake up, they'd attack each other to death in three seconds flat. I scoop them out, put them all in an empty yogurt container, and snap the lid on. They weigh almost nothing. I take them to bed with me and wrap myself in the quilt. And though I don't want to let myself cry, I do, because they're dead beyond the reach of hope or science, and Sage is the one who did it, and no matter what I do

67

to get back at him—burn his room, trash his car—he'll just find a way to get me back worse.

That night, after a quiet dinner at which Sage does not appear and at which I pretend to my parents that nothing is wrong, I take the yogurt container and walk the mile to the pond, which isn't even a real natural pond but an ornamental small lake near the east entrance of Gettyswood. I crouch in the grass near a fake dock and unwrap the fish and throw them into the water, one by one. It doesn't take me long to realize how ridiculous I must look, hurling tiny fish into a pond. They float on top, dark shapes against the moonlit surface, and I know they will probably be eaten by birds or by other fish.

It's the first time I've been to the pond since the accident. Things look almost the same as they did that night, the trees without leaves, the grass patchy and frozen. In the weeds beside me I find a piece of thick glass, blue at the edge, and I can't help wondering if it belonged to the Toyota windshield. Though I know the car was dragged out months ago, I imagine it there beneath the surface of the water, Isabel still trapped inside. It's impossible to believe how gone she is, how untouchable. She's the only one who doesn't have to know what it's like here on Earth without her.

The next day I'm waiting for my dad to take me to school, thinking maybe I'll tell him about the fish, but at the last moment Sage comes down with his car keys in hand. He looks exhausted after his long headache.

"I'll drive," he says, his voice scratchy and low.

"You sure?" our dad says.

Sage nods. I kiss our dad goodbye and follow Sage to the car. All the way to school he seems to be getting ready to say something to me. He keeps giving me a squinty look, as if he's trying to figure out what I'm feeling, but I'm not about to let him know. I keep my face still as stone, just as he did when we were driving home from scuba class. School is not far from our house. We get there before he manages to talk.

"See you at three?" he says as we climb out.

"Whatever," I say.

I wait for him to say something else, to confess or apologize, but he just turns and lopes across the parking lot.

When we get home from school I find a blue plastic bag on my bed. I open it to find the swim fins and mask I'd admired at Arbor Valley Sea and Ski. There's no note, but at the bottom of the bag I find a credit card receipt with my mother's signature. The fins look even better in person than they did in the store window, the translucent blue plastic shot through with green swirls, the glass of the mask almost iridescent. I kick off my shoes and pull the fins on. They fit.

I am so happy, clomping around the room in my new Sea-Quest Thrusters, that it's a fresh shock to pass by my experimental fish and see the empty containers among them. I take off the fins and mask and put them back in the bag. I pull the experimental notebook from my backpack. I have not recorded blood pressure data in two days, and it almost seems not worth continuing the experiment. Out of habit, though, I feed the fish their flakes and vitamins and take their blood pressures with the HP device. Everyone's blood pressure is slightly high today. It makes me wonder if they can sense that something went wrong, that they themselves have only narrowly escaped disaster. As I sit down on the bed to record my results, there is a soft knock at the door. "Come in," I say, hoping it will be Sage. Instead it is my mother.

"You look nice today," I say, and she does, in black pants and a gray sweater and scarf. Her cheek feels cold when she kisses me, as if she has just come in from outside.

"How are they?" she says, looking into the plastic fish containers. Because she was the one who drove me to Detroit to buy the eggs, and helped me set up the experiment with its control and experimental groups, she knows something's wrong when she sees the empty containers. She gives me a puzzled look.

"Some of the research subjects died," I say.

"Why?" she says. "What happened?"

"I don't know." I could tell her it was Sage's doing, but I don't. What happened is between him and me.

She has me walk her through the water temperatures and chemistry, the blood-pressure sensing mechanisms, the fish's diet. Of course she can find nothing that would have caused the random deaths. She stands there looking into the containers as if an answer might emerge from the water. If it occurs to her that Sage might have killed the fish, she doesn't say so.

"I'm sorry, Maddy," she says finally. "You took such good care of them."

I don't respond, because I know I will cry if I try to speak.

"Maybe they got some kind of virus," she says. "That can happen. You just have to carry on with the experiment. Note the deaths in your log and move on."

"I'll try," I tell her.

"You know," she says, fingering the edge of one of the containers, "I had lunch with your father today. Afterward he cleaned my teeth and bleached them." She smiles, and her teeth are as white as sleet.

"Nice," I say.

"We wondered if you were going to go to class again tonight."

"I wasn't planning to. But those are excellent fins." I take them out of the bag again and put them on, flopping around the room to demonstrate. Then I put on the mask. "How do I look?" I ask her.

She takes me by the shoulders, turning me back and forth. Despite the dead fish, despite my failure in the swimming pool, despite everything that has happened in the past four months, she looks almost proud of me. "Très Jacques Cousteau," she says. "Très magnifique."

On the way to scuba that night I watch Sage as he drives and eats, the grease shining on his fingers. He steers with one hand and grabs chicken nuggets with the other. If he had another hand, he would be using it to smoke. He seems to want to keep his mouth full so he doesn't have to talk to me. I don't eat anything. Usually he'd finish my nuggets and fries too, but tonight he leaves my food alone.

We pull into the parking lot and find our space, and then we get out so Sage can have a cigarette. It is cold and windy March, still frozen, without a hint of spring. Sage has a hard time getting the lighter to stay lit, but finally his cigarette catches. He takes a drag and then extends the pack toward me.

"Yeah, right," I say.

He blows out a plume of smoke, throwing his head back to get his hair out of his eyes—a gesture Isabel once told me she loved, but which to me seems like the kind of thing people do when they're trying to look cooler than they really are. "I know you steal them sometimes," he says.

I take the pack from him and swizzle the cigarettes around inside. Their smell reminds me of the lunch I spent out on the loading dock. I tell him I'll pass.

As Sage smokes he shoots quick glances at my fins, trying to look at them without being obvious. I lean against the car and slap them against my leg. Finally he says, "How come I didn't get any fins?"

"I don't know," I say. "Maybe because you're such a dickhead."

He takes the pack of cigarettes from me and stuffs it into his pocket.

"You can't just not mention the fish, Sage." I look him hard in the eye. "You can't pretend nothing happened."

He leans against the car and crosses his arms. Very quietly he says, "I'll get you some replacement fish."

"Do you know how ridiculous that is? I raised those fish

71

from eggs, just for the experiment. Under controlled conditions. It took months!"

"Okay, okay."

My throat goes tight. I sling my towel over my shoulder and begin to walk toward the door of the Y. Already I can hear the sound of little kids inside, playing as they wait to be picked up. Sage comes up behind me and grabs my wrist, but I whick it away.

"Maddy," he says, and I turn to look at him. He's so cold I can see him shivering. Behind him the Y glows with yellow light, its entryway toothed with icicles. "I wouldn't have to get you fish for your experiment," he says. "I could get you some pet fish."

"Just forget it, Sage."

"Listen to me," he says. "I'm an asshole. I admit it."

"You didn't use to be," I say. "Not such a major asshole, anyway."

Cars sweep by, honking for the kids waiting inside. When the door of the Y opens, the sound of the kids' voices grows sharper. Somewhere farther inside is the pool with its tiled depths.

"You make me wish I died instead of her," I say.

He stands there staring at me as if I've hit him. A fine dry snow has begun to fall, speckling his jacket with flakes. He drops his cigarette and grinds it into the asphalt with his heel. "I followed you the other night," he says. "When you went to the pond."

"You followed me?"

"You went sneaking out of the house. I didn't know what you were going to do."

I hate the thought of him watching as I threw my fish into that pond. It seemed a stupid enough thing to do when I thought I was unobserved. "Don't follow me around, Sage," I say. "If I want you to go somewhere with me, I'll ask you."

"No, you won't," he says. "Why would you?" He takes out another cigarette, then puts it back in the pack. Finally he speaks again, so quiet I have to lean close to hear him. "I can't believe I turned out to be such a shitty person," he says. "I wasn't even nice to *her*."

"What are you talking about?"

"I was a terrible boyfriend. I got mad at her for no reason during band practice. I didn't listen to her enough. I forgot her birthday. I made fun of her car."

"You weren't a terrible boyfriend," I say. "Isabel loved you."

"How do you know?"

"I just do," I say. "I could see it."

Just then the girl from last week walks by, swinging a gym bag over her shoulder. She lifts a hand and waves as if she's never seen me coughing out water on the side of the pool. I wave back.

"We're going to be late," Sage says.

I follow him into the Y, and we split off toward our separate locker rooms.

Among the rows of yellow lockers I unpack my suit and towel, my new mask. As I change clothes, the girl in red comes over and picks up my swim fins.

"SeaQuests," she says in her Romanian accent. "Very professional."

"My mom got them for me."

"They match you," she says, holding them up against my bathing suit.

"You can try them later if you want," I say, and she looks pleased.

When I see the pool again, the place where I went down last time, nausea slams me. I try to take some slow breaths. Out on the bleachers some kids are talking about different kinds of equipment, single tanks versus double, but Sage is sitting off to one side, scratching his ankle. The blond swim-team-looking instructor whose name I have forgotten is hauling complete scuba sets and wetsuits out of a storeroom. No one's bothering to help her. The red-suit girl and I go down there and start hauling out tanks, and by the time we're finished my nausea has gone away.

"All right," the instructor says, dusting off her hands. "Who wants to dive?"

People yell and clap. Even Sage looks interested.

She says we're going to do a five-minute ten-foot dive, and tells everyone to get into wetsuits. The suits are the one-piece back-zip kind; the Romanian girl and I zip each other in. The instructor gives us each a weight belt and a scuba set and shows us how to fasten the tanks to the buoyancy control device. We learn how to attach the regulator to the tank, how to turn on the air, and how to test the regulator by pushing the purge button. We learn that we're supposed to use the hang-ten sign to say *cool* to each other, because the thumbs-up sign means to go to the surface. We lift the gear onto each other's backs and secure all the buckles. Then we stagger toward the deep end and take practice breaths just standing on the side of the pool. The air from the tank is metallic and very dry. The last thing we do before going in is to put on fins and masks. My new flippers look sleek and aqua blue against the white tiles of the floor.

Finally it is time again for all of us to get into the water. Sage moves close to me as we line up to splash in, him shivering, me trying not to look over the edge into the mouth of the water.

"Quit thinking about last time," he says. "It's going to be different."

"We'll see," I say.

"Practice measuring your breaths, like she told us."

I practice measuring my breaths, and it calms me a little. We watch our classmates line up and fall backward into the pool. I see them down there beneath the surface, not coming up for a breath, and all of a sudden a great excitement fills me. Although I know it is stupid, I feel as if we're going to find ourselves in the ocean when we splash down, surrounded by coral reefs and fish, seeing things we'd never even imagined. When I crouch for my roll entry, Sage crouches beside me. Together we fall back and splash down. At first I forget to breathe. We're underwater, after all. But when my lungs start getting tight I suck in a breath. The air is cold and surprising in my lungs, and suddenly I'm scuba diving, shooting out bubbles of used breath into the pool, and Sage is finning beside me.

When I think of Isabel this time it's not as a mermaid but as the living girlfriend of my brother, wearing blue jeans, playing bass in the garage, telling me to try singing. She would have liked to see us diving, Sage and me, going down into the richest blue of the bottom. We tread water, watching each other through our masks. I cannot see his eyes through the glass, but I can see, reflected small and blue, a girl wearing swim fins and a metal tank, self-contained and breathing underwater.

Note to Sixth-Grade Self

On Wednesdays wear a skirt. A skirt is better for dancing. After school, remember not to take the bus. Go to McDonald's instead. Order the fries. Don't even bother trying to sit with Patricia and Cara. Instead, try to sit with Sasha and Toni Sue. If they won't let you, try to sit with Andrea Shaw. And if Andrea Shaw gets up and throws away the rest of her fries rather than sit with you, sit alone and do not look at anyone. Particularly not the boys. If you do not look at them, they may not notice you sitting alone. And if they don't notice you sitting alone, there is still a chance that one of them will ask you to dance.

At three-thirty stand outside with the others and take the number seven bus uptown. Get off when they all get off. Be sure to do this. Do not stare out the window and lose yourself. You will end up riding out to the edge of town past the rusted gas-storage tanks, and you will never find the right bus home. Pay attention. Do not let the strap of your training bra slip out the armhole of your short-sleeved shirt. Do not leave your bag on the bus. As you cross the street, take a look at the public high school. The kids there will be eating long sticks of Roman candy and leaning on the chain-link fence. Do they look as if they care who dances with whom, or what steps you'll learn this week? News flash: They do not. Try to understand that there's a world larger than the one you inhabit. If you understand that, you will be far ahead of Patricia and Cara.

For now, though, you live in this world, so go ahead and follow the others across the street to Miggie's Academy of Dance. There is a low fence outside. Do not climb on it in your skirt. Huddle near the door with the other girls. See if anyone will let you listen. Do not call attention to yourself. Listen as Patricia, with her fascinating stutter, describes what she and Cara bought at the mall. Notice how the other girls lean forward as she works through her troublesome consonants: *G-G-Guess Jeans and an Esp-p-prit sweater.* They will talk about the TV shows they watch, who killed whom, who is sleeping with whom; they will compare starlets' hairstyles. None of this talk is of any importance. For God's sake, don't bother watching those TV shows. Keep reading your books.

At four o'clock, go inside with the others. Line up against the wall with the girls. Watch how the boys line up against their wall, popular ones in the middle, awkward ones at the sides. Watch how the girls jockey to stand across from the boys they like. Watch Brittney Wells fumble with the zipper of her nylon LeSportsac. Don't let her get next to you with that thing. Try to stand across from someone good. Do not let yourself get pushed all the way out to the sides, across from Zachary Booth or Ben Dusseldorf. Watch how Patricia and Cara stand, their hips shot to one side, their arms crossed over their chests. Try shooting your hip a little to one side. Rest your weight on one foot. Draw a circle on the wooden floor with one toe. Do not bite your fingernails. Do not give a loud sniff. Think of the word *nonchalant*. Imagine the eleventh-graders, the way they look when they smoke on the bus. Let your eyes close halfway.

When Miss Miggie comes out, do not look at her enormous breasts. Breasts like those will never grow on your scarecrow body. Do not waste your time wanting them. Instead, watch how she moves in her low-cut green dress: chin high, back straight, hips asway. Listen to the way she talks: Fawx Trawt, Chaw-chaw, Wawtz. Love how she talks, but do not pick it up. When you move north in three years, you cannot afford to say *y'all*. Listen as Miss Miggie describes what y'all will learn that day. Watch how her hand traces the dance steps in the air. Now that the boys are occupied, staring at her breasts, you can look openly at Eric Cassio. Admire his hair and eyes, but quickly. Like all boys he will feel you looking.

The first dance will always be a cha-cha. On the record they will sing in Spanish, a woman trilling in the background. It will start a thrill in your chest that will make you want to move. Watch Miss Miggie demonstrate the steps. Practice the steps in your little rectangle of floor. Watch how Patricia and Cara do the steps, their eyes steady in front of them, their arms poised as if they were already holding their partners. Now concentrate on dancing. Avoid Sasha and Toni Sue with their clumsy soccer-field legs. Ignore Brittney and that purse. When Miss Miggie looks at you, concentrate hard. Remember practicing with your father. Do not throw in an extra dance step that you are not supposed to know yet. Do not swish your skirt on purpose. Do not look at the boys.

Long before it is time to pick partners, you will feel the tightness in your stomach. Do not let it break your concentration. You have too many things to learn. Remember, if you want to have the most gold stars at the end of the eight weeks, you are going to have to work hard. Imagine dancing in a spotlight at the end-of-class ball, with the best boy dancer from all the seven private schools. On the Achievement Record, next to your name, there are already five stars. Patricia and Cara also have five stars. Everyone else has two or three. Think of the stars in their plastic box. You can almost taste the adhesive on their backs. Two more stars can be yours today, if you do not let yourself get nervous.

When it is time for the boys to pick, do not bite your hangnails. Do not pull at your skirt. Watch how Patricia and Cara lean together and whisper and laugh, as if they don't care whether or not they get picked. Watch how Miss Miggie brings her arms together, like a parting of the Red Sea in reverse, to start the picking. The boys will push off with their shoulder blades and make their way across the floor. Do not make eye contact! If you make eye contact you will drown. Do not, whatever you do, look at Eric Cassio. You do not care which one of those other girls he picks. You know it will not be you.

When the picking is over, hold your chin up and wait for Miss Miggie to notice you standing alone. She will take Zachary Booth by the shoulder and steer him over to you. When he is standing in front of you, look down at his white knee socks. Stand silent as he asks, with his lisp, if he can have thith danth. Ignore the snorts and whispers of your classmates. Do not think about Zachary Booth's hand warts. Let him take your right hand and put his left hand stiffly at your waist. Be glad you are dancing with a boy at all, and not with Brittney Wells, as you did last week.

When Miss Miggie starts the music, raise your chin and look Zachary Booth in the eye. Make sure he knows that even though he is the boy, you will be the one to lead. As much as he hates to dance with you, he will be grateful for that. It will be up to you alone to make sure you don't both look like fools. Squeeze his hand when it is time to start. Whisper the steps under your breath. When he falters, keep right on going. Let him fall back in step with you. Out of the corner of your eye, watch Miss Miggie drifting through the room as she claps the rhythm, her red mouth forming the words *one two*. When she looks your way, remember your father's advice: head high, shoulders back. Smile at Zachary Booth. Ignore the grimace he makes in return. If you dance well you may be picked to demonstrate.

And you know which boy will be picked. You know who is picked to demonstrate nearly every time, who Miss Miggie always *wants* to pick, even when she has to pick one of the others just to mix things up. Eric Cassio is not just great in *your* opinion. Already the world understands how excellent he is. The music swells toward its final cha-cha-cha and Miss Miggie's eyes scan the room. Her red lips come together like a bow. She raises her rack of breasts proudly and lifts her finger to point. The finger flies through the air toward Eric Cassio, and Miss Miggie calls his name. He scowls and looks down, pretending to be embarrassed, but there is a smile at the corner of his mouth. Patricia bites a fingernail. Understand that she is nervous. This gives you power. Do not flinch when Zachary Booth pinches your arm; do not let the burning in your eyes become tears. He does not concern you. The only thing that concerns you is who Miss Miggie will point to next. It could be anyone. It could be you. Her finger flies through the air. Is it you? Oh, God, it is.

Do not look at Patricia and Cara as they extend their tongues at you. Ignore Zachary Booth's explicit hand gesture. Forget you weigh sixty-nine pounds; stop wanting breasts so badly. So what if you wear glasses? So what if your skirt is not Calvin Klein? For this one moment you have no hangnails, no bony knees, and there is a secret between you and Eric Cassio. When the others clear the floor, look him square in the eye and share that secret. The secret is, you know he likes to dance. It goes back to the day when you were punished together for being tardy, when you had to transplant all the hybrid peas from the small white plastic pots to the big terra-cotta ones. Your hands touched, down in the bag of potting soil. When you got cold he gave you his green sweater. Later, as you were cleaning up—the water was running, no one could hear him—he told you he *liked* to dance. Remember these things. The fact that he ignored you at lunch that day, at recess, and every day afterward—even the fact that he is now Patricia's boyfriend—does not matter. He *likes* to dance. Look into his eyes, and he will remember he told you.

Let his arm come around you, tanned and slim. Take his hand; it is free of warts. The dance requires that you maintain eye contact with him almost constantly. Do not be afraid to meet his blue eyes. Smile. Remember what your father has taught you: Cuban motion. It is in the hips. A white boat rocking on waves. The half-hour demonstration with your mother, her hair upswept, was not for nothing. Here you are. Miss Miggie lowers the arm onto the record, and the maracas shake into action.

When you dance with Eric Cassio, communicate through your hands. A press here, a sharp squeeze there, and you'll know what he wants you to do, and he'll know what you want him to do. As you change directions, catch Patricia's eye for one moment. Give your hips the Cuban motion. Make her watch. When you twirl, twirl sharp. Listen to Miss Miggie clapping in rhythm. Let all the misery fall out of your chest. Smile at Eric. He will smile back, just with the corner of his mouth. He is remembering transplanting the peas. He does not smile at Patricia that way; that is a smile for you.

Do the special pretzel thing with your arms, that thing Miss Miggie has only shown you once; pull it off without a hitch. End with your back arched and your leg outstretched. Listen to the silence that comes over the room like fog. Remember the way they look at you. No one will applaud. Five seconds later, they will hate you more than ever.

The next day, watch out. You will pay for that moment with Eric. Wear pants, for God's sake. Take no chances. In gym you will play field hockey; remember that this is not one of your better games. You are on the red team, Patricia and Cara are on the blue. You are left wing forward. When you get the ball, pass it as quickly as you can. What will happen is inevitable, but it will be worse if you make them mad. It will happen at the end of the game, when you are tired and ready for gym to be over. As you race down the side of the field toward the ball, halfback Cara's stick will come out and trip you. You will fall and sprain your wrist. Your glasses will fly off and be broken in two at the nosepiece. You will cut your chin on a rock.

Lie still for a moment in the trampled clover. Try not to cry. The game will continue around you as if you do not exist. Only the gym teacher, leathery-skinned Miss Schiller, will notice that anything is wrong. She will pick you up by the arm and limp you over to the bench. Do not expect anyone to ask if you are okay. If they cared whether or not you were okay, this would never have happened. Let this be a lesson to you about them. When Patricia scores a goal they cluster around her, cheering, and click their sticks in the air.

At home, seek medical assistance. Do not let anything heal improperly. You will need that body later. As your mother binds your wrist in an Ace bandage, you will tell her you tripped on a rock. She will look at you askance. Through instinct, she will begin to understand the magnitude of your problem. When she is finished bandaging you, she will let you go to your room and be alone with your books. Read the final chapters of *A Little Princess*. Make an epic picture of a scene from a girls' boarding school in London on three sheets of paper. Push your brother around the living room in a laundry basket. That night, in the bath, replay in your head the final moment of your dance with Eric Cassio. Ignore the fact that he would not look at you that day. Relish the sting of bath-water on your cuts. Tell yourself that the moment with Eric was worth it. Twenty years later, you will still think so.

That weekend something will happen that will seem like a miracle: Patricia will call you on the phone. She will tell you Cara's sorry for tripping you in gym. Look down at your purple swollen wrist, touch the taped-together bridge of your glasses. Say it's no big deal. Patricia will ask what you are doing that afternoon. You will whisper, "Nothing." She will ask you to meet her and Cara at Uptown Square.

—We're going shopping for d-d-dresses for the Miggie's B-ball, she'll say. Wanna come?

Now, think. *Think.* Do you really believe Cara could be

sorry, that suddenly she and Patricia could crave your company? And even if they did, would you want these girls as friends? Try to remember who you're dealing with here. Try to tell Patricia you will not go shopping.

Of course, you will not refuse. You will arrange a time and place to meet. Then you will spend half an hour picking out an outfit, red Chinese-print pants and a black shirt, matching shoes and earrings. You will ask your mother to drive you to the mall, and she will consent, surprise and relief plain on her face. She will even give you her credit card.

When you arrive at the entrance to Uptown Square, with its marble arches and potted palms, you will pretend to see Patricia and Cara inside. You will kiss your mother and watch her drive away. Then you will stand beside the potted palms and wait for Patricia and Cara. You will take off your broken glasses and put them in your pocket, and adjust the hem of your shirt. You will wait there for ten minutes, fifteen, twenty. When you run inside to use the bathroom you will hurry your way through, afraid that you're keeping them waiting, but when you go outside again they will still not be there.

You will wonder whether Patricia meant *next* week. You will bite your nails down to the quick, then continue biting.

Stop this. They are not coming.

Go inside. Wander toward the fountain with the alabaster naked ladies. Sit down at the fountain's edge and look at the wavering copper and silver circles beneath the water. Don't waste time thinking about drowning yourself. Don't bother imagining your funeral, with your classmates in black clothes on a treeless stretch of lawn. If you die you will not be there to see it, and your classmates probably won't be either.

Instead, take a nickel from your pocket and make your own wish: Patricia and Cara strung upside-down from the tree in the schoolyard, naked for all the world to see. Kiss your nickel and toss it in. Feel better. Dry your eyes. Here you are in Uptown Square with your mother's credit card. Go to Maison Blanche, past the children's department, straight to

Preteens. Tell the glossy-haired woman what kind of dress you want: something short, with a swirly skirt. Look through all the dresses she brings you; reject the ones with lace and flounces. On your own, look through all the others on the rack. You will almost give up. Then, at the very back, you will find your dress. It is midnight-blue with a velvet spaghetti-strap bodice and a satin skirt. Tell yourself it is the color of Eric Cassio's eyes. Try it on. Watch it fit. Imagine yourself, for a moment, as a teenager, an eleventh-grader, the girls you see in the upper school bathroom brushing their hair upside down and flipping it back. Flip your hair back. Twirl in front of the mirror. The dress costs fifty-eight dollars, with tax. Pay with your mother's credit card. The woman will wrap it in white tissue and seal it with a gold sticker, then slide it into a white store bag. By the time your mother comes to pick you up, you'll have almost forgotten about Patricia and Cara. When she asks you how your afternoon went, lie.

School this next week will be hell. Everyone will know about Patricia and Cara's trick on you, how you went to the mall and waited. Now you will have to pay a price. People will come up to you all day and ask you to their birthday parties and family picnics and country clubs. Do not dignify them with a response, particularly not crying. This will be extremely difficult, of course. Try to understand what's going on: You got to dance with Eric Cassio, and he refused to act as if you made him sick. This is a threat to the social order.

By Tuesday afternoon, things will become unbearable. It is a dull week—preparations for a spring pageant, the history of the Louisiana Purchase, sentence diagramming in Language Arts—and people have nothing better to talk about. After lunch, on the playground, they gather around you as you try to swing. They needle you with questions: How many hours did you wait? Did you cry? Did you make believe you had a pretend friend? Did you have to call your mommy?

Get out of the swing. Be careful. You are angry. Words do not come easily around your classmates, particularly not at times like these. But you cannot let them continue to think that they have made you miserable. Tell them you went to Maison Blanche and bought a blue velvet dress.

—Liar! You can't afford a dress from Maison Blanche.

—I did.

—No, you d-didn't. I think you bought a d-d-d—

—A *diaper,* Cara finishes.

—It's a blue velvet dress. With spaghetti straps.

—They don't even h-h-h-have a dress like that there. You n-never went in there, you liar. You were too b-busy crying. *Waah-aah!* No one likes me! You bought a d-d-d-d-dirty baby diaper. You're wearing it right now! Ew, ew.

Ew, ew, ew. They run away from you, holding their noses, and tell their friends you had to wear a diaper because you kept stinking up your pants. Back in the classroom, before the teacher gets back, they push their desks into a tight little knot on the other side of the room. Finally you understand the vocabulary word *ostracize.* Look away from them. Stare at the blackboard. Swallow. Out of the corner of your eye, glance at Eric Cassio. He will be watching you, not laughing with the others. Patricia will lean over and whisper in his ear, and he will answer her. But he will not—not once—laugh at your expense.

When the teacher comes in and asks what on earth is going on, everyone will start moving the desks back without a word. Soon you will all get lost in the angles and word shelves of a sentence diagram. After that, Math. Then the bus ride home. Now you can spend all evening sulking in the alcove of your bedroom. When your parents come to tell you it's time for dinner, you will tell them you have a headache. You will cry and ask for orange children's aspirin. Half an hour later your little brother will come to you with a plate of food, and he will sit there, serious-eyed, as you eat it.

Later that night you will hear your parents in their bedroom, talking about sending you to a different school. Your father is the champion of this idea. When your mother argues that things might be getting better for you, you will secretly take her side. You tell yourself that leaving the school would mean giving up, letting the others win. You will not have that. You will not go to the schools your father suggests: Newman, your rival, or Lakeside, a religious day school. You will get angry at him for mentioning it. Doesn't he believe you can prove yourself to them, get friends, even become popular?

You blind, proud, stupid, poor dunce.

Next day, you will take the dress to school. Why, for God's sake? Why? Won't they see it at the Miggie's Ball anyway? But you insist on proving to them that it's real, despite the obvious danger. You will carry it in the Maison Blanche bag to show you really bought it there. When it's time for morning recess, you will casually take the bag out of your locker as if you have to move it to put some books away. Patricia and Cara will stop at your locker on their way out. You will pretend not to see them. Notice, however, that Eric Cassio is standing in the doorway waiting for them.

—Look, she b-brought a bag of baby d-d-d-d—

—You're stinking up the whole place, Cara says.

You pick up the bag so that the tissue inside crinkles, then steal a glance inside and smile to yourself.

—Is that your K-mart dress for the Miggie's Ball?

—Can I b-borrow it? Patricia takes the bag from you and holds it open. You feel a flash of fear, seeing it in her hands. Look at Eric Cassio. He is staring at his shoes. Patricia takes out the tissue-wrapped dress and tears the gold sticker you have kept carefully intact. As she shakes it out and holds it against herself, she and Cara laugh.

—Look at me. I'm Cinderella. I'm Cher.

Tell her to give it back.

—Oh, sure. C-come and g-get it. Patricia lofts the dress over your head in a blur of blue; Cara catches it.

—Don't you want it, stinky baby? Cara shakes it in your face, then throws it over your head again to Patricia.

Patricia holds the dress over your head. She is three inches taller than you. You jump and catch the hem in one hand and hold on tight. When Patricia pulls, you pull too. Finally she gives a sharp yank. There is a terrible sound, the sound of satin shearing, detaching itself from velvet. Patricia stumbles back with half your dress in her hands. Her mouth hangs open in a perfect O. Outside, kids shriek and laugh at recess. A kickball smacks against the classroom wall.

Cara will be the first to recover. She will take the half-dress from Patricia and shrug. Oh, well, she says. It was just an ugly dress.

—Yeah, Patricia says, her voice flat and dry. And a stupid b-brand.

Cara will throw the piece of dress at you. Let it fall at your feet. Suppress the wail of rage inside your rib cage. Do not look at Eric Cassio. Do not move or speak. Wait for them to leave. When the classroom door closes behind them, sit on the floor and stuff the rags of your dress back into the paper bag. Stare at the floor tile, black grains swirling into white. See if you can make it through the next five minutes. The next ten. Eventually, you'll hear the class coming back from recess. Get to your feet and dust off your legs. Sit down at your desk and hold the bag in your lap.

You will remember a story you heard on the news, about a brother and sister in Burma who got caught in a flood. As they watched from a rooftop, the flood stripped their house of its walls, drowned their parents against a bamboo fence, and washed their goats and chickens down the road. Their house is gone. Their family is gone. But they hold on to a piece of wood and kick toward dry land. Think how they must have felt that night, kicking into the flood, the houses all around them in splinters, people and animals dead.

On Saturday, wear something good: a pair of white shorts and a red halter and sandals. Put your hair in a barrette. Try not to think about the dress in its bag at the bottom of your closet. That does not concern you. Go downstairs and get something to eat. You will not erase yourself by forgoing meals. After breakfast, when your mother asks if you'd like to make cookies, say yes. Look how much this pleases her. You have not felt like doing anything in weeks. Take out the measuring cups and bowls and all the ingredients. Mix the dough. Allow your brother to add the chocolate chips.

Put the cookies in the oven. Check them at three minutes, and at five. Your brother claps his hands and asks again and again if they are ready yet. When they are ready, open the oven door. A wash of sugary heat will hit your face. Pull on the mitts and take out the cookie sheet. Just then, the doorbell will ring.

Listen as your mother gets the door. You will hear her talking to someone outside, low. Then she'll come into the kitchen.

—There's a boy here for you, she says, twisting her hands in her apron. He wants to ride bikes.

—Who?

—I don't know. He's blond.

Do not drop the tray of cookies on the kitchen tile. Do not allow your head to float away from your body. The familiar tightness will gather in your throat. At first you will think it is another joke, that when you go to the door he will not be there.

But then there he is, in the doorway of the kitchen. It is the first time in years someone else your age has stood inside your house. And this is Eric Cassio, in his blue-striped oxford shirt and khaki shorts, his hair wild from the wind. Watch him stare at your brother, who's gotten a handful of cookie dough. Try talking. Offer him some cookies and milk. Your mother will take your brother, silently, out into the yard, and in a few moments you will hear him shrieking as he leaps through the sprinkler.

Now eat a cookie and drink milk with Eric Cassio. Do not let crumbs cling to your red halter. Wipe the line of milk from your upper lip. Watch Eric eat one cookie, then another. When he's finished he will take a rumpled white package from his backpack and push it across the table. You will be extremely skeptical. You will look at the package as if it were a bomb.

—I told my mom what happened at school, he says. She got you this.

Turn the package over. It is a clothing bag. When you open it you will find a dress inside, a different one, dark red with a jewel neckline and two small rosettes at the hip.

—I know it's not the same as the other one, he says.

Look at him, hard, to make sure this is not a joke. His eyes are steady and clear. Stand up and hold the dress up against you. You can see it is just the right size. Bite your lip. Look at Eric Cassio, speechless. Try to smile instead; he will understand.

—Patricia won the Miggie's thing, he says. She told me last night.

For a moment, you will feel bludgeoned. You thought it would be you. You and Eric Cassio. It was supposed to make all the difference. Patricia couldn't possibly have more stars than you. Then remember there's another important thing to ask him.

—Who's the boy?

He looks down into his lap, and you understand that the boy is him. When he raises his eyes, his expression tells you that despite the dress, despite the hybrid peas, things are not going to change at school or at Miss Miggie's. He will not take walks with you at recess or sit next to you at McDonald's. You can see he is apologizing for this, and you can choose to accept or not.

Get to your feet and pull yourself up straight; raise your chin as your mother has shown you to do. Adjust the straps of your sandals, and make sure your halter is tied tight. Then ride bikes with Eric Cassio until dark.

The Smoothest Way
Is Full of Stones

We aren't supposed to be swimming at all. It is Friday afternoon, and we're supposed to be bringing groceries home to Esty's mother so she can prepare Shabbos dinner. But it's the middle of July, and heat radiates from every leaf and blade of grass along the lake road, from the tar-papered sides of the lake cottages, from the dust that hangs in the air like sheer curtains. We throw our bikes into the shade behind the Perelmans' shed, take off our socks and shoes, and run through warm grass down to their slip of private beach, trespassing, unafraid of getting caught, because old Mr. and Mrs. Perelman won't arrive at their cottage until August, according to my cousin. Esty and I stand at the edge of the lake in our long skirts and long-sleeved shirts, and when the water surrounds our ankles it is sweetly cold.

Esty turns to me, grinning, and hikes her skirt. We walk into the water until our knees are submerged. The bottom is silty beneath our toes, slippery like clay, and tiny fish flash around our legs like sparks. We are forbidden to swim because it is immodest to show our bodies, but as far as I know there's no law against wading fully clothed. My cousin lets the hem of her skirt fall into the water and walks in all the way up to her waist, and I follow her, glad to feel water against my skin.

This is the kind of thing we used to do when we were little—the secret sneaking-off into the woods, the accidental wrecking of our clothes, things we were punished for later. That was when Esty was still called Erica, before her parents got divorced, before she and her mother moved to Israel for a year and became Orthodox.

Now there is a new uncle, Uncle Shimon, and five little step-cousins. My Aunt Marla became Aunt Malka, and Erica became Esther. Erica used to talk back to her mother and throw bits of paper at the backs of old ladies' necks in synagogue, but in Israel she spent months repenting her old life and taking on a new one. This summer we've done nothing but pray, study Torah, cook, clean the lake cottage, and help Aunt Malka take care of the children. As we walk into the lake, I wonder if Erica still exists inside this new pious cousin.

I follow her deeper into the water, and the bottom falls away beneath us. It's hard to swim, heavy and slow, and at times it feels almost like drowning. Our denim skirts make it impossible to kick. Ahead is the Perelmans' old lake float, a raft of splintering boards suspended on orange plastic drums, and we pull hard all the way to the raft and hold on to the ladder.

"We're going to be killed when your mom sees our clothes," I say, out of breath.

"No, we won't," Esty says, pushing wet hair out of her face. "We'll make up an excuse. We'll say we fell in."

"Yeah, right," I say. "Accidentally."

Far down below, at the bottom of the lake, boulders waver in the blue light. It's exciting to think we've come this far in skirts. The slow-moving shadows of fish pass beneath us, and the sun is hot and brilliant-white. We climb onto the raft and lie down on the splintering planks and let the sun dry our clothes. It is good just to lie there staring at the cottage with its sad vacant windows, no one inside to tell us what to do. In a few more weeks I will go home to Manhattan, back to a life in which my days are counted according to the American calendar and prayer is something we do once a year, on the High Holidays, when we visit my grandparents in Chicago.

Back in that other world, three hundred miles from here, my mother lies in a hospital bed still recovering from the birth and death of my brother. His name was Devon Michael. His birth weight was one pound, ten ounces. My mother had a problem with high blood pressure, and they had to deliver him three months early, by C-section. It has been six weeks since Devon Michael lived and died, but my mother is still in the hospital, fighting infection and depression. With my father working full-time and me out of school, my parents decided it would be better for me to go to the Adelsteins' until my mother was out of the hospital. I didn't agree, but it seemed like a bad time to argue.

My cousin says that when I go home I should encourage my parents to keep kosher, that we should always say b'rachot before and after eating, that my mother and I should wear long skirts and long-sleeved shirts every day. She says all this will help my mother recover, the way it helped her mother recover from the divorce. I try to tell her how long it's been since we've even done the normal things, like go to the movies or make a big Chinese dinner in the wok. But Esty just watches me with a distant enlightened look in her eyes and says we have to try to do what God wants. I have been here a month, and still I haven't told her any of the bad things I've done this year—sneaked cigarettes from my friends' mothers' packs, stole naked-lady playing cards from a street vendor near Port Authority, kissed a boy from swim team behind the bleachers after a meet. I had planned to tell her all these things, thinking she'd be impressed, but soon I understood that she wouldn't.

Now Esty sits up beside me on the raft and looks toward shore. As she stares at the road beyond the Perelmans' yard, her back tenses and her eyes narrow with concentration. "Someone's coming," she says. "Look."

I sit up. Through the bushes along the lake road there is a

flash of white, somebody's shirt. Without a word we climb down into the water and swim underneath the raft, between the orange plastic drums. From the lapping shade there we see a teenage boy with copper-colored hair and long curling peyos run from the road to the bushes beside the house. He drops to his knees and crawls through the tangle of vines, moving slowly, glancing back over his shoulder. When he reaches the backyard he stands and brushes dead leaves from his clothes. He is tall and lanky, his long arms smooth and brown. Crouching beside the porch, he opens his backpack and takes out some kind of flat package, which he pushes deep under the porch steps. Then he gets up and runs for the road. From the shadow of the raft we can see the dust rising, and the receding flash of the boy's white shirt.

"That was Dovid Frankel," Esty says.

"How could you tell?"

"My mother bought him that green backpack in Toronto."

"Lots of people have green backpacks," I say.

"I know it was him. You'll see. His family's coming for Shabbos tonight."

She swims toward shore and I follow, my skirt heavy as an animal skin around my legs. When we drag ourselves onto the beach our clothes cling to our bodies and our hair hangs like weeds.

"You look shipwrecked," I tell my cousin.

"So do you," she says, and laughs.

We run across the Perelmans' backyard to the screened-in porch. Kneeling down, we peer into the shadows beneath the porch steps. Planes of light slant through the cracks between the boards, and we can see the paper bag far back in the shadows. Esty reaches in and grabs the bag, then shakes its contents onto the grass. What falls out is a large softcover book called *Essence of Persimmon: Eastern Sexual Secrets for Western Lives*. On the cover is a drawing of an Indian woman draped in gold-and-green silk, reclining on cushions inside a tent. One hand disappears into the shadow between her legs, and in the other she holds a tiny vial of oil. Her breasts are high and round, her eyes tapered like two slender fish. Her lips are parted in a look of ecstasy.

"Eastern sexual secrets," Esty says. "Oh, my God."

I can't speak. I can't stop staring at the woman on the cover.

My cousin opens the book and flips through the pages, some thick with text, others printed with illustrations. Moving closer to me, she reads aloud: "One may begin simply by pressing the flat of the hand against the open yoni, allowing heat and energy to travel into the woman's body through this most intimate space."

"Wow," I say. "The open yoni."

Esty closes the book and stuffs it into the brown paper bag. "This is obviously a sin," she says. "We can't leave it here. Dovid will come back for it."

"So?"

"You're not supposed to let your fellow Jew commit a sin."

"Is it really a sin?"

"A terrible sin," she says. "We have to hide it where no one will find it."

"Where?"

"In our closet at home. The top shelf. No one will ever know."

"But *we'll* know," I say, eyeing her carefully. Hiding a book like this at the top of our own closet is something Erica might have suggested, long ago.

"Of course, but we won't look at it," Esty says sternly, her brown eyes clear and fierce. "It's *tiuv*, abomination. God forbid anyone should ever look at it again."

My cousin retrieves her bike from the shed and stows the book between a bag of lettuce and a carton of yogurt. It looks harmless there, almost wholesome, in its brown paper sack. We get on our bikes and ride for home, and by the time we get there our clothes are almost dry.

Esty carries the book into the house as if it's nothing, just another brown bag among many bags. This is the kind of ingenious technique she perfected back in her Erica days, and it works equally well now. Inside, everyone is too busy with Shabbos preparations to notice anything out of the ordinary. The little step-cousins are setting the table, arranging the Shabbos candles, picking up toys, dusting the bookshelves. Aunt Malka is baking challah. She punches down dough as she talks to us.

"The children need baths," she says. "The table has to be set. The Handelmans and the Frankels are coming at seven, and I'm running late on dinner, as you know. I'm not going to ask what took you so long." She raises her eyes at us, large sharp-blue eyes identical to my mother's, with deep creases at the corners and a fringe of jet-black lash. Unlike my mother she is tall and big-boned. In her former life she was Marla Vincent, a set dresser for the Canadian Opera Company in Toronto. Once I saw her at work, hanging purple velvet curtains at the windows of an Italian palazzo.

"Sorry we took so long," Esty says. "We'll help."

"You'd better," she says. "Shabbos is coming."

I follow my cousin down the hall and into our bedroom. On the whitewashed wall there is a picture of the Lubavitcher Rebbe, Menachem Schneerson, with his long steely beard and his eyes like flecks of black glass. He's on the east wall, the wall my cousin faces when she prays. His eyes seem to follow her as she drags the desk chair into the closet and stows *Essence of Persimmon* on the top shelf.

"What do we say to Dovid Frankel tonight?" I ask her.

"Nothing," she says. "We completely ignore him."

I make one last phone call to my mother before Shabbos. It's always frightening to dial the number of the hospital room because there's no telling what my mother will sound like when she answers. Sometimes she sounds like herself, quick and funny, and I can almost smell her olive-aloe soap. Other times, like today, she sounds just like she sounded when she told me Devon Michael had died.

"I can hardly hear you," she says, her own voice small and faint, somewhere far off down the line. The phone crackles with static.

"We went swimming today," I tell her, trying to speak loud. "It was hot."

Far away, almost too quiet to hear, she sighs.

"It's nearly Shabbos," I say. "Aunt Malka's baking challah."

"Is she?" my mother says.

"How are you feeling?" I ask her. "When can you come home?"

"Soon, honey."

I have a sudden urge to tell her about the book we found, to ask her what we're supposed to do with something like that, to find out if she thinks it's a sin. I want to tell her about Dovid Frankel, how we saw him sneaking along the lake. I tell my mother things like this sometimes, and she seems to understand. But now she says to send her love to Aunt Malka and Uncle Shimon and Esty and all the step-cousins, and before I have a chance to really feel like her daughter again, we're already saying goodbye.

At six-thirty, the women and girls arrive. They bring steaming trays of potato kugel and berry cobbler, bottles of grape juice and sweet wine. The men are at shul, welcoming the Shabbos as if she were a bride, with the words *bo'i kallah.* Here the women do not go to synagogue on Fridays. Instead we arrange the platters of food and remove bread from the oven and fill cups with grape juice and wine. We are still working when the men and boys arrive, tromping through the kitchen and kissing their wives and daughters *good Shabbos.*

My cousin, her hands full of raspberries, nudges me and nods toward a tall boy with penny-brown hair, and I know him to be Dovid Frankel, the boy from the lake, owner of *Essence of Persimmon.* I watch him as he kisses his mother and hoists his little sister onto his hip. He is tall and tanned, with small round glasses and a slender oval face. His mouth is almost girlish, bow-shaped and flushed, and his hair is close-cropped, with the exception of his luxuriously curled, shoulder-length peyos. He wears a collarless blue shirt in a fabric that looks homemade. I don't realize I'm staring at him until Esty nudges me again.

Everyone gathers around the dinner table, which we've set up on the screen porch. The men begin singing "Shalom Aleichem," swaying with the rise and fall of the melody. I feel safe, gathered in, with the song covering us like a prayer shawl and the Shabbos candles flickering on the sideboard. I pray for my mother and father. Dovid Frankel stands across from me, rocking his little sister as he sings.

Uncle Shimon, in his loose white Israeli shirt and embroidered yarmulke, stands at the head of the table. His beard is streaked with silver, and his eyes burn with a quick blue fire. As he looks around the table at his friends, his children, his new wife, I can tell he believes himself to be a lucky man. I think about my previous uncle, Walter, who has moved to Hawaii to do his astronomy research at a giant telescope there. Once he brought the family to visit us at Christmastime, and in his honor my mother set up a tiny plastic tree on our coffee table. That night we were allowed to eat candy canes and hang stockings at the fireplace, and in the morning there were silver bracelets for Esty and me, with our names engraved. Esty's bracelet said *Erica,* of course. I wonder if she still has it. I still have mine, though it is too small for me now.

Beside me, Esty looks down at her plate and fingers the satin trim at the waist of her Shabbos skirt. I catch her looking at Dovid Frankel, too, who seems oblivious to us both. From the bedroom, *Essence of Persimmon* exerts a magnetic pull I can feel in my chest. I watch Esty as we serve the soup and the gefilte fish, as we lean over Dovid Frankel's shoulder to replace his fork or remove his plates. My cousin's cheeks are flushed and her eyes keep moving toward Dovid, though sometimes they stray toward pregnant Mrs. Handelman, her belly swollen beneath the white cotton of her dress. Mrs. Handelman is Dovid Frankel's oldest sister. Her young husband, Lev, has a short blond beard and a nervous laugh. During the fish course, he tells the story of a set of false contractions that sent him and Mrs. Handelman running for the car. Mrs. Handelman, Esty whispers to me, is eighteen years old. Last year they went to school together.

We eat our chicken and kugel, and then we serve the raspberry cobbler for dessert. The little step-cousins run screaming around the table and crawl underneath. There is something wild and wonderful about the disorder of it all, a feeling so different from the quiet rhythms of our dinner table at home, with my mother asking me about my day at school and my father offering more milk or peas. Here, when everyone has finished eating, we sing the Birkat Hamazon. By now I know all the Hebrew words. It's strange to think that when I go home we will all just get up at the end of the meal and put our plates in the sink, without singing anything or thanking anyone.

When the prayer is over, my uncle begins to tell a story about the Belkins, a Jewish family some thirty miles up the lake whose house burned down in June. "Everything destroyed," he says. "Books, clothes, the children's toys, everything. No one was hurt, thank God. They were all visiting the wife's brother when it happened. An electrical short in the attic. So when they go back to see if anything can be salvaged, the only thing not completely burnt up is the mezuzah. The door frame? Completely burnt. But the mezuzah, fine. A little black, but fine. And so they send it to New York to have the paper checked, and you'll never believe what they find."

All the men and women and children look at my uncle,

their mouths open. They blink silently in the porch light as if my uncle were about to perform some holy miracle.

"There's an imperfection in the text," my uncle says. "In the word *asher*. The letters aleph-shin are smudged, misshapen."

Young Mr. Handelman looks stricken. "Aleph-shin," he says. "Aish."

"That's right. And who knows what that means?" Uncle Shimon looks at each of the children, but the children just sit staring, waiting for him to tell them.

"I know," Dovid Frankel says. "It means fire."

"That's right," says Uncle Shimon. "Fire."

Around the table there is a murmur of amazement, but Dovid Frankel crosses his arms over his chest and raises an eyebrow at my uncle. "Aish," he says. "That's supposed to be what made their house burn down?"

My uncle sits back in his chair, stroking his beard. "A man has to make sure his mezuzah is kosher," he says. "That's his responsibility. Who knows how the letters got smudged? Was it the scribe, just being lazy? Was it his assistant, touching the text as he moved it from one worktable to another? Maybe a drop of water fell from a cup of tea the scribe's wife was bringing to her husband. Should we blame her?"

"For God's sake, don't blame the wife," my aunt says, and all the women laugh.

"I like to have our mezuzot checked every year," says my uncle. He leans back in his chair and looks at Dovid, crossing his fingers over his belly. "We alone are responsible for our relationship with Hashem. That's what Rebbe Nachman of Breslov taught us in the eighteenth century."

"We should have our mezuzah checked," Mr. Handelman says, squeezing his wife's hand. He looks with worry at her swollen belly.

"I made a mezuzah at school," says one of the little step-cousins, a red-haired boy.

"You did not," his older brother says. "You made a mezuzah *cover*."

Esty and I get up to clear the dessert plates, and Dovid Frankel pushes his chair away from the table and stands. As we gather the plates, he opens the screen door and steps out into the night. My cousin shoots me a significant look, as if this proves that he has sinned against Hashem and is feeling the guilt. I take a stack of dessert plates into the kitchen, trying to catch a glimpse of Dovid through the window. But it is dark outside, and all I can see is the reflection of the kitchen, with its stacks and stacks of plates that we will have to wash. When the men's voices rise again, I go to the front of the house and step outside. The night is all around me, dew-wet and smelling like milkweed and pine needles and lake wind, and the air vibrates with cicadas. The tall grass wets my ankles as I walk toward the backyard. Dovid is kicking at the clothesline frame, his sneaker making a dull hollow *clong* against the metal post. He looks up at me and says, "Hello, Esty's cousin," and then continues kicking.

"What are you doing?" I ask him.

"Thinking," he says, kicking the post.

"Thinking what?"

"Does a smudged mezuzah make a family's house burn down?"

"What do you think?"

He doesn't answer. Instead he picks up a white stone from the ground and hurls it into the dark. We hear it fall into the grass, out of sight.

"Don't you believe in Hashem?" I ask him.

He squints at me. "Do *you*?"

"I don't know," I say. I stand silent in the dark, thinking about the one time I saw my brother before he died. He was lying in an incubator with tubes coming out of every part of his body, monitors tracing his breathing and heartbeat. His skin was transparent, his eyes closed, and all I could think was that he looked like a tiny skinny frog. Scrubbed, sterilized, gloved, I was allowed to reach in through a portal and touch his feverish skin. I felt terrible for him. *Get better, grow, kick,* I said to him silently. It was difficult to leave, knowing I might not see him again. But in the cab that night, on the way home with my father, I was imagining what might happen if he did live. The doctors had told us he could be sick forever, that he'd require constant care. I could already imagine my parents taking care of him every day, changing his tubes and diapers, measuring his tiny pulse, utterly forgetting about me. Just once, just for that instant, I wished he would die. If there is a God who can see inside mezuzahs, a God who burns people's houses for two smudged letters, then he must know that secret too. "Sometimes I hope there's not a God," I say. "I'm in a lot of trouble if there is."

"What trouble?" Dovid says.

"Bad trouble. I can't talk about it."

"Some people around here are scared of you," Dovid says. "Some of the mothers. They think you're going to show their kids a fashion magazine or give them an unkosher cookie or tell them something they shouldn't hear."

I have never considered this. I've only imagined the influence rolling from them to me, making me more Jewish, making me try to do what the Torah teaches. "I didn't bring any magazines," I tell him. "I've been keeping kosher all summer. I've been wearing these long-sleeved clothes. I can hardly remember what I'm like in my normal life."

"It was the same with your cousin," he says. "When she and your aunt first came here, people didn't trust them."

"I can't believe anyone wouldn't trust them," I say. "Or be scared of me."

"I'm not scared of you," he says, and reaches out and touches my arm, his hand cool and dry against my skin. I know he is not supposed to touch any woman who is not his mother or his sister. I can smell raspberries and brown sugar on his breath. I don't want to move or speak or do anything that will make him take his hand from my arm, though I know it is wrong for us to be touching and though I know he wouldn't be touching me if I were an Orthodox girl. From the house comes the sound of men laughing. Dovid Frankel steps closer, and I can feel the warmth of his chest through his shirt. For a moment I think he will kiss me. Then we hear a screen door bang, and he moves away from me and walks back toward the house.

That night, my cousin won't talk to me. She knows I was outside with Dovid Frankel, and this makes her furious. In silence we get into our nightgowns and brush our teeth and climb into bed, and I can hear her wide-awake breathing, uneven and sharp. I lie there thinking about Dovid Frankel, the way his hand felt on my arm, the knowledge that he was doing something against the rules. It gives me a strange rolling feeling in my stomach. For the first time I wonder if I've started to *want* to become the girl I've been pretending to be, whose prayers I've been saying, whose dietary laws I've been observing. A time or two, on Shabbos, I know I've felt a kind of holy swelling in my chest, a connection to something larger than myself. I wonder if this is proof of something, if this is God marking me somehow.

In the middle of the night, I wake to find Esty gone from her bed. The closet door is closed, and from beneath the door comes a thin line of light, the light we leave on throughout Shabbos. From inside I can hear a shuffling and then a soft thump. I get out of bed and go to the closet door. "Esty," I whisper. "Are you in there?"

"Go away," my cousin whispers back.

"Open up," I say.

"No."

"Do it now, or I'll make a noise."

She opens the closet door just a crack. I slide in. The book is in her hand, open to a Japanese print of a man and woman embracing. The woman's head is thrown back, her mouth open to reveal a sliver of tongue. The man holds her tiny bird-like hands in his own. Rising up from between his legs and entering her body is a plum-colored column of flesh.

"Gross," I say.

My cousin closes the book.

"I thought you said we were never going to look at it again," I say.

"We were going to ignore Dovid Frankel, too."

"So what?"

My cousin's eyes fill, and I understand: She is in love with Dovid Frankel. Things begin to make sense—our bringing the book home, her significant looks all evening, her anger. "Esty," I say. "It's okay. Nothing happened. We just talked."

"He was looking at you during dinner," she cries.

"He doesn't like me," I say. "We talked about you."

"About me?" She wipes her eyes with her nightgown sleeve.

"That's right."

"What did he say?"

"He wanted to know if you'd ever mentioned him to me," I lie.

"And?"

"I said you told me you went to school with his sister."

My cousin sighs. "Okay," she says. "Safe answer."

"Okay," I say. "Now you have to tell me what you're doing, looking at that book."

My cousin glances down and her eyes widen, as if she's surprised to find she's been holding the book all this time. "I don't know what I'm doing," she says. "The book was here. I couldn't sleep. Finally I just got up and started looking at it."

"It's a sin," I say. "That's what you told me before."

"I know."

"So let's go to bed, okay?"

"Okay," she says.

We stand there looking at each other. Neither of us makes a move to go to bed.

"Maybe we could just look at it for a little while," I say.

"A few minutes couldn't hurt," my cousin says.

This decides it. We sit down on the wooden planking of the closet floor, and my cousin opens the book to the first chapter. We learn that we are too busy with work, domestic tasks, and social activity to remember that we must take the time to respect and enjoy our physical selves and our partners' physical selves, to reap the benefits that come from regular, loving, sexual fulfillment. The book seems not to care whether "the East" means Japan, China, or India; the drawings show all kinds of Eastern people in sexual positions whose names sound like poetry: "Bamboo Flute," "The Galloping Horse," "Silkworms Spinning a Cocoon." My cousin's forehead is creased in concentration as she reads, her eyebrows nearly meeting.

"What's the orgasm?" my cousin says. "They keep talking about the orgasm."

"I don't know," I say. "Check the index."

She flips to the index, and under *orgasm* there is a long list of page numbers. We choose one at random, page 83. My cousin reads in a whisper about how to touch oneself in order to achieve the word in question. We learn that one can use one's own fingers or any object whose shape and texture one finds pleasing, though the use of electronic vibrating devices is not recommended. These can cause desensitization, the book tells us. But certain Eastern devices, such as *ben wa* balls or the String of Pearls, can greatly enhance a woman's pleasure.

"Sick," my cousin says.

"I still don't get it," I say.

"What do you think they mean by the *clitoris*?"

Though I have a vague idea, I find myself at a loss for words. My cousin looks it up in the index, and when she learns what it is she is amazed. "I thought that was where you peed from," she breathes. "How weird."

"It's weird, all right," I say.

Then she says, "I can't believe Dovid Frankel has read all this. His hands probably touched this page." She lets the book fall into her lap. It opens to a glossy drawing of a woman suspended in a swinglike contraption from the roof of a pavilion, high above a turbaned man who gazes up at her with desire and love. Two servants in long robes hold the cords that keep the woman suspended.

"Oh, my God," my cousin says, and closes the book. "We have to repent tomorrow, when we say Shacharit in the morning. There's a place where you can tell God what you did wrong."

"We'll repent," I say.

We stow the book on its high shelf and leave the closet. Our room is cold, the light coming in from outside a ghostly blue. We climb into our twin beds and say the Shema and the V'ahavta. The V'ahavta is the same prayer that's written in the text of a mezuzah, and when I say the word *asher* a sizzle of terror runs through me. Has God seen what we have just done? Are we being judged even now, as we lie in bed in the dark? I am awake for a long time, watching the cool air move the curtains, listening to the rushing of the grasses outside, the whir of the night insects. After some time I hear a change in the rhythm of breathing from my cousin's bed, and a faint rustle beneath the sheet. I pretend to be asleep, listening to the metallic tick of her bedsprings. It seems to go on for hours, connected with the sound of insects outside, the shush of grass, the wind.

The next morning I am the first to wake. I say the Shema and wash my hands in the basin we leave on the nightstand, cleansing myself as I open my eyes to this Shabbos morning. My cousin sleeps nearly sideways, her long legs hanging off the bed, covers pushed back, nightgown around her thighs. Though her limbs have not seen the sun all summer, her skin is a deep olive. There is a bruise on her knee the size of an egg, newly purple, which I know she must have gotten as we climbed the metal ladder onto the Perelmans' float.

In sleep her face is slack and flushed, her lips parted. It has never occurred to me that my cousin may be beautiful the way a woman is beautiful. With her cropped brown hair and full cheeks, she has always looked to me like a tall, sturdy child. But this morning, as she sleeps, there is a womanliness to her body that makes me feel young and unripe. I dress quietly so as not to wake her, and tiptoe out to the kitchen to find my uncle standing on the screen porch, beside the table, folding his tallis into its velvet bag so he can go to shul for morning services. Sunlight falls in through the screen and covers him with its gold dust. He is facing Jerusalem, the city where he and Aunt Malka found each other. I open the screen door and step out onto the porch.

"Rebecca," he says. "Good morning, good Shabbos." He smiles, smoothing his beard between both hands.

"Good Shabbos," I say.

"I'll be at Torah study this afternoon. After lunch."

"Okay."

"You look tired," he says. "Did you sleep?"

"I slept okay."

For a moment we stand looking at each other, my uncle still smiling. Before I can stop myself, I'm asking the question that pushes its way to the front of my mind. "After a person dies," I say, "is the family supposed to have the mezuzah checked?"

My uncle's hands fall from his beard. He regards me sadly, his eyes deep and grave. "When my first wife, Bluma Sarah, died," he says, "I had everything checked. Our mezuzah, my tefillin, our ketubah. The rebbe found nothing. Finally I asked him to examine my soul, thinking I was the bearer of some imperfection. Do you know what the rebbe told me?"

"No," I say, looking at my feet, wishing I hadn't asked.

"He told me, 'Sometimes bad things just happen. You'll see why later. Or you won't. Do we always know why Hashem does what he does? *Neyn*.'"

"Oh."

"I think God wanted me to meet your aunt," says Uncle Shimon. "Maybe He wanted me to meet you, too." He tucks his tallis bag under his arm and buttons his jacket. "Bluma Sarah had a saying: *Der gleichster veg iz ful mit shtainer.*"

"What's it mean?"

"The smoothest way is sometimes full of stones," he says.

All day I keep the Shabbos. This means I do not turn on a light or tear paper or write or bathe or cook or sew or do any of the thirty-nine kinds of work involved in building the Holy Temple. It is difficult to remember all the things one cannot do; as I sit in the tall grass, playing a clumsy round of duck-duck-goose with the little step-cousins, I am tempted to pull a grass blade and split it down its fibrous center, or weave a clover chain for one of the girls. But the Shabbos is all around us, in the quiet along the road and the sound of families in their yards, and I remember and remember all day. My cousin spends most of the day alone. I see her praying in a sunlit patch of yard, swaying back and forth as she reads from her tiny Siddur; then she lies in the grass and studies Torah. When she disappears into the house I follow her. She's closed herself into our closet again, the door wedged tight against intruders. I imagine her undoing this morning's work of repentance, learning new body-part names, new positions. When I whisper through the door for her to come out, she tells me to go away.

All day I'm not allowed to use the telephone to call my mother. I walk around and around the yard, waiting for the sun to dip toward the horizon. Aunt Malka watches me from the porch, looking worried, and then she calls me over.

"What's all this pacing?" she says.

"I'm keeping Shabbos," I say.

"You can keep it right here with me," she says, patting the step beside her.

I sit down. Before us the older children are trying to teach the younger ones how to do cartwheels. They fly in awkward arcs through the long grass.

"Your mother sounds much better," she says. "You'll be going home soon."

"Probably," I say.

"There's a lady I know who lives near you," she says. "I'll give you her number. She and some other women run a mikveh near your house, on Twenty-second and Third."

"What's a mikveh?"

"It's the ritual bath," she says. "It cleans us spiritually. All women go. Men, too. Your mother should go when she gets out of the hospital. You can go with her, just to watch. It's lovely. You'll see." One of the little boys runs up and tosses a smooth black pebble into Aunt Malka's lap, then runs away, laughing. "We're commanded to go after childbirth," she says.

"Commanded by who?"

"By Hashem," she says, turning the pebble in her fingers. Through its center runs a translucent white ribbon of quartz.

"Even if the baby dies?" I ask her. "Do you have to go then?"

"Yes," she says. "Especially then. It's very important and beautiful. The bath is very clean, and this particular one is tiled all in pink. The women will help your mother undress and brush her hair, so the water will touch every part of her. Then she'll step down into the bath—it's very deep and large, like a Jacuzzi—until she's completely covered. They'll tell her what b'rachot to say. Then she'll be clean."

"Everyone's supposed to do this?" I ask her.

"We're commanded to," she says. "Adults, anyway. For women, it's every month unless we're pregnant. When I'm here I do it right in the lake. There's a woman who had a special shed built on her property, and that's where we go in."

"What if my mother doesn't want to go?" I ask.

"If you tell her how important it is, I'm sure she'll go," she says, and hands me the black pebble. I rub it with my thumb, tracing the quartz.

My aunt gathers the little step-cousins for a walk down the lake road, smoothing their hair, retrieving their lost shoes, securing their *kippot* with metal clips. I imagine her walking into the lake, her dark curls spreading out behind her, and my skin prickles cold in the heat. When she invites me to come along on the walk, I tell her I will stay home. I lie down in the grass and watch her start off down the road, the little step-cousins circling her like honeybees.

Real bees weave above me through the grass, their bodies so velvety I want to touch them. For what feels like the first time all summer, I am alone. I rub the pebble with my thumb, imagining it to be a magic stone that will make me smaller and smaller in the tall grass. I shrink to the size of a garter snake, a leaf, a speck of dust, until I am almost invisible. There is a presence gathering around me, an iridescent light I can see through my laced eyelashes. I lie still against the earth, faint with dread, and I feel the planet spinning through space, its dizzying momentum, its unstoppable speed. It is God who makes the shadows dissolve around me. He sharpens the scent of clover. He pushes the bees past my ears, directs the sun onto my back until my skin burns through the cotton of my Shabbos dress. I want to know what He wants and do what He wants, and I let my mind fall blank, waiting to be told.

When three stars come into the sky, the family gathers for Havdalah. We stand in a circle on the grass outside, all nine of us, and we light the braided candle and sing to God, thanking Him for creating fire, *aish*. According to the tradition, we examine our fingernails in the light of that candle, to remind us of the ways God causes us to grow. Then we smell spices and drink wine for a sweet week, and finally we sing the song about Eliyahu Hanavi, the prophet who will arrive someday soon to bring the Messiah. I stand with one arm around a little step-cousin and the other around Esty. As

Havdalah ends she drifts off toward the house, one hand trailing through the long grass.

Now that Shabbos is over, the first thing I do is call my mother. Standing in the kitchen, I watch my aunt and uncle carrying children toward the house as I dial. For the first time it occurs to me that it might be awful for my mother always to hear children in the background when I call her, and I wonder if I should wait until they go to bed. But by that time the phone's ringing, and it's my father who answers anyway.

"Hey, son," he says. It's an old game between us; he calls me *son* and I call him *Pa,* like in the Old West. This is the first time we've done it since Devon Michael was born, though, and it sounds different now.

"Hi, Pa," I say, playing the game even so, because I miss him.

"Still out on the range?"

"Indeedy."

"How's the grub?"

"Grub's not bad," I say. "How's Ma?"

He sighs. "Sleeping."

"Not good?" I say.

"I think she needs you home," he says. "She's not feeling well enough now to do much, but I'll bet if she saw her kid she'd shape up pretty fast."

"When can I come home?"

"It looks like a couple of weeks," he says. "She's had some problems. Nothing serious, but the doctor thinks she might need IV antibiotics for a little while still."

"Aunt Malka says she should go to a ritual bath," I say. "To get spiritually clean."

There's a silence on my father's end, and I wonder if I've said something wrong. In the background I hear a woman's voice on the intercom but I can't make out what she's saying. "You there, Dad?" I say.

"I'd like to talk to your aunt," he says. "If she's around."

Something about his tone gives me pause. Even though

Aunt Malka's just a few steps away, talking quietly out on the screen porch with Uncle Shimon, I tell my father she's gone out for milk. Silently I promise myself to repent this lie tomorrow, during Shacharit.

I can hear my father scratching his head, sharp and quick, the way he sometimes does. "You have her give me a call," he says. "All right?"

"All right," I say. "Tell Mom I love her."

He says he will.

That evening, my cousin disappears during dinner. We're all eating tomatoes and cottage cheese and thick slices of rye bread with whipped butter, the kind of meal we always eat after Shabbos, and in the middle of spreading my third slice of bread I look over and Esty's gone.

"Where's your cousin?" Aunt Malka says. "She didn't touch her food."

"I'll find her," I say. I go to our room and open the closet door, but the closet is empty. The book is gone from its high shelf. I glance around the room, and it takes me a few moments to see my cousin's huddled shape beneath her bedclothes.

"Esty," I say. "What are you doing?"

She lifts her head and looks at me, her cheeks flushed. In her hand she holds a flashlight. "Reading," she whispers.

"You can't just leave dinner," I say.

"I wanted to look something up."

"Your mom wants to know what's wrong."

"Tell her I have a headache," Esty says. "Say I took some aspirin and I'm lying down."

"You want me to lie?"

She nods.

"It's against the Ten Commandments."

Esty rolls her eyes. "Like you've never lied," she says.

"Maybe I don't anymore."

"Tonight you do," she says, and pulls the bedclothes over her head, rolling toward the wall. I go out to the dinner table and sit down, pushing at my slice of rye with a tomato wedge.

"Nu?" my aunt says. "What's the story?"

"She's reading," I say.

"In the middle of dinner?"

"It's all right," Uncle Shimon says. "Let her read. I wish some of these would read." He casts a hand over the heads of his own children.

"I read," says one of the little girls. "I can read the whole aleph-bet."

"That's right," her father says, and gives her another slice of bread.

I finish my dinner, and then it's left to me to do all the dishes while Aunt Malka bathes the step-cousins and gets them ready for bed. I stand there washing and looking out into the dark yard, seeing nothing, angry at my cousin and worried about her. I worry about my mother, too, lying in the hospital with intravenous antibiotics dripping into her arm, spiritually unclean. I've always assumed that my brother's death was somehow meant to punish *me,* since I was the one who imagined it in the first place, but now I wonder if we are all guilty. After all, we've been walking around doing exactly what we want, day in and day out, as if what God wants doesn't matter at all, as if God were as small and insignificant as the knickknacks on my grandmother's shelves, the porcelain swans and milkmaids we see when we go to her house for the High Holidays.

A thin strand of fear moves through my chest, and for a moment I feel faint. Then, as I look out the window, I see a white shape moving across the lawn, ghostly in the dark. I stare through the screen as the figure drifts toward the road, and when it hits the yellow streetlight glow I see it's my cousin.

Drying my hands on a dish towel, I run out into the yard. Esty is far away in the dark, but I run after her as fast as I can through the wet grass. When I get to the road she hears me coming and turns around.

"What are you doing?" I say, trying to catch my breath.

"Nothing," she says, but she's keeping one hand behind her back. I grab for the hand but she twists it away from me. I see she's holding a white envelope.

"What is it?" I say. "You're going to the post office in the middle of the night?"

"It's not the middle of the night."

"You snuck out," I say. "You don't have to sneak out just to mail a letter."

"Go inside," Esty says, giving me a little shove toward the house.

"No," I say. "I'm not going anywhere. I'll scream for your mother if you don't tell me what you're doing."

"You would," she says, "wouldn't you?"

I open my mouth as if to do it.

"It's a note to Dovid Frankel," she says. "It says if he wants to get his book back, he has to meet me at the Perelmans' tomorrow night."

"But you can't. It's forbidden."

"So what?" my cousin says. "And if you tell anybody about it, you're dead."

"You can't do anything to me."

"Yes I can," she says. "I can tell my mother this was *your* book, that you brought it from New York and have been trying to get us to read it."

"But she'll know you're lying," I say. "Dovid will tell her it's a lie."

"No he won't."

I know she's right. Dovid would never own up to the book. In the end he would think about how much he has to lose, compared to me. And so I stand there on the road, my throat tightening, feeling again how young I am and how foolish. Esty smooths the letter between her palms and takes a deep breath. "Now turn around," she says, "and go back into that house and pretend I'm in bed. And when I come back, I don't want to see you reading my book."

"*Your* book?" I say.

"Mine for now."

I turn around and stomp back toward the house, but when I get to the screen door I creep in silently. The little cousins are sleeping, after all. There is a line of light beneath my aunt and uncle's door, and I hear my uncle reading in Hebrew to Aunt Malka. I go to our bedroom and change into my nightgown and sit on the bed in the dark, trying to pray. The eyes of the Lubavitcher Rebbe stare down at me from the wall, old and fierce, and all I can think about is my cousin saying *You would, wouldn't you,* her eyes slit with spite. I brush my teeth and get into bed, and then I say the Shema. Saying it alone for the first time, I imagine myself back home in my own bed, whispering to God in the silence of my room, and the thought makes me feel so desolate I roll over and cry. But it isn't long before I hear Esty climbing through the window and then getting ready for bed, and even though I still feel the sting of her threat, even though I know she's ready to betray me, her presence is a comfort in the dark.

I struggle awake the next morning to find that Esty is already out of bed. From the kitchen I can hear the clink of spoons against cereal bowls and the high plaintive voices of the step-cousins. Aunt Malka's voice rises over theirs, announcing that today we will all go blueberry picking. I sigh in relief. Blueberry picking is what I need. I say the Shema and wash my hands in the basin beside the bed.

My cousin is in a fine mood today, her short bangs pulled back in two blue barrettes, a red bandanna at her throat. She sings in the van on the way to the blueberry farm, and all the little cousins sing with her. My aunt looks on with pleasure. At first I'm only pretending to have a good time, but then I find I no longer have to pretend. It feels good to swing a plastic bucket and make my slow way down a row of blueberry shrubs, feeling between the leaves for the sun-hot berries. My cousin acts as if nothing happened between us last night, as if

we had never fought, as if she never went down the road to
Dovid Frankel's house in the dark. When her pail is full she
helps me fill my pail, and we both eat handfuls of blueberries,
staining our shirts and skirts and skin.

Back at home the cousins study Torah with Uncle Shimon,
and Aunt Malka and Esty and I bake blueberry cake. Esty
keeps glancing at the clock, as if she might have to run out
any minute to meet Dovid. When the telephone rings she
gives a jolt, then lunges to pick it up.

"Oh, Uncle Alan," she says. "Hi."

Uncle Alan is my father. I stop stirring the cake batter and
try to get the phone from my cousin, but she's already hand-
ing it to Aunt Malka.

"Hello, Alan," Aunt Malka says. I watch her face for bad
news, but none seems to be forthcoming. "Yes," she says.
"Yes. . . . Yes, we certainly are." Holding the phone between
her cheek and shoulder, she walks out of the kitchen and into
the little girls' bedroom and closes the door behind her.

"What's going on?" Esty says.

"I don't know." I pour the cake batter into the floured pan
Esty has prepared, and we slide it into the oven. Through the
wall I can hear Aunt Malka's voice rising and falling. "I think
it has to do with the mikveh," I say. "I told my dad yesterday
that my mom should go, and he had a strange reaction."

"She does have to go," my cousin says. "You're supposed to
go to the mikveh after you've given birth or had your period.
Your husband can't touch you until you do."

"Your mom already told me about that."

"There are hundreds of rules," she says, sighing. "Things
we're supposed to do and not supposed to do. Maybe you'll
learn about them when you're older."

"What rules?" I say. "I'm old enough."

"I can't just say them here in the kitchen."

"Yes, you can. What are the rules? What are you supposed
to do?"

My cousin bends close to my ear. "You can't do it sitting or standing," she says. "You can't do it outside. You can't do it drunk. You can't do it during the day or with the lights on. You're supposed to think about subjects of Torah while you do it. Things like that."

"You're supposed to think about subjects of Torah?"

Esty shrugs. "That's what they say."

Through the wall we hear Aunt Malka's voice approaching, and my cousin moves away from me and begins wiping flour and sugar from the countertop. Aunt Malka comes out of the bedroom, her face flushed, her brows drawn together. She's already hung up the phone.

"How's my mother?" I ask her.

"Recovering," she says, gathering the cup measures and mixing bowls.

"Am I in trouble?"

"No." She sends hot water rolling into the sink and rubs soap into the dish sponge, then begins scrubbing a bowl. She looks as if she's the one who's been punished, her mouth drawn into a grim line. "You have to do what you think is right, Rebecca," she says, "even when the people around you are doing otherwise."

"Okay," I say.

"It's not a problem right now," she says, "but when you go home it may be."

I glance at Esty. She's looking at her mother intently. "Do you really believe that?" she says. "About doing what you think is right?"

"Absolutely," her mother says. "I've always told you that."

Esty nods, and Aunt Malka continues washing dishes, unaware of what she's just condoned.

At twelve-thirty that night my cousin dresses in a black skirt and shirt and covers her hair with a black scarf.

She wraps *Essence of Persimmon* in its brown paper bag and tucks it under her arm. The house is dark and quiet, everyone asleep.

"Don't do this, Esty," I whisper from my bed. "Stay home."

"If you tell anyone I'm gone, you're dead," she says.

"At least take me along," I say.

"You can't come along."

"Try and stop me."

"You know how I can stop you."

The dread eyes of the Lubavitcher Rebbe stare down at me from the wall. *Protect your cousin,* he seems to say, and though I don't know what I am supposed to protect her from, I climb out of bed and begin dressing.

"What are you doing?" Esty says.

"I'm coming along."

"This has nothing to do with you, Rebecca."

"I was with you when you found the book," I say.

Esty looks down at the brown paper bag in her hands. Her face, framed by the black scarf, is dark and serious. Finally she speaks. "You can come," she says. "But there's one condition."

"What condition?"

"If we get caught, you have to take the blame. You have to take the blame for everything."

"But that's not fair."

"That's the way it is," she says. "You decide."

We sit for a moment in the silence of our room. The curtains rise and fall at the window, beckoning us both into the night. "All right," I say.

"Get dressed, then," my cousin says. "We're already late."

I finish dressing. My cousin slides the bedroom window as far open as it will go, and we crawl out silently into the side yard. We creep through the grass and out to the road, where no cars pass at this time of night. When I look back, the house is pale and small. I imagine Bluma Sarah hovering somewhere above the roof, keeping watch, marking our progress toward the lake.

We walk in the long grass at the side of the road, keeping out of the yellow pools of light that spill from the streetlamps. In the grass there are rustlings, chatterings, sounds that make me pull my skirt around my legs and keep close to my cousin. We do not talk. The moon is bright overhead. The few houses we pass yield no sign of life. Tree frogs call in the dark, the rubber-band twang of their throats sounding to me like *God, God, God.* The road we walk is the same road we traversed on Friday afternoon, our bicycles heavy with Shabbos groceries. I can almost see the ghosts of us passing in the other direction, our faces luminous with the secret of the book, our clothes heavy and damp with lake water. Now we are different girls, it seems to me, carrying a different kind of weight.

By the time we emerge into the Perelmans' backyard, our skirts are wet with dew. Our sneakers squelch as we tiptoe toward the screen porch. We pause in a stand of bushes, listening for Dovid Frankel, hearing nothing.

We wait. The hands on my cousin's watch read twelve fifty-five. The lake lies quiet against the shore like a sleeping animal, and the shadows of bats move across the white arc of the moon. At one o'clock we hear someone coming. We both suck in our breath, grab each other's arms. We see the shadow of Dovid Frankel moving across the dew-silvered lawn. We wait until he comes up, breathing hard, and sits down on the porch steps. Then we come out of the bushes.

Dovid jumps to his feet when he sees us. "Who's that?" he says.

"It's okay," my cousin whispers. "It's just us. Esty and Rebecca."

"Quiet," Dovid says. "Follow me."

We follow him up the steps and enter the moonlit darkness of the screen porch. For a long moment, no one says anything. It is utterly silent. All three of us seem to be holding our breath. Dovid looks at my cousin, then at me. "Where's my book?" he says.

Esty takes the brown paper bag from under her arm. She slides out *Essence of Persimmon.*

Dovid lets out a long sigh. "You didn't tell anyone, did you?"

"Are you kidding?" Esty says.

Dovid reaches for the book, but Esty holds it away from him.

"It's a sin," she says. "Looking at pictures like these. You know you're not supposed to do anything that would make you . . . that would give you . . ."

"That would make you what?" Dovid says.

"I mean, look at these people," she says, stepping into a shaft of moonlight and opening the book. She takes Dovid's flashlight and shines it on a drawing of two lovers intertwined on an open verandah, watching tigers wrestle in the tiled courtyard. She stares at the drawing as if she could will herself into the scene, touch the lovers' garments, their skin, the tiles of the courtyard, the tigers' pelts.

"There are laws," my cousin says. "You can't just do it on a porch, with tigers there. You can't do it in a garden."

"I know," Dovid says.

"I'm serious," Esty says. She moves closer to Dovid. "There are rules for us. We have to be holy. We can't act like animals." She looks up at him, so close their foreheads are almost touching. "We can't have books like this."

"What do you want me to do?" he says. "What am I supposed to do?"

My cousin rises onto her toes, and then she's kissing Dovid Frankel, and he looks startled but he doesn't pull away. The book falls from her hand. Quietly I pick it up, and I open the screen door and step out into the Perelmans' backyard. I walk through the long grass to the edge of the water and take off my shoes and socks. The water is warmer than the air, its surface still. I take one step into the lake, then another. I am all alone. I pull off my long-sleeved shirt and feel the night air on my bare skin. Then I step out of my skirt. I throw my clothes onto the shore, onto the grass. Still holding the book, I walk into the water and feel it on all parts of my body, warm, like a mouth, taking me gently in. When the sandy bottom drops away I float on my back, looking up at the spray of stars, at the dense gauze of the Milky Way. The moon spreads its thin white sheet across my limbs. In my hand the book is heavy with water, and I let it fall away toward the bottom.

Care

Tessa knows how to cross the street with a six-year-old: You take her hand, look both ways, and wait until it's safe. Then you stay within the crosswalk as you cross. She does all these things as she guides Olivia, her niece, across the street toward the cable-car stop. There's a right way to take care of a child, she knows, and a wrong way. Many wrong ways. What you do *not* do: Take the drugs that are in your pocket, the Devvies and Sallies in their silver pillbox. She can make it through the day without them. Even bringing them was wrong—another wrong thing. But it makes her feel better to have them close by.

The heel of Tessa's left shoe is coming loose, so she's been walking on the ball of her foot ever since she left her apartment. She has a blister already. At the stop she sits on a bench and examines the broken shoe. The tips of tiny nails glint in the space between heel and sole. Olivia sits next to her, zipping and unzipping her lavender jacket.

"What's wrong with your shoe?" Olivia asks.

"Nothing," Tessa says, straightening the heel. She stuffs her hands into the pockets of her leather jacket—Kenji's jacket, actually, heavy and worn and smelling of his cigarettes—and feels for the pillbox. There it is in the right-hand pocket, round and familiar, a relief.

"Can I get a souvenir?" Olivia says, eyeing a shop across the street.

"Maybe later. We have to wait for the cable car."

"Can we just look for a second?"

Tessa glances down the street in the direction of the car turnaround. A cable car is just beginning to make the climb up the hill. "We have to stay here."

"I want a T-shirt and a light-up snow dome," Olivia says.

"You'll get what I give you," Tessa says, and Olivia goes silent. She slides down the bench, as far away from Tessa as possible.

Tessa tries to concentrate on the distant clang of the bell. She wills the cable car to hurry up. All her joints feel dry and sore, her mind whitely empty. She bites the inside of her cheek just for the distraction.

The cable car glides uphill through the intersection of Post and Powell and comes to rest at their stop. It's packed with tall boys in green-and-white sweatshirts that read BONN JUNGENCHOR. The boys are belting out a peasant tune in three-part harmony. Tessa and Olivia squeeze onto the side rail and grab the brass pole as the cable car begins to move. All around them the boys sing the lilting chorus with its repeating nonsense line: *O-di-lon tee-lee, o-di-lon tee-lee.* Tessa's head begins to pound. She wonders if Olivia is too young to be standing on the side rail of a cable car, hanging on to a pole as they ascend Nob Hill. Maybe they should be inside the car, not standing here, where Olivia could fall onto the tracks or be jostled to the pavement. The bell of the cable car is like a pickax inside Tessa's head. "Clay Street, Clay," the driver calls, yanking the wooden brake. For a long moment, a metallic screech drowns out the German boys' song.

They roll through Chinatown, with its dead-eyed fish on ice and its mysterious herb stores, its smells of frying meat and fruity garbage and wet boxes. Farther along, the German boys stop singing. Olivia knocks and knocks her toe against the brass pole. Tessa wants to make her stop, but she can't move. There's a hot fast clawing inside her chest. She takes one hand off the pole and feels for the silver pillbox. With her thumb she flicks the lid open. She can feel the difference between a Devvie and a Sallie, the Devvie like a chalky little submarine, the Sallie hexagonal and coated. She works a Devvie out with her index finger. It calms her just to hold it. Clenching it in her hand, she wraps her arm around the pole and braces herself for the next hill.

Her shoes keep slipping on the smooth side rail, and the narrow skirt she's wearing makes it hard to get her balance. God, if only her mind had been working that morning, she would have worn something different, more casual. Her plan had been to dress as if she'd otherwise be spending the day at a job. When she got to the hotel, though, her sister Gayle was busy zipping Olivia into her jacket and folding her socks down and putting her hair up into a ponytail. She'd hardly glanced at Tessa's clothes. It was a good thing, too, because Tessa hadn't gotten it right. She couldn't find any stockings or a convincing jacket. And if she *had* a job, and this were really her day off, wouldn't she just be wearing jeans and a T-shirt? But Gayle had her mind on the lecture she was going to deliver that afternoon, something about *Mrs. Dalloway,* and Tessa left before she could notice much of anything.

The German youths move on to another song, this one in English. Tessa doesn't recognize it, but it has the predictable swelling cadences of a show tune. One of the teenagers beside her belts out the baritone. Olivia stares at the rows of pink and yellow houses, at the blue expanse of bay opening before them. They can see an antique sailing vessel docked near Ghirardelli Square, and the white masts of fishing boats bobbing alongside a pier. The cable car is going downhill now, mashing Olivia against the brass pole and Tessa against Olivia.

"You're hurting me," Olivia says.

Tessa pushes herself away, feeling the Devvie like a smooth pebble in her fist. "We're almost there," she says. "We can get some ice cream, okay?"

Olivia rubs a hand under her nose. "I'm not allowed," she says. "It'll spoil my appetite."

"Not today it won't. Not while you're with me."

Olivia gives her a skeptical look.

"I'm your adult today," Tessa says. "I make the rules."

At last the cable car reaches its turnaround. Tessa and Olivia get off and walk toward Ghirardelli Square, leaving the German choirboys behind. Each step sends a burning jolt through Tessa's foot. She'll never make it through the day in these shoes. There's a line at the ice-cream shop entrance, of course, and they have to wait outside in the wind and the blinding sun. The other people in line are parents and children, shivering in their bright T-shirts and shorts. They're all strangely quiet. They edge against the brick wall of the ice-cream shop, away from a man with dun-colored dreadlocks and milky eyes. Around his neck is a sign that reads, simply, AIDS. He moves in Tessa's direction, shaking a coffee can. Tessa takes a crumpled dollar from her pocket. When the man reaches her, she drops it in his can. He grins and says, "Thank you, beautiful." Though she's never seen him before, something seems to pass between them, a kind of uneasy recognition. Tessa pulls Kenji's jacket tighter around herself as the man moves off down the line.

"He smelled like pee," Olivia says.

"You would too, if you were him," Tessa says. It gives her a strange satisfaction to see how much this disturbs her niece. Olivia takes another look at the man and then moves behind Tessa, out of sight.

It's another fifteen minutes before the host shows them to a booth. As soon as he leaves, Tessa slides her shoes off and tucks her throbbing feet under her thighs. Olivia seems nervous, glancing at the families in other booths, humming a tight little song to herself. Will no one quit singing? Tessa lowers her forehead onto her fist.

When the waiter comes and asks what they'll have, Olivia shakes her head and looks down at the table. Tessa orders a hot-fudge-and-Oreo sundae for Olivia and coffee for herself. As they wait, Tessa takes sugar packets from the little ceramic sugar holder and rips them open one by one, lining them up on her napkin. She's not thinking about it, just getting into the rhythm of it, the feeling of paper in her hands, the sound of tearing. Olivia stares at her. Tessa looks down at the row of sugars, the little nest of torn-off strips of paper. This is not normal behavior. She puts a hand in her pocket and rolls the Devvie between her fingers, thinking how easy it would be to take this one white pill. Olivia would never even notice. It couldn't hurt anyone. In fact, she'd be worse off without it. And Olivia would be worse off. Olivia needs her to take this Devvie. Who knows what will happen otherwise?

The waitress brings the ice cream and the coffee, and Olivia seems relieved. She picks up the long spoon and lifts a delicate peak of whipped cream from the sundae. When she tastes it, she smiles and then scoops up a bite of ice cream and hot fudge. Quickly, with a feeling of inevitability, Tessa puts the Devvie on her tongue and washes it down with coffee. She takes a long breath and leans back in her chair. In a few minutes she'll begin to feel it. She glances at her wrist where she once wore a watch. She remembers the watch, an oversized Swiss Army chronometer, and wonders how it got away from her.

Across the table, Olivia eats her ice cream with deliberation, spooning hot fudge and whipped cream with each bite. Tessa watches her, waiting for the first quickening of the drug, that flutter at the center of her chest. Soon she will be able to handle anything, including taking care of her niece, her sister's child. She squints at Olivia, trying to imagine her as a six-year-old Gayle. But Gayle was a thin sly-eyed girl, her mouth full and pink, her hands agile. This girl is sturdy and round-faced. Pure Henry.

Oh, her brother-in-law is valiantly good, doesn't smoke or drink; he is devoted to the study of imaginary numbers and to the building of handy gadgets. In his house, each family member's preferred bathwater temperature is programmed into a special faucet, and the toaster oven responds to voice commands. "Black," Tessa said, last time she visited, and the toaster complied. Henry is responsible and compassionate, a good father. Right now he's back home taking care of Ethan, the younger child, who has the chicken pox. He's the kind of husband who can be trusted to take care of a sick child. Tessa can almost stand him, though for a long time she wanted to kill him. Gayle had met him in college. For years Tessa felt like he was the one who'd taken Gayle away, made Gayle forget that she and Tessa were supposed to go to Barcelona when they finished school, get a tiny apartment there, teach English, go out with dark-eyed men, give the world of careers and babies and husbands a grand and permanent *adiós.*

Of course, if it hadn't been Henry, it would have been someone else. Or something else. Tessa understands that now. Gayle started talking about graduate school when Tessa was still a freshman. She applied and got in right out of college. Stupidly, Tessa kept talking about Barcelona as if they might still go, as if Gayle might ditch her boyfriend and her Ph.D. in favor of a wild life in Catalonia. When Tessa was a senior herself, she asked Gayle what she was supposed to do next. She'd majored in computer programming, but she couldn't imagine getting a normal job, working in an office. Gayle suggested that Tessa go to Barcelona and teach English, just like they'd talked about. But that wasn't what they'd talked about, and Gayle knew it. Instead, Tessa dropped out of school and moved to San Francisco. And just look at her now.

Tessa can feel the Devvie coming on, the flush in her face that means her veins are dilating, the flutter in her diaphragm as the drug gets down to business. She can't avert her eyes from Olivia, sated and pale, the empty ice-cream bowl in front of her. They'll go look at the sea lions, they'll shop for souvenirs. She can do these things.

She pays the bill and wipes Olivia's face with a napkin, and then they're back out into the wind and sun. The light has become brighter and hotter and she's drinking it in like milk. Now she's the one who's singing, a hand-clapping song from when she and Gayle were little girls, *Miss Lucy had a steamboat, the steamboat had a bell.* It's a song where you say all the bad words but not really, *Miss Lucy went to heaven, the steamboat went to hell-o operator, please give me number nine. . . .* She and Gayle used to sing it at the top of their lungs when their father wasn't home. She should teach it to Olivia. *Behind the 'frigerator there lay a piece of glass; Miss Lucy sat upon it and broke her little ass me no more questions, tell me no more lies . . .* but she can't remember what comes after that. And these shoes are killing her. Why is she still wearing them? She pauses to take them off, and the sidewalk is mercifully cold against her burning feet.

"You're barefoot," Olivia says. "You can't go barefoot."

"Why not?"

"You might step on glass. Or a bee. Or doody."

"I'm not going to step on doody," Tessa says. "Believe me."

"You could get an infection," Olivia says, pausing at the door of a crowded T-shirt shop. On a tall rotating stand beside the door, pink and turquoise and yellow novelty flip-flops hang on individual hooks. Tessa turns the stand, looking. Maybe Olivia is right. Maybe what she needs is a new pair of shoes.

"What do you think of these?" Tessa pulls off a pair of pink flip-flops with palm trees stenciled in black on the footbed. *California Dreamin',* they say in looping script.

"You should get them," Olivia says. "And I could get a souvenir."

"I just got you ice cream," Tessa says.

"I'm going to look in here," Olivia says vaguely, and wanders inside toward a shelf of plush toys. Tessa glances at the price tag on the flip-flops: twelve dollars, but maybe they're worth it. She goes to the register and waits in line, shifting from foot to foot, biting her nails. When she gets to the front of the line, she pays for the shoes with the twenty Kenji gave her that morning. There are still a couple of crumpled bills in her pocket. How much does she have left? Ten bucks? Fifteen? She doesn't even want to check. She still has to buy a present for Olivia and lunch for both of them and the cable-car ride back, and her bank account is history, and her credit card won't accept new charges ever again. The rush in her chest becomes a pounding, the beginning of panic.

Tessa takes her flip-flops and goes to get Olivia, who's struggling with another child at the rack of plush toys. The child is a blond boy, perhaps three inches taller. He pulls a toy otter away from Olivia and holds it against his chest.

"I want that bear," Olivia says.

"That's not a bear," Tessa says.

"I want him," Olivia says, her voice low and dangerous. The boy takes a step back, holding the otter. His hair is cut like a hockey player's, short and scruffy on top, long in back. A thin blond woman rushes toward him and grabs him by the wrist.

"Wayne Christopher," the woman says. "You put that thing back where you got it."

Baring his teeth at Olivia, the boy shoves the otter back onto its shelf, deep behind the other animals. His mother pulls him out of the store, scolding. Olivia goes to the shelf and digs through the animals until she's found the otter, a glossy brown thing with deep, live-looking eyes. "I want him," she says, holding the toy against her chest.

There's no way Tessa can afford the otter. She's sure it must cost fifteen dollars at least. But she doesn't feel like arguing about it. What she wants is to get outside and put on her new flip-flops. She glances around the store and takes Olivia's hand. Nothing is going to make her drop the otter.

Tessa leads her toward the door, through a group of women in sun visors, past the racks of magnets and postcards, then out onto the sidewalk.

Olivia glances back over her shoulder toward the store. "Hey," she says. "Stop."

Tessa pulls her along. Without a word, they walk toward Pier 39, Tessa still barefoot, the new flip-flops in a plastic bag in her hand, the broken pumps forgotten somewhere inside the store. When they've gone two blocks, Tessa sits down on a bench and puts on the flip-flops. They feel so much better she wants to cry. Olivia looks down at the otter she's still holding in her arms.

"You made me steal him," she says.

"No, I didn't," Tessa says. "You stole him all by yourself."

Olivia draws her eyebrows together. "You made me leave while I was holding him."

"You could have dropped him," Tessa says.

Olivia says nothing, looking down at the otter. Tessa feels a kind of triumph.

"It's time to go now," she says. "We have to go see the sea lions."

"I have to put him back," Olivia says.

"No, you don't. You said you wanted him. Now you have him. Give him a name or something." Tessa stands and puts a hand on the back of Olivia's neck. "Let's go," she says.

"You're pinching me," Olivia says, squirming out of her grasp. She hides the otter under her jacket and holds it there as they make their way down the wharf.

The flip-flops do the trick. It's crazy how much better Tessa feels. She could walk for miles, for hours. Olivia trots beside her, trying to keep up, the otter concealed beneath her jacket. She keeps glancing back in the direction of the store as if someone might still come after them. Tessa knows she should be worried about what Olivia will tell her mother, and what Gayle will believe. But she almost *wants* Olivia to tell her mother. It feels good to know she's made Olivia do something her parents would punish her for. This is not right, she knows—not the way to take care of a six-year-old. There's no time to think about it, though; the Devvie has filled her with shimmering urgency. They need to see the sea lions and think about lunch and maybe she should take a Sallie. There's nothing quite like a Sallie after a Devvie, that lucent pink infusion that makes her almost come, every time. They've spent hours doing this, she and Kenji. At first it was just on Sundays in the Arboretum, but after they quit their jobs at Oracle they started doing it every day. One Devvie, then a Sallie, then another Sallie, and another Devvie. Then the feeling of each other's bodies. It's better than Ecstasy, cheaper than meth. She wasn't going to do it today, not both, not even a Devvie, but now that she's started maybe she should go ahead and take the Sallie.

Pier 39 is teeming with parents and children and teenagers and cops and vendors. There's the smell of hot dogs, waffle cones, saltwater taffy. Above the accordion music and children's shouts, Tessa can hear the frantic braying of sea lions. Olivia should be loving this. Instead she's looking anxious and pinched, her hand cold in Tessa's. They make their way down to the end of the pier, where families have gathered at the railing to watch the sea lions down in the bay. They lie on wooden floats in a protected cove, hundreds of them, molasses-brown, their glossy bodies heaped upon the floats and upon one another. They smell like elephants in the zoo. Fat with fish, they drowse in the sun or crow at the tourists, their faces small and canine. Spoiled, Tessa thinks. Tame. Hardly even animals anymore. Olivia sidles up to the railing, staring. Behind her there's a free spot on a bench. Tessa sinks into it, stretching her legs out in the sun. It's too hot for Kenji's jacket now. She takes it off and holds it on her lap. She cannot close her eyes to feel the crescendo of her buzz, as much as she wants to. She has to watch Olivia.

The Devvie surges in her, flushing her cheeks, and she concentrates on the dark brush of her niece's ponytail. Olivia's sea-green ponytail holder matches the green edging of her socks. She is a child cared for in great detail. Tessa likes the sound of that in her mind: *cared for in great detail.* She wonders what Olivia would look like if she were *her* kid, if Tessa were the one responsible for raising her. Worse, maybe. No matching ponytail holder, no cute windbreaker. But she'd be happier, Tessa's sure of that. She wouldn't be worrying about everything she ate and everything she might step on and this rule and that rule. She'd be a girl, a little girl, not a tiny cramped adult.

Olivia seems completely absorbed in the sea lions now, ready to stand there at the railing for a long time. Long enough, maybe, for Tessa to do what she wants to do. She works a hand into the pocket of Kenji's coat. There, like a promise, is the pillbox, the Sallies waiting inside. She flips the top and slides one out. The smoothness of it. The regularity of its six corners. She lays it on her tongue to taste the sweet coating before she swallows. Olivia crouches at the railing now, poking a finger through the wooden slats. Beside her, other children scream and laugh and point.

Tessa closes her eyes, letting the sun come down upon her. She can feel the waves of the Devvie still breaking over her, the flutter in her chest that means it's working, and it's lovely, and it's making her lovely and gone. The Sallie will take a little while to work, but when it does work, what joy. She will sit here and wait. She will let her niece watch those braying dogs of the sea. But she can't sit still or get comfortable, and she can't help thinking about what they'll have to do next, and after that, and after that, and she can't help thinking about Gayle back at the hotel, her sister, who seems so far from her now.

She opens her eyes. Olivia's pulling on her hand. "Stand up," she says.

"What is it?"

"I have to go bathroom."

"Right now?"

In answer, Olivia presses a hand between her legs.

"Okay, okay," Tessa says. When she stands, her vision crowds with blue sparks. She steadies herself against the bench. "We'll find one," she says. "Come on."

They weave through the tourists, looking. Olivia's mouth is pursed with the effort of holding it in. Tessa keeps forgetting what they're looking for—not ice cream, they've had that, not the sea lions, not souvenirs. She sees a line of girls and women extending from a door and suddenly she remembers, but this is not the bathroom, it's a fudge shop. She looks for signs and finds none. She asks a small woman with a broom and dustpan, but the woman shrugs and says, "No speak." Olivia is dancing now, making urgent noises in her throat. Finally, coming around a corner, they find it: the women's bathroom, a blue door and then a long silver cavern of stalls. Olivia breaks away from Tessa and locks herself inside one of them.

Tessa takes a stall nearby and closes the door behind her. She leans against the door, trying to slow her breathing. She doesn't have to pee. What she wants is to feel that Sallie. If she can get it, just the beginning of it, right here alone in the stall, it will be perfect. She will receive the shock of it in her groin, the tightening heat of it in her belly. She puts Kenji's jacket on again, trying to think about being in bed with him when this day is over. Instead she imagines Henry with his hands on Gayle. His broad white face, his small damp mouth. The chalkdust smell of him. She imagines him panting and sweating, whispering equations to stave off his orgasm.

Tessa sits down on the toilet and puts her head in her hands. From all up and down the row of stalls comes the roar of flushing, the banging of metal against metal, the raised voices of mothers and children. What would her own mother think if she saw Tessa now? Sometimes it almost seems better that she died when she did, when Tessa was four. Tessa remembers her mother playing with her in a kiddie pool, holding her on her knees as Tessa splashed. She's sure she remembers this, though Gayle always said she only *thought* she remembered it because they had a picture of it. It was one of the photographs they'd had in their secret closet altar, back in their room at home. They also had a pair of their mother's dancing shoes, silver; an old pink plastic hairbrush with strands of her hair; an empty wallet with a broken snap; a pair of malachite earrings. For years they kept finding small things of hers around the house, and at night they'd sneak into the closet and add them to the altar. There, crouched in the dark, they'd talk about her in whispers and see who could remember more. Gayle always won, of course.

There were times when Tessa would go into the closet by herself and look at the photos, try on the shoes and earrings, feeling as if that might help her remember something. It was hopeless, though. Tessa could never catch up. And after a while it all began to seem beside the point. As Gayle grew older she seemed to think about their mother less and less. Instead of creeping into the closet with Tessa, she would stay up late with their father in his study. She'd brew weak tea, which Tessa wasn't allowed to drink yet, and she'd sit on the leather ottoman and talk about what had happened at school or what she'd read in the newspaper that day. Their father would talk to Gayle almost as if she were another adult, asking her opinions and listening to her responses. A few times he even let Gayle come to the political science classes he taught at the university. When Tessa had finally asked him, a few years ago, why he'd never taken *her* to his classes, he'd looked at her with surprise and said he never knew she was interested.

Tessa can feel the Sallie beginning to come on, but it's coming on wrong because she's sitting here in a bathroom stall and thinking about the wrong things. The Sallie ices her veins and makes her toes cramp up. She needs some water. She needs money. Her skin prickles cold. Something is happening and she cannot make it stop.

From outside the stall Olivia calls something, words Tessa cannot make out. *Hold on,* she tries to say, but her voice is not working properly. A wave of shudders breaks over her, and then another, and then they keep on coming. She has to get her niece and get out of there. They need to go someplace quiet and alone. She is ready for that. She will open the door on three.

One.

Two.

Three.

But where is Olivia?

Not in the corridor between the line of stalls, and not in the open stalls, and not by the sinks washing her hands or by the dryers drying them. Not hiding under the Changin' Station or in the utility closet. She must be outside, waiting by the entrance. That is where she has to be. Tessa steps into a blinding crush of sun, a cataract of men and women and children. She looks beside the restroom door, behind the trash can a few feet away, behind the planter with its tiny sick palm. She sits down on the bench beside the palm. Under the surge of the Sallie she can feel the rhythmic thwick of panic in her chest, the wingbeats of an insect. Maybe this is a game. *Ass me no more questions, tell me no more lies.* Tessa goes back into the restroom and makes her way up and down the row of stalls. Women are staring at her, she realizes, giving her looks of concern or fear, pulling their children away. They think she's crazy, and why not? Her hair is a wind-nest, her jacket a bulky male thing, her shirt half untucked from her tweed skirt, her feet dirty in pink flip-flops.

"Olivia," she screams. "This is not a joke!"

The noise and bustle of the restroom continue around her. She waits, but her niece does not appear.

She has to look outside again. She shoulders through the

door and out into the wind. The fronds of the sick palm tree rustle like paper. What color jacket is Olivia wearing? Is it blue? Purple? Is that her, standing by the rail? No, a different child, an older child. The sea lions. She must have gone back to see them, to wait for Tessa there. How to get back to that place? She remembers a confusion, a frantic search for restrooms. Where did they end up? She can hear the sea lions' sound, their fretful barking, and she follows it through a twist of shops and wooden staircases and restaurant patios, looking for that jacket all the while, the jacket that might have been light blue or lavender or pale green; something green, maybe the dress underneath. She should never have let Olivia go into a stall alone. How could she keep it straight, what you were and weren't supposed to do? There are things she should be doing now, smart ways of trying to find Olivia. She has to think of what they are. If she could just lie down somewhere, in a cool dark room. But she cannot lie down.

Olivia is not standing by the rail watching the sea lions. Tessa leans forward over the rail, staring into the lapping water. A child, leaning out too far, could fall in. Would anyone notice? Would anyone notice if she, Tessa, dropped herself into that black-blue, if she let herself sink to the bottom?

What about the otter, that toy she made Olivia steal from the T-shirt shop? That must be where she is, in the shop, putting that thing back on the shelf. That can be the only place. She knows where it is. Back in the direction of the cable car. Olivia would have remembered. And Tessa can find it. It's the only T-shirt shop in San Francisco that has her broken shoes. She slaps along the pier in the direction of the shop, her flip-flops threatening to fly off her feet, the rubber thongs cutting into her skin. Get out of her way. She is a woman in a hurry, a person trying to beat fate. She scans the crowds for a glimpse of purple, for a head of tight dark curls, a ponytail, a sea-green ponytail holder. Her sister, sitting in a conference room in a hotel downtown, has no idea what is happening. Perhaps Olivia is headed there right now, running to tell her mother what Tessa's done. Here's what Tessa knows: No child of hers would run off into a crowd, lose herself in a strange city.

All along Beach Street there are T-shirt shops and T-shirt shops and T-shirt shops. Three of them have flip-flops displayed out front. Two of these have stuffed animals inside. One of these has otters. None of them has Olivia. Tessa stands on the sidewalk, looking out toward the bay. There, passing between the shore and Alcatraz, is a rust-red oil tanker with the word TANAKA on the side in high white letters. A million gallons of oil. She can almost taste it, bitter and black.

Tessa shuffles along Beach Street. She should tell the cops. She needs help. But look at her, in her crazy outfit, with Devvies and Sallies in her pocket. They'll think she's a kidnapper, a criminal. They'll handcuff her and throw her into a cell. Then they'll search the apartment. Kenji will be arrested too. She has to call him. Maybe he can make it all stop. Up ahead there is a pay phone, a little man shouting into it. She bounces on her toes, waiting, looking, willing Olivia to walk by. She'd like to take her by the shoulder, shake her, wake her up: *This* is the world, not what your parents have told you. This is what exists just outside the borders of your pretty life. It's what she's had to learn herself, the hard way, through Gayle's slow and steady pulling away, through all that time since college when she didn't know what to do with herself, the hated jobs in offices, her father's quiet disappointment, those deadened months at Oracle, and the months since she quit, months of her and Kenji in the apartment during the day, fucking and fighting and tweaking and reading the paper and watching movies and lying to everyone. She knows she's getting closer to a new kind of truth, a real discovery, a kind of knowledge Gayle will never have.

The little man gets off the phone and runs down the street, cursing. Tessa picks up the phone. She can smell food, sweet and greasy, on the receiver. She can't speak into the hum of the dial tone or decide which buttons to press. Her head feels like it's hurtling in fast-forward, her breath coming so fast her vision is going black at the edges. She can't explain why she's standing on the street holding this phone instead of searching for Olivia. A recording comes on and tells her what to do if she'd like to make a call.

"Get Kenji," she says to the voice. "Dial Kenji."

Please hang up and try again.

Try what? She can't hang up. Someone else is already waiting for the phone. *If you'd like to make a call.*

She jams the receiver onto the hook, then picks it up again and presses numbers. *Please deposit thirty-five cents.* She digs in her pocket for change and finds a quarter and a dime. She fumbles them into the slot and dials again. Seven numbers. She can manage them. She does. The phone is ringing, and then, like a reprieve from everything, Kenji's voice. She can hardly believe he still exists in this world. She tries to say something but all she can do is cough out sobs.

"Tessa? Is that you?"

"It's not my fault!" she cries into the receiver.

"Hey," he says. "Come home. Where did you go?"

"You have to come get me," she says.

He gives a faint, panicked laugh. "Come get you? I can't come get you! I'm extremely fucked up at the moment."

"You have to come," she says. "Olivia's gone."

"Who?"

She hangs up and sits down on the curb. Behind her, someone else picks up the phone and begins punching numbers. There are cars passing in the street just beyond Tessa's flip-flops, almost running over her feet as they pass. Crushed bones, blood, a wreck. She almost wants it.

She stands and crosses the street, making the cars swerve around her. There's a small park sloping down toward the water, with pigeons coming down like shattering slate. Weathered green benches stand between beds of blue and yellow pansies. She sits down on a bench, looking out toward the flat metallic expanse of the bay. She feels something going wide and empty in her chest, the Devvie slipping out from beneath the Sallie, the cartoon moment just before you fall, when the cliff's already gone but gravity has not yet got you. A horror goes through her: a child somewhere, screaming, lost. Not just a child, her own niece. She takes the pillbox from her pocket, looks inside. Two Devvies, one more Sallie. She looks at the flower bed beside the bench, then kneels on the grass. With her finger she digs a hole in the loose soil of the flower bed, turning up dirt and curled-up bugs and roots. Then she packs the pillbox into the hole and tamps the soil down on top of it. She fixes this spot in her mind: the park with its beds of pansies, the flower bed near the center of the park. She picks the dirt from beneath her fingernails, then walks down to the beach and washes her hands in the cold water of the bay.

The waiting room is plastered with posters of missing children, of wanted men and women wearing numbers. She sits in an orange plastic chair, looking down at her wrists. Uncuffed. Beside her on the floor is a cup of black police-station coffee. This is where the police brought Olivia when they found her wandering the wharf alone, crying for her mother, and it is where they brought Tessa when she told them what had happened. She, Tessa, has not been treated like a criminal; she's been allowed to sit here while someone goes to get Olivia. She cannot shake the feeling that someone might come in at any minute and take her roughly by the back of the neck and shove her into a cell. Her policeman acted as if things like this happened all the time: children wandering away from their harried guardians at Pier 39, everyone reunited soon afterward. Now the policeman carries Olivia into the waiting room, her small face grim and scrubbed, her pale purple jacket torn at the sleeve, the stolen otter tucked under her arm. When the officer sets her down she looks at Tessa with shamed, fearful eyes. Tessa pulls her close and holds her there. The girl's arms come around her. It amazes her to think Olivia would trust her after what has happened.

"See that?" the officer says to Olivia. "I told you she wouldn't be mad."

She feels Olivia's breath, quick and hot, against her neck. "I'm sorry," Olivia says.

"It's okay," Tessa says. "It's okay."

They step back out into the sun, into the blinding afternoon, and walk down Bay Street back toward the water. Olivia is stunned and silent, holding Tessa's hand. She seems uninterested in the shops and houses. There are no tourists on this part of Bay Street, only women and men going about the business of their lives. Now would be the time to take Olivia back to the hotel, to get her cleaned up in Gayle's hotel room, to wait for her sister to be finished with her conference. Tessa and Olivia could both pretend everything was fine, and maybe Gayle would believe them. Or maybe she wouldn't, and everything would begin to change—the nightmare that has become Tessa's life might crack open and begin to fall away. Part of her wants to surrender to that, to let Gayle know at last what has happened to her life, to make her have to recognize it and do something about it, finally. Maybe that's what she's been hoping for all day, maybe that's why she let herself lose Olivia: to make things so terrible they'd have to change. But Olivia is back now, and Tessa feels almost as if she's been tricked. She feels as if she doesn't have the power to decide anything anymore, as if she's being pulled along slick tracks by a strong and twisted steel rope underground, like the cable car. All she can think about are the pills in their silver box, dark and safe beneath the soil. She has to have them, and she has to keep having them. She feels like she'll die if she doesn't. The Devvie is long gone now, and her nerves crackle with the afterburn of the Sallie. A cold white pain gathers behind her eyes. She hurries Olivia along the sidewalk, toward the park.

"I went to put my animal back," Olivia says. "I went back to that store."

"But you didn't put him back," Tessa says. "You decided to keep him."

Olivia looks down at the otter, saying nothing. At an intersection she and Tessa stop to watch the cars pass. Olivia fingers the ripped sleeve of her jacket, trying to hold the edges of the fabric together. "I tore this," she says. "My mom's going to be mad."

"Maybe she won't be," Tessa says, not really listening.

"Yes, she will."

Tessa is at the end of kindness. Her temples pulse with pain. As she looks down at Olivia, a fine sharp cruelty gathers in her chest. "At least you *have* a mother," she says. "When I was your age, my mother was dead."

Olivia's mouth opens and closes. Tessa will not watch her start to cry. When the light changes, she takes Olivia's wrist and pulls her across the street. As they enter the park, Tessa walks faster. Her flip-flops make their muffled slap against the pavement. In the distance she can see the bay, bright-scaled with afternoon light. She heads toward the row of benches along the park path, each with its crowd of pigeons, each separated by a bed of pansies. The benches are empty now. Tourist families hurry along the path, looking as if they mean to get somewhere before the sun gets any lower.

At a flower bed near the center of the park, Tessa gets to her knees to examine the soil. She can't tell if this is the right place or not. The bench beside the flower bed looks familiar, but they all have the same weathered green paint, the same brass plaques. She scrabbles through the loose soil. Nothing. She moves to the next flower bed, kneeling down to dig again while Olivia watches, holding the otter.

"What are you doing?" Olivia asks, her voice a dry whisper.

"Looking for something," Tessa says. She turns up clods of dirt, but her pills are not there. She leads Olivia along the path, then stoops beside the next flower bed. She thinks she remembers these flowers at the edge, these yellow pansies with their dark velvet hearts. Olivia sits down on the grass and holds the otter, her eyes glassy with fatigue. The wind is sharp against Tessa's neck as she kneels beside the flower bed. Her fingers are going numb, her nails are packed with soil, but she lowers her head and digs.

Stars of Motown
Shining Bright

Lucy waited in her room for Melissa to arrive from Cincinnati. They would drive in Melissa's old Cadillac, that sleek white boat, forty miles east to Royal Oak, where they would spend the night with Jack Jacob. Lucy was fifteen and no longer a virgin. The teen magazine articles pondering the question of whether one was ready to give it up no longer applied to her. She could, at that very moment, be pregnant. Not that she was pregnant. She had been careful, and so had Jack Jacob. Still, there was a possibility. And now she was off to see him again, to spend the night with him in Royal Oak, and it was all right with her parents because he was a boy she'd met in youth group, and because they were staying at his parents' house, and because Melissa would be there too. These friendships were important, her parents had told her. These friendships could last a lifetime.

The trip had been Melissa's idea. She liked road trips and she liked adventures in which she and Lucy did something they could tell everyone about afterward, with lots of dramatic detail. But she didn't know about what had happened between Lucy and Jack. Lucy hadn't told her. It felt too private to talk about over the phone. Maybe if Melissa had lived closer, Lucy would have gone over to her house and whispered it to her in the dark. On the other hand, maybe she wouldn't have. She wasn't sure how Melissa would react. Melissa liked Jack too. She and Jack had even fooled around once at a youth group convention. While everyone else was busy at the Saturday-night dance, Melissa and Jack had snuck away to the high-vaulted sanctuary and made out for half an hour on the floor between two rows of pews. Lucy knew because she'd been there, guarding the door in case any of the youth leaders came along. She remembered trying not to listen but listening anyway. She remembered the bronze Eternal Light flickering in the half-dark. At one point Melissa sat up to twist her hair into a ponytail, and she shot Lucy a self-satisfied smile. Lucy knew what that smile was about: Jack, a senior, liked *her*, Melissa. Not tonight, though. Things were different now. Lucy was the one Jack wanted, and Melissa would have to live with that.

There was the white Cadillac at last, rolling long and smooth into the driveway. It had once belonged to Melissa's mother, but now it had daisy decals on the hood and a Barbie dangling from a tiny noose on the rearview mirror. Lucy watched Melissa climb out, tall and lank in a short white skirt and sling-back shoes, her hair caught in a high ponytail. There was something about the sheen of her legs, the slowness of her walk, that made Lucy sick with envy.

Lucy went downstairs and tiptoed to the door. Through the peephole she could see Melissa practicing nonchalance, swinging her keys on one finger and moving her hips from side to side as if to music. She tilted her head back, blew a pink gum bubble, and sucked it in as it burst. Lucy opened the door.

Melissa leaned forward coolly and kissed Lucy first on one cheek and then the other, European style. She smelled of nail polish remover and black-cherry lip gloss and beauty salon shampoo. At her feet was a large black shoulder bag stuffed with clothes.

"Where are your parents?" she said.

"Gone," Lucy said. "Neighborhood Watch meeting."

"Good." Melissa brushed past Lucy and led her upstairs as if this were *her* house, as if she owned Lucy's room and everything in it. She threw her bag on the bed and opened the doors to Lucy's closet, flicking her way through Lucy's shirts and pants and skirts. Every now and then she would extract a garment and regard it with distaste, then replace it on the bar and shove it aside. "You have no clothes," she concluded.

"Don't remind me," Lucy said.

Melissa sat down on the bed, just inches from the place where Lucy had slept with Jack Jacob, and then she opened her overnight bag and pulled out something that looked like a clot of black yarn. When she unrolled it, Lucy saw that it was a crocheted dress with short sleeves and no back.

"I couldn't wear it over here," Melissa said. "Your parents would freak." She peeled off her shirt and skirt and tossed them to Lucy. She was wearing white stockings that ended at the thigh with a band of elastic lace. These too she took off and tossed to Lucy. "You can wear my clothes if you want," she said. "Don't spill anything on them, though." From her bag she pulled out another pair of stockings, black with lace at the top, and put them on. In stockings, panties, and brassiere she posed in front of Lucy's full-length mirror, bending forward to look at her cleavage. She was the only girl Lucy knew who actually loved her body.

Lucy pulled on the stockings and stretched them up to her thighs. They were a tight fit around the tops. She struggled into Melissa's skirt and shirt. When she looked in the mirror, she thought she hardly looked like herself at all.

"Much better," Melissa told her. "Though you should have straightened your hair or pulled it back or something." She herself was cool and lean in the black crocheted dress, the tops of her stockings and her pale thighs visible through the fabric. "We don't have time now, though," she said. "Do you have your stuff?"

Lucy had packed an overnight bag. In it was a pair of satin

pajamas she'd bought without telling her parents. She imagined entering Jack's room in those pajamas, his eyes traveling
over her, Melissa looking at her in envy. Was it possible that
Melissa could envy her? Maybe when she told her what had
happened.

They'd become friends at last year's Regional Convention, when Melissa had told her about the date with Adam
Moskovitz. She and Melissa had found themselves sitting
next to each other in the synagogue social hall during a long
panel discussion about Tikkun Olam, which meant Healing
the World. Adam, a senior and the vice president of Midwest
Region, had been one of the panelists. Every time he made a
point about how important it was to spend time helping out at
your local soup kitchen or collecting clothes for Russian immi-
grants, Melissa would roll her eyes and make a little sarcastic
huff. Finally she took Lucy by the sleeve and they went to the
ladies' lounge. This was a big Cincinnati-synagogue ladies'
lounge, with tailored chintz sofas in a pink-carpeted ante-
room. It smelled of rose soap and ammonia, and the plumbing
hummed in the walls. Melissa unfolded herself onto a sofa
and closed her eyes. Then she told about the date with Adam,
how he'd taken her out to a Japanese restaurant and then to
his parents' private box at the symphony, where he'd shoved a
hand under her skirt and told her he wanted her *right then*.
He'd pulled her up against the wall, in a tiny space between
the box door and a velvet curtain, and he lifted her skirt and
did it, not even using a condom. Melissa cried a little as she
told the story, though the way she described the sex itself,
with anatomical details and language that sounded like a
porno magazine, made Lucy feel as if she were bragging—or
lying.

In comparison, Lucy's night with Jack would sound plain
and undramatic. She had wanted to do it, first of all. She'd
known Jack since she was twelve and had always thought he

was nice and not unattractive, though maybe slightly greasy, with his hair gelled back and his dance-club shirts in every color. He was even famous, in a small way: He'd been in a movie, *Streets of Detroit*. In his one scene, Jack, the troubled younger brother, had gotten shot by mistake. Still alive, he lay on the sidewalk looking tragic and vulnerable. The stricken older brother knelt beside him. Jack looked up at him, eyes clouding. *It's not your fault, Tommy,* he said.

The problem was, Melissa had always liked him too. It was obvious she couldn't wait to see him tonight. Lucy had never seen her acting so nervous. As she drove along I-94 toward Detroit, she did not sing with the radio or talk to Lucy. She drove with one hand on the wheel and the other clenched around a small pearl-gray box in her lap. The way she kept opening it just a little and peeking inside seemed calculated to create mystery, so Lucy forced herself not to ask what was in it. Instead, she leaned over and turned up the radio. It was DJ Baby Love, at WLUX.

"The stars are shining bright above Motown tonight," said DJ Baby Love in his plush baritone, "and it's Diana Ross with 'Ain't No Mountain High Enough.' " Lucy sang along, making up lyrics when she didn't know them.

"You're loud," Melissa said. "And bad."

"Yeah, that's right." Lucy rolled her shoulders and sang with Diana.

"You are so not black."

"But I'm beautiful," Lucy said. She tried acting carefree and fifteen, entirely uninterested in Melissa and that pearl-gray box. She had other things to think about, things of greater importance. Somewhere beneath the stars of Motown, Jack was waiting.

That night with Jack, she'd known exactly what was going to happen. They'd gone to see *The Birds* at the Michigan Theater, and they'd shared a bowl of mint chip at the

Home Dairy. And then they'd gone back to her house and sat in the driveway in Jack's Continental for what seemed like hours, taking burning swigs from Jack's silver flask. She hated the taste of whatever it was, so most of the time she was just taking pretend swigs, tipping the flask up to her mouth and blocking the liquor with her tongue. She tried acting like she was getting a little drunk. Jack had a hand on her thigh, just in the same place, for a long time. It was early June and cool, the crickets making their shrill dry sound in the box elders beside the driveway. Upstairs the light in her parents' bedroom was still on. Jack told her about California, about the women at the fitness club in Bel Air where he taught Pilates and weight training. A few of the women had offered him money for special favors, which he'd declined to perform. He talked about trying out for sitcoms. He talked about looking for an agent. He talked about living in a shitty bungalow three blocks from the beach, and about going to Compton on Saturday nights with a black friend from Detroit, and almost getting his ass shot off, and consequently having to buy a gun for self-protection. It was a double-action Kel-Tec .32. He had it with him, in fact, and he showed it to her. It was brushed steel, blunt-nosed, small enough almost to disappear in his closed hand. He pulled the slide back to show her a cartridge in the chamber. This gun had no external safety, he said, so she should never touch it unless they were in Detroit some night and she had to protect herself. She'd held guns before, had taken riflery at summer camp, but it frightened her to see this small sleek pistol in his hand, right there in the driveway of her house. She didn't want to touch it. He put it in the glove compartment, and she tried to forget it was there.

She told him about how she was volunteering at a shelter for runaway teen girls and their babies, a place where her parents would never have let her work in a million years. She'd lied to them, saying she was working as a candy striper at the hospital, and her father would drive her downtown and she'd go into the hospital and wait until he drove away before walking to the shelter. She told him about finding packets of crack stashed in diapers, which hadn't actually happened to her but to Lynette, one of the other volunteers. Jack removed his hand from her thigh.

"You're too serious," he said. "You should try to act like a fifteen-year-old sometimes."

"How?"

"You could kiss me," he said. "You could climb right onto my lap."

She laughed. "Is that what fifteen-year-olds do?"

"Sometimes."

"And then what would happen?"

"And then I'd take you inside and make love with you. Nice and sweet."

She said she'd think about it. She was trying to act casual, though really she'd been thinking about it for nearly a month, ever since she'd gotten the postcard saying he was coming back from California for a visit. She'd even taken condoms from the shelter. So she was ready to do it, and here he was. Her parents' light was off now. They'd have to be quiet. She climbed into his lap and kissed him.

Later they went inside and upstairs to her room, where she locked and double-locked the door and got undressed, folding her clothes neatly on a chair as if she were at the doctor's office. She listened for movement from the direction of her parents' room and heard nothing, so she crawled into her bed and waited. She expected it to be painful and brutal, like the unprofessional extraction of a tooth. But when Jack was in bed with her, breathing quiet into her hair, touching her everywhere, getting her to touch him, she forgot to worry about the pain.

When it was over, she felt good. Not a virgin anymore, but better. He kissed her goodnight and went to sleep on the couch downstairs. The next morning he thanked her parents for their hospitality and took Lucy out for pancakes and eggs.

As they were leaving the diner, they passed a plant nursery where tiny fir trees stood in a row along a wooden fence. Jack said he wanted to buy one for Lucy to commemorate their night together. She laughed, but he said he was serious, and so they bought the tree and planted it beside a rock garden in Lucy's backyard. The whole time she moved as if through syrup, feeling warm in all her limbs. Now he was planning to leave for California sometime that week. She hadn't thought it would make her sad, but it did.

She'd been waiting to tell Melissa the whole story in person, but now she didn't feel like talking about it at all. How could she describe it, anyway? She didn't want to use the kind of details Melissa had used when she'd talked about Adam Moskovitz, and she didn't want to make it sound romantic, either. But she wanted to talk about it. She wanted to say his name.

"What do you think Jack's doing right now?" she said, trying to sound bored.

"I don't know," Melissa said, rubbing the pearl-gray box with her thumb. "Showering, maybe. I'm always asking myself that same question. I'm always like, 'I wonder what he's doing right now?' I think about him all the time."

"You think about him all the time?"

"There's something I should tell you, actually," Melissa said. "Something important." With a serious look, eyes flinty and small, she put a hand on Lucy's arm. "You have to swear you won't tell anyone about this."

"What?" Lucy said. Her scalp prickled with sudden cold.

"I mean *swear*. Not your parents, not my parents, not the police. Even if they torture you."

"Okay, I swear! Just tell me!"

"Jack and I are getting married," said Melissa. "We're leaving tomorrow morning to drive out to California, and on the way we're getting married in Vegas. And then we're getting an apartment in LA and he's going to introduce me to this magazine guy he knows. I'm going to get this job working at the magazine. I'll be a model at first, but later on they're going to teach me how to do design and layout."

Lucy stared. A semi blasted by, rocking the car.

"We don't care what people say about us being too young," Melissa said. "We're in love. Plus I have a fake birth certificate saying I'm eighteen."

"But you can't *marry* him. You're not even going out with him."

"We are," Melissa said. "We hooked up a couple of times before he went out west, and he's been writing to me. We didn't want to broadcast our relationship to the whole world."

Lucy thought of how he'd gone into her, deliberate and quiet. He'd waited forever, just on the verge. Then she'd raised her hips and they were rocking together.

"It won't be easy at first," Melissa said. "But I had to get away from home. I couldn't stand it anymore, with my stepmom treating me like I'm in elementary school. And always making me baby-sit for her own kids, those brats. And acting like she owns my dad. And everyone pretending like *my* mom doesn't exist anymore." Melissa paused, giving Lucy the dare-you-to-pity-me look that came on whenever she mentioned her mother, who'd left the family three years earlier for a Minneapolis real-estate entrepreneur. "I can get my GED out there, and when I start learning graphic design I can make some money. This magazine guy Jack knows, he's very artistic. He does films, too. The modeling's just for a while, anyhow, before I get into the design side."

"What modeling?" Lucy said.

"You know, artistic modeling."

"You mean nude."

"It's not *porn*," Melissa spat. "Most of it's just partial nudity, and you don't even have to touch anyone. You'd never understand, though. No offense, Lucy, but you're so immature. I never should have told you."

Outside, trees flashed lean and dark against the distant glow of Detroit. The corn was shoulder-high in the fields, its tassels ghostly silver. "Ha-ha," Lucy said. "Right? You're completely shitting me."

"I am so not shitting you," said Melissa. "I'm so serious I could fucking kill myself for telling you. You'll run home and tell your mom and everything will be ruined." She stared ahead at the highway.

Lucy couldn't believe it. She kept waiting for Melissa to give her a cross-eyed look and then start laughing. But Melissa was fierce and determined, her face flushed, her hands tight on the steering wheel. "I knew you'd be a baby about it," she said. "But you've got to get your shit together because you're going to help us. That's why you're on this trip."

"No, it's not," Lucy said.

"You're going to be our accomplice," Melissa said. "We're going to take his car, and you're going to drive this one back to my mom's and leave it in the driveway."

"Like fuck I am."

"You have to. It's part of the plan."

"There's no plan," Lucy said. "You're completely lying."

"I'm not lying," said Melissa. "Look." She opened the pearl-gray box. Lucy took it from her and switched on the dome light. Inside was a plain gold band with a Tiffany-style setting. The diamond was clear and fiery and small enough to be convincing. Lucy took it out and turned it over and over in her fingers, feeling the chill of the gold.

"Okay," Melissa said. "Give it back."

Lucy put the ring back into the box, handed it to Melissa, and turned off the dome light. She looked down at her own hands, which were bare. "If you're really engaged," she said, "why don't you wear your ring?"

"Are you joking? It's not exactly stealth."

Melissa changed the radio station. On all the presets there were commercials. Lucy wondered what Melissa would do if she grabbed the ring box and threw it out the window.

"He gave me something else, too," Melissa said, "but I can't tell you what it is."

"Why not?"

"Because look at yourself. Everything I tell you, you're like, *Oh, my God!*"

"Fine," Lucy said. "I don't care."

Melissa pulled off the highway toward a gas station, where a red-and-blue sign advertised Icees. She drove up beside a vacant pump and turned to Lucy.

"Do you have any money?" she asked.

"For what?"

"I'll give you a hint: This is a *gas* station, where they sell *gas*."

"I'm not giving you money."

"I'm engaged," Melissa said. "This can be your engagement present to me." She grabbed Lucy's purse and fished out a twenty, then went to pump the gas. Lucy watched her as she stood against the gas pump and fiddled with the elastic of her stocking. She did a little hip grind to the bass thrumming from a low-slung Crown Vic. The two boys inside, their hair shaved close and their teeth flashing with gold, watched her like zombies. When the tank was full, Melissa went into the convenience store.

Lucy looked through her purse for quarters. She could call someone from the shelter to come get her—her friend Lynette, maybe. Or she could just grab her bag and hitch a ride home. She imagined herself standing beside the highway in her short white skirt. It seemed like an image from a slasher movie. When she looked through the window, trying to see Melissa inside the store, one of the boys in the Crown Vic waved.

The pearl-gray box was still on the seat where Melissa had left it. Lucy picked it up and shook the ring out onto her palm. Something else was rattling around inside the box, something heavier than the ring. She pried out the velvet insert and a key fell into her lap. It was a Cadillac key but with a round head: a glove compartment key. Turning it over in her hand, she looked toward the convenience store with its racks of chips and magazines. Melissa was nowhere in sight. She fitted the key into the glove compartment lock. It turned, and the compartment fell open. There, on top of the maps and old Midas receipts, was Jack's gun.

Before, in Jack's car, it had frightened her. Now she wanted to hold it in her hand. It was cold and heavy and small enough to fit her palm. The muzzle was clean and oiled, and there was the trigger, a smooth place for an index finger. She pulled back the slide like Jack had showed her. The gun was still loaded. She pointed it into the foot well and said, "Freeze!"

She could do anything now. Not that she'd *do* anything. But here she was, no longer a virgin, and in her hand she had this gun. They were going to Detroit. They were going to see Jack Jacob. She put the gun back into the glove compartment and waited for Melissa to come out.

The rest of the way to Detroit, Lucy didn't say a word. She knew Melissa wanted her to ask questions, to act interested in what was going to happen, but she refused to do it. Beside her on the Cadillac seat, Melissa tried to act like she didn't care. She sang along with the radio as the suburbs of Detroit rushed by, their shopping malls and car showrooms and soaring Methodist churches glowing alongside the highway. They passed the eighty-foot-high Uniroyal tire and the old New Silver Rolladium of Southfield, with its spotlit fake palm trees and its mural of a freestyle skater in silhouette. Then they pulled off the highway into Royal Oak. The houses there were cramped little castles of white or pink brick, each with its green cropped lawn. Jack's house was a small Tudor in a row of Tudor houses. It was shabbier than the others, somehow—its shutters peeling, its plaster lawn gnome missing the peak of his cap. But the lawn had been mowed recently, and a pair of Jack's grassy sneakers stood beside the door.

"You have to promise you won't do anything stupid," Melissa said as she killed the motor. "You've got to stop freaking right now. Think of yourself as my maid of honor. Your job is to help me stay calm before my wedding."

"Okay," Lucy said. She felt prickly-skinned and powerful, ready to commit reckless deeds. She'd replaced the key in the pearl-gray box but left the glove compartment unlocked.

They got out of the car with their things and went to the door, and Melissa rang the bell. She made an attempt at door-waiting nonchalance, smacking her gum and twirling the keys, but it didn't last long. After a minute she got up on her toes and tried to look through the tiny sheer-curtained window at the top of the door.

"Where is he?" she said. "He'd better be here."

Then he was there, opening the door for them, welcoming them into the living room, with its slipcovered gold couches and its smell of old chicken soup. Melissa jumped at him and he picked her up, swinging her. One of her black shoes fell off. Lucy tried to get him to look at her, but he kept avoiding her eyes. Her stomach lurched and she had to sit down on a couch. A curl of torn plastic bit into her thigh. "Jesus fucking Christ," Jack was saying. "Look at you two." Lucy adjusted her thigh-highs and crossed her legs. She told herself to relax. She stared at the carpet with its pattern of gold scrolls and turquoise roses, a terrible carpet, perhaps the world's worst.

"Don't sit there," Jack said. "Come upstairs. See my room."

He started up the stairs and Melissa followed. "Come on," she called to Lucy.

Lucy went, dragging her overnight bag. She followed Jack and Melissa down the hall, down a strip of olive-colored carpet, past the pictures of Jack's family and Jack himself as a kid with dark eyes and pin-straight black hair. They passed a closed bedroom door. Inside, someone was snoring loudly.

"My mom," Jack said. "Out cold."

In his room, white Christmas lights blinked around the ceiling and Pink Floyd's *Delicate Sound of Thunder* played on the stereo. There was a ratty football-helmet rug half covered by an air mattress, which smelled new, as if purchased for the occasion. The air mattress was made up in black sheets. A TV sat near it on the rug. Beside the TV, on a boy-sized desk, stood a glossy black ice bucket, three glasses, and bottles of gin and peach schnapps and tonic water and vodka. On a bookshelf were some dusty baseball trophies and a framed bar mitzvah certificate. The air was heavy with the smells of vinyl and sandalwood incense.

"The luxury lounge," Jack said.

Melissa threw her bag onto the floor. "Let's go out," she said. "There must be a party or something."

"A party?" Jack said. He seemed disappointed.

"It's early. I want to go out. Lucy does too, don't you, Lucy?"

"Sure," Lucy said. Anything to get away from that room, with its terrible smell and its giant mattress.

"This town's dead," Jack said. "The party's right here tonight."

"I know what we should do!" Melissa said. "The Silver Rolladium. We passed it on the way here. We *have* to go."

"I don't skate," Jack said. "As a rule."

"We have to," Melissa said. "Please, please. We can leave if it sucks."

"Jesus Christ," Jack said, holding the back of his neck with one hand. "Okay. But just for a little while. I don't want to spend all night there."

Melissa gave Lucy a look of triumph. Then she took her tiny makeup bag and disappeared into the bathroom, down the hall. Lucy stood on the football-helmet rug and looked at Jack.

"What?" Jack said.

When Lucy didn't respond, he said, "Let's go downstairs. Let's have a talk." He took her hand and led her downstairs to the kitchen, where Lucy sat on a yellow stool at the breakfast bar. Jack opened the refrigerator and took out a carton of orange juice. He opened it, sniffed it, put it away. He took out a can of Fanta Grape. "You want a Fanta Grape?" he said.

Lucy shook her head.

"How about a real drink? I know I could use one." Jack went into another room and came back with a cut-glass decanter. "This is Scotch," he said. "Is Scotch okay?"

"I don't care," Lucy said. It was hard to make her voice sound the way she wanted it to, steady and glacier-cold. Maybe a drink would help.

Jack put ice cubes into a glass and poured Lucy an inch of Scotch. He set the glass before her. It smelled like sweetened nail polish remover. She lifted the glass and drank. It was horrible, bitter, burning. She coughed and wiped her mouth.

"Shit," Jack said. "That's some drinking." He took the empty glass and poured some for himself. "You look hot in that skirt," he said. "You really do."

"Fuck you," she said.

Jack took a drink of Scotch. "Lucy," he said, "I have to explain a few things."

"No need. Melissa told me everything."

"You don't understand, though."

"What's to understand? You're engaged. Congratulations."

He gave her a moist smile. "Let's not worry about all that tonight. We should just have a good time. We know how to have a good time together, don't we?" He put a hand on her arm and rubbed the inside of her wrist with his thumb.

Lucy pulled away. "I'm going to tell Melissa about last weekend."

"I don't think that's a good idea."

"I think it's a fabulous idea."

"Okay," Jack said. "Tell her. I'll say it's not true. Who do you think she's going to believe?" He tilted his head at her and smiled.

Lucy sat back, feeling the heat of the Scotch in her blood. A hum like bees filled her head. Now Melissa was coming down the stairs, crossing one foot in front of the other like a Miss America contestant, singing "Ready for skating, ready to go roller skating" to the tune of "Getting to Know You." In the kitchen she leaned over the bar to give them a look down her shirt. Lucy could see the black bow at the center of her bra.

"Ouch, baby," Jack said. "Put those away."

"Are we going?" said Melissa.

They were.

At the skating rink the air was thick with smoke-machine smoke, and the skaters shot through beams of flashing light. The floor was packed. All the girls were dressed in small tight clothes, their hair done in elaborate braids or ponytails. It was house night, and Lucy could feel the drums at the center of her chest. Jack draped one arm around her shoulders and the other around Melissa's. He steered them through the crowd toward the skate-rental booth, looking as if he were loving this.

"Check out these walls," he said, and Lucy did. The walls were lined with sparkly black carpet, meant as a crash guard for the skaters. "It's like a porno movie," he said. "It's like we could all just lie down and fuck anywhere, if gravity suddenly went haywire."

Melissa giggled and gave him a slap on the arm. "You're so bad," she said.

They rented skates and put them on. Before Lucy could get the feel of them, Melissa took her by the hand and pulled her out onto the wooden skating floor. Lucy stumbled along, trying to keep her balance. She'd hated skating ever since she was a kid. She'd never wanted those white skates with pink pom-poms like the other kids had. She'd never tried to win the games at skating parties. Now her arms and legs felt numb from the whiskey, and the music was a dull throb inside her head. Jack kept giving her a heavy-lidded look as they skated, a half smile meant to be sexy. She wanted to jab her fingers right into his eyes and watch him double over in pain. The worst part was that when she let her mind go, she was still imagining him apologizing to her, on his knees even, telling her how sorry he was, what an asshole he was, and it was really Lucy he wanted to marry and take to California.

Lucy caught up with Melissa and pulled her toward the girls' room. Melissa was laughing, pushing strands of her pony-tail out of her face and adjusting the lace tops of her thigh-highs. They both skidded when their skates hit the girls' room tiles.

"These tights are going to be totally wrecked," Melissa said, "but it's worth it." She leaned against the wall and pulled a crumpled cigarette from her pocket. When she tried to straighten it out, it broke. "Fuck," she said. "Do you have any?"

"No," Lucy said.

Melissa threw the cigarette away and checked her eye-brows in the mirror. Then she turned to Lucy and smoothed her curls with one cool hand. "You look like shit. And you smell like whiskey." She laughed. "You know what I always thought?" she said, leaning against a sink. "I thought I could take you and make you into a totally new girl. When I met you at that convention, I said to myself, That girl's kind of pretty but she dresses lame and acts immature. I bet I could make her so cool."

"I'm not immature," Lucy said.

"Oh, I know, I know," Melissa said. "Your job and all that, doing good deeds for the pregnant teens. Plus I think you lost some weight lately."

Lucy thought about the gun, about the weight of it in her hand, and the smooth sheen of the barrel, and the arc of the trigger against her index finger. She imagined aiming, squeez-ing, then the explosion and the peppery smell of gunpowder, like when she used to shoot rifles at summer camp.

"Our friends are *so* going to freak when you tell them," Melissa said. "Think about two weeks from now at Nationals!

Everyone's going to be like, She did *what*? Oh, my *God*. Her and *Jack*? You have to tell everyone we were seeing each other for months and it was this big secret."

The restroom door banged open and a group of younger girls skated in. They wore tight glitter jeans and pastel-colored tank tops, and they were all talking about someone named Connie: Connie better get her hands off Trey. Connie didn't know who she was messing with. Connie was going to regret she ever came here. The girls leaned toward the mirror to reapply their lip gloss. Every now and then they glanced at Lucy and Melissa as if to make sure they were paying attention.

"Any of you have a cigarette?" Melissa asked.

"Are you crazy?" Lucy said. "They're like twelve."

One of the girls rolled her eyes. "We're fourteen," she said.

Another girl opened the door. "Come on, you guys," she said. "It's the couples' skate." The lights had dimmed, and there was a slow song playing. The younger girls finished putting on their makeup and filed out.

"There's no way those girls are fourteen," Melissa said.

"I know," Lucy said. "It's depressing." She thought of a girl she'd been tutoring earlier that week at the shelter, a skinny, dark-eyed girl named Tiana Woods. She was trying to pass pre-algebra, but her baby had an ear infection and wouldn't stop crying. The girls in the glitter jeans had looked about Tiana's age. "Listen to me," Lucy said. "Just don't go out to California. I know what I'm talking about."

Melissa sighed. "How could you understand?" she said. "Imagine if your mom had run off with some asshole. Imagine if your dad was married to the world's biggest bitch-on-a-stick, who always tried to treat you like a nine-year-old. Imagine your house feeling like a jail." She looked at Lucy, her eyes large and dramatic.

Lucy wondered if anyone could feel sorry for Melissa. She'd been to Melissa's house, that iced white cake on a cul-de-sac in Cincinnati. She'd met Melissa's stepmother, a small harried woman with two children of her own. Melissa's stepmother had made a low-fat vegetarian stir-fry for Melissa so she wouldn't have to wreck her diet with manicotti, which was what everyone else was eating that night.

"I guess I can't imagine," Lucy said.

"Now, here's what's going to happen. I'm going to fix my lipstick, and then I'm going back out there to skate. And then we're going back to Jack's house, and maybe we'll have a few drinks and watch a movie. In the morning Jack and I are going to load my stuff into his car and get on the road, and you're going to drive my car back to my house, and then you're going to take the Greyhound home." Melissa opened her purse and took out a folded envelope, from which she pulled two twenties and put them into Lucy's hand. "And you're going to do it so no one sees you, and if they do see you you're going to have sudden total amnesia."

"And then what?" Lucy said. "What happens tomorrow night, when your parents start to freak?" She thought about Melissa's father, who'd come to pick her up from youth group conventions—a narrow man in a beige golf shirt and gold glasses, huffing as he carried Melissa's suitcases. Hanging from the rearview mirror of his car was a Lucite photo holder with a picture of Melissa as a kid, playing a tiny violin.

"Are you going to help me?" Melissa said. "Or are you going to fuck it all up?"

"Let's just go home now," Lucy said. "*Home* home. Come on."

Melissa leaned toward the mirror and redid her lipstick. "Don't fuck it all up, Lucy. I mean that so seriously, you have no idea."

Lucy went into a stall and sat down. She heard the music swell as Melissa opened the restroom door, and then go quiet again as the door swung closed. She couldn't believe how stupid they all were. She should call Melissa's father right now. She should kick Jack's ass or shoot it off. What was she doing in this roller-rink bathroom? She stared at the back-of-the-door nail salon advertisement, at the gritty tile floor, at the smoked plastic Rollmastr with its eternal roll. All she wanted was to get out of there. She flushed and washed her hands and went to find Melissa.

There she was, on the far side near the railing, holding Jack's hand, leading him out onto the polished floor. He staggered a little at first, but then got his balance and began to skate. The Lurex fibers in his shirt caught the light. Melissa skated beside him, her ponytail swaying. Lucy stepped out onto the rink, meaning to catch up with them, do something, pry them apart, but as she started to skate another girl plowed into her. They both stumbled into the carpeted wall of the rink, trying to keep their balance. High-pitched shrieks of laughter came from the sidelines. There, pointing and calling out, were the younger girls from the restroom. The girl who ran into Lucy took a step back and straightened her pink tank top, her face streaked with tears. Lucy wondered if this was Connie, the Connie who had better watch out. "It's okay," she said to the girl. "We didn't even fall."

"Fuck you," the girl said, and skated away.

At Jack's house the volume of his mother's snoring had increased to a roar. Even with the door of Jack's room closed, Lucy could hear her going. She listened to the snore as they sat on a sleeping bag on the air mattress, drinking peach schnapps and watching a soft-core movie called *Wet and Wild West*. Lucy's head felt stuffed with wool. She couldn't take her eyes from the TV. Onscreen, two women in cowboy boots and Western shirts stood naked in a barn, licking each other's breasts and rubbing against each other. They looked bored enough to fall asleep. The sound was turned down low in case Jack's mother woke up, but not so low that they couldn't hear the soundtrack of sighs and moans. Jack had a hand up Melissa's skirt. Lucy could see it moving beneath the fabric. Melissa's eyes were closed and she was breathing fast, but Jack wasn't watching her. He was watching Lucy, giving her a secret smile. He put his other hand on her thigh and made a slow circle with his thumb. Lucy stared at his hand.

"I want to make you both happy," he said. "I want to make you both feel good."

Melissa's eyes snapped open. She looked at Jack's hand on Lucy's thigh. "What the fuck?" she said.

Jack removed his hand from Lucy's thigh.

"What the fuck, Lucy? Were you going to sit there and let him do that?"

Lucy shrugged. It was a good question.

"Shit, Jack," Melissa said. "Can't we go somewhere private?"

"But we're all comfortable here," Jack said.

"Not me," said Melissa. She got up and left the room, and Jack followed her. Lucy heard the bathroom door click shut. They were inside together, talking in low voices. Then Melissa began moaning, as if she were performing in the movie herself. Lucy rolled herself into the sleeping bag and closed her eyes. The snores echoed in the hall. Onscreen, the girls climbed coarse-looking ropes. From the bathroom came a series of sharp cries, Melissa's, rising in pitch. Lucy sat up and drank a glass of water with some ice. She knew why she was there that night: She was there because Melissa wanted a spectator. What good was it to elope to California if no one watched it happen, if no one could go to Nationals and spread the news? It would be the most spectacular thing anyone they knew had ever done. And who better to tell everyone than Lucy, that less-than-pretty girl who had no life of her own?

It wasn't just about telling their friends, though; Lucy knew that too. It was about Melissa's family. When her parents had been fighting, they'd been fighting over her: who would get custody, who had hurt her worse. Now, no one was fighting over her. Her mom was happy with the Minnesota businessman. Her dad had his new wife. Melissa was just one of their kids now, a picky teenager worried about her diet.

Lucy pulled herself to her feet. She found Melissa's keys and her own bag of unacceptable clothes, including the satin pajamas she'd bought to tantalize Jack. She went down to the car. Outside everything was dead silent, the small Tudor houses stretching along the curve of the street. She could hear the highway a few blocks away, a constant riverlike hum. The windows of the car were fogged. She opened the door and climbed into the driver's side, then slid the key into the ignition.

She thought about what would happen if she turned the key, if she pulled out into the street, if she drove all the way to Cincinnati and then took the bus home. She thought about what that would mean for Melissa. Melissa would have to go to California. There could be no backing out, after she'd made all those plans and then bragged about them. Lucy wanted to make her do it. She thought about how things would go for Melissa once she was living in Jack's ratty bungalow near the beach. Within weeks they'd hate each other. If they lasted, it would be worse. She imagined Melissa with a crying baby on her hip. Meanwhile, Lucy would have graduated from high school and gone on to college. Maybe Melissa would send a postcard from some miserable town out West. Lucy would spread the word, all right. She couldn't wait to do it.

Then she thought of the girl who'd crashed into her at the skating rink, the girl in the pink tank top who might or might not have been Connie. How Lucy had tried to let the girl know it was okay. How the girl had glared at her and said *fuck you.* That was what happened when girls treated each other the way those girls had treated Connie. They got to the point where they couldn't recognize help, where every other girl seemed like an enemy.

Lucy slid over to the passenger seat and opened the glove compartment. Inside, cool and solid, was the gun. She took it in her hand. It made her feel better just to hold it. What strange power, to be sitting there in a car on a quiet street, sleeping neighbors all around, with a gun in her hand and millions of things to shoot. She opened the door and aimed at a light post, at a bush beside the drainpipe of Jack's house, at the weathervane on the roof. *Bang,* she whispered. *Bang, bang, bang.* She put her hand up under her sweater, pressing the gun flat against her belly. She had to remind herself that it was real, a weapon, a thing that could make someone die. She imagined aiming at the ceiling of Jack's room, the pistol jolt and then plaster falling.

She got out of the car and went up the walk, into the house, and stood in the middle of the living room on the turquoise-rose and gold-scroll carpet. The house was quiet now. Outside, a streetlamp flickered. Squares of yellow light fell through the window and onto the carpet like scattered cards. Lucy climbed the stairs, the gun cocked before her, and edged down the hallway toward the bathroom. The sex noises had stopped. There was just the sound of the shower and of Jack talking. She listened. He was describing a problem he'd been having with his toenails. She could hear Melissa's faint *uh-huh*. They both sounded exhausted.

She went into Jack's room and lay down on the air mattress, holding the gun tight against her chest, beneath her shirt. The porno tape had ended, and the TV screen glowed blue. It had been hours since Lucy had eaten. She wondered what kind of food Jack's mother kept in the house, if there was cereal or a bagel. She would eat lox and cream cheese when she got home, lots of lox, lots of cream cheese, on an everything bagel with capers. Oh, she was tired. Maybe she could just take a little nap.

But down the hall there was the sound of a door opening and closing, and all the muscles in Lucy's back went tight. She pulled the covers over herself, keeping one eye half open. Jack came in, a towel around his waist, his hair wet from the shower. He knelt beside Lucy and touched her face. She breathed in through her nose in a way she hoped suggested deep sleep. There was a soft dull thump, his towel hitting the bedroom floor, and he climbed in beside her, naked. He was saying her name, shivering, pressing himself hard against her thighs.

"Wake up," he said into her hair. "Melissa's in the shower. It's our last chance." He reached under her skirt and wedged a hand between her legs.

She moved away from him, toward the wall, but he followed, trying to move his hand around inside her panties. She jerked away and stood up on the air mattress, bracing herself against the wall. In her other hand, still hidden beneath her shirt, she held the gun.

"Hi," he said, and gave her a weak smile.

"Get up," she said. "Now."

"Why?" he said.

She pulled the gun from beneath her shirt and pointed it at his head.

His smile fell away. He got to his feet. She could see his thighs contracting as if he meant to jump at her, and she lowered the gun until it pointed at his penis. "Don't make any fast moves," she said. "I could shoot you accidentally."

"Please tell me it's not loaded."

"It's loaded," Lucy said. "I checked, just like you showed me." She could shoot him right now. She imagined him lying on the ground, his eyes clouding, saying *It's not your fault*.

Jack's mouth opened. He pointed to a pair of shorts hanging off the back of a chair. "Okay if I put those on?" he said, trying to smile again.

"No," she said. "Just get into the closet."

He opened the closet door. The closet was crammed with papers, clothes, model cars, letters—hundreds of things. Jack had to climb on top of a crate of laundry in order to fit inside. He crouched in the semi-dark, staring at Lucy. "It's you I love," he said. "I made a mistake."

"Bullshit," Lucy said.

"I mean it. I told Melissa everything."

"Right," Lucy said. "After you fucked her."

"Please, Lucy. Give me the gun."

Lucy closed the closet door. She took the desk chair and wedged it underneath the doorknob the way she'd seen it done in movies. It seemed to work; he pushed on the door from inside but it didn't open. She wedged the chair in even tighter. "Stop pushing," she said, "or I'll shoot right through this door."

He stopped pushing.

"You are one greasy motherfucker," she told him. "Anyone can see it."

"But I love you."

"I'll shoot your ass off," she said, pointing the gun at the closet door.

"You know, it's dark in here, Lucy. And it smells bad."

"It's your closet, not mine."

There was a scream. Melissa stood in the doorway, a towel clutched to her chest.

"Be quiet," Lucy said, and pointed the gun at her. "Jack's mom is sleeping."

"The gun," she said.

"Get your stuff," Lucy said. "Hurry up."

"Oh, shit, Lucy, don't point that thing at me. I mean it."

"We're going home," Lucy told her. "Get some clothes on."

"I'm not going home."

"Yes you are," Lucy said.

"What are you going to do, shoot me?"

"Is that a dare?"

"This is ridiculous, Lucy."

"No it isn't. You're getting your stuff, and we're going home." Lucy picked up Melissa's bag and threw it at her, trying to remember if she'd ever once before told Melissa what to do. It felt clean and right. "Pack your clothes," she said. She had to get them out of there, because in another minute she was going to start to freak.

Melissa struggled into her black crocheted dress and high heels. She stuffed the thigh-highs into her overnight bag and looked up at Lucy.

"Stand up," Lucy said. By this time the gun felt as if it were part of her hand, a magic finger she could point to make things happen. Melissa stood. Lucy took her by the arm and led her out into the hall.

"All right, all right," Melissa said, twisting her arm away from Lucy. "You don't have to pinch me like that."

Jack rattled the closet door again. Lucy let him do it. It was time to go now, down the hall, past the door of Jack's mom's bedroom and the photographs of Jack as a little kid, and then down the stairs to the scroll-and-rose living room and out the front door and into the yard. All along the street the sad Tudor houses were jaundiced with morning sun. Melissa stumbled down the front walk, the black bag bumping against her hip.

"Come on," Lucy said, and took her around to the passenger side of the car. Lucy got in on the driver's side, throwing their clothes into the back seat. When she started the car, the roar of the engine felt sweet and strong. She pulled out and drove toward the highway, cranking DJ Mellow B on WLUX. He was playing Marvin Gaye, "What's Going On?" The gun was in Lucy's lap, within plain sight of anyone who wanted to look into the car. She tucked it into the waistband of her skirt. Melissa sat huddled against the passenger-side door and stared through the windshield, unblinking.

The sounds of Motown followed them, the Supremes and the Four Tops and the Marvelettes crooning them all the way onto the open highway. After a few miles Melissa reached for a cigarette and lit it, rolling down the window to blow smoke.

"Jack told me about going to see you," she said, wiping her nose on her sleeve. "He told me everything you did."

Lucy squinted at the road. "He did?"

"Yeah." She made a short harsh sound in her throat, half laughter, half disgust, and tapped a bit of ash out the window. "He said he didn't want any secrets between us. But it sounded more like he was bragging about how great you thought he was."

"He wasn't so great."

"God, what an asshole. Who knows who else he would have fucked before we made it to LA?"

"He tried to have sex with me this morning," Lucy said. "After he took a shower. That's why I put him in the closet."

"I'm not surprised," Melissa said. "He's got a serious dick problem. He's got hyperdickia."

"Yeah," Lucy said. "He's terminal."

Melissa put an elbow against the window and stared out at the passing rows of corn. "I feel sorry for our parents," she said. "They have no idea what goes on."

"At least you're not running away to California."

"Not this week."

Five minutes from Lucy's neighborhood, they stopped at a gas station and changed into jeans in the restroom. They fixed their makeup in the mirror and brushed their teeth. Lucy extracted the gun from the waistband of her skirt, where it had pressed painfully against her side. She and Melissa wrapped it in a paper towel and buried it in the garbage can. Silent and exhausted, they drove toward Lucy's house. As they rounded the corner of her street, Lucy could already imagine the way the house would smell when she opened the door: clean and dry, like fresh laundry. She could enter that house and go upstairs. She could take a shower. She could crawl into bed.

When they pulled up in front, her parents were planting flats of marigolds in the flower beds along the driveway. They wore gardening clogs and Michigan visors, and her mother had on her I DIG GARDENING T-shirt. Seeing them made Lucy want to cry with relief. Her mother lifted her trowel and waved.

Lucy touched Melissa's arm. "Go straight home," she said.

"I will," Melissa said. "I'll call you when I get there."

Lucy got out of the car and took her bag from the back seat. She slammed the door and watched the long white Cadillac ease away from the curb. After the car had turned the corner, she kissed her mother and father and went upstairs to her room. She threw her overnight bag into the closet. She turned down the covers of her bed, where Jack Jacob had touched her but would never touch her again. Then she went to the bathroom to take a shower, and when she took off her clothes she could still see the outline of the gun, plain as a photograph, against her skin.

What We Save

From the monorail Helena could see topiary cut into the shapes of giraffes and elephants and birds. Her sister Margot pressed her nose against the glass, watching, but their mother didn't even look out the window. Instead she sat with her chin on her hands, staring into the empty aisle. They shot past a lake full of flamingoes, then threaded their way through what seemed like an endless parking lot. Near the ticket gates, a voice announced that they had reached their final stop. Helena had to touch her mother's shoulder to bring her back from wherever she'd gone in her mind. They stood and moved toward the monorail doors with all the other families. The doors slid open to admit a blast of thick wet heat, and Helena and her mother and sister stepped out into it.

It was nine o'clock already. By now the Sewalds would be waiting for them at the landscaped Mickey Mouse head, but there was a long line at the ticket counter. As they joined the back of the line, Helena's mother straightened her wig and looked at her watch, and Margot jumped in place, her brown curls flapping against her neck. Blood thrummed in the backs of Helena's legs. She wished she were back in the hotel with her father, listening to him prepare his lecture on T-cells. The last thing she felt like doing right now was walking around a theme park with her mother's high school boyfriend and his family. Her mother had been in love with Brian Sewald and had gone to the prom with him nineteen years earlier. Every year at Christmas they received a postcard from the Sewald family: blond Brian, his wife, and their twin sons, in bathing suits on the beach, with the caption *Holiday greetings from Florida!*

This past winter, Helena's mother had studied the post-card for a long moment before putting it up on the refrigerator. In the photo Brian was almost bald. "He used to have such beautiful hair," she said to Helena.

Helena sat quiet and looked at her mother's own hair, sparse and feathery as the down of a baby bird.

"It's always nice to get a postcard," her mother said, staring out into the frozen garden. In high school, when Brian was failing History, Helena's mother had tutored him so he could stay on the swim team. His grades improved, he led the team to a state championship, and after dinner one night he asked Helena's mother to the prom. She tried to hide her surprise, but then she overturned her plate of blackberry pie into the lap of her yellow dress. Helena had seen the dress with its faded blue stain. Her mother kept it in the attic, packed away in mothballs.

Now Brian was an engineering professor at the University of Miami and had a small boat he sailed on the weekends with his family. The postcard showed the two Sewald boys, tanned and wearing turquoise bathing trunks, sitting on the edge of the beached sailboat, holding its rudder and ropes. They were sixteen now, two years older than Helena. She liked their sharp looks—their flat slim muscles and high cheekbones and the near-white hair hanging blunt against their foreheads. One of the boys grinned into the camera, his eyes narrowed by the sun. The other boy's eyes were shadowed beneath the fall of his hair, and his upper lip was curled. He seemed about to say something mean to his mother, who was crouched in the hollow of the boat. Nora Sewald, a slim brunette in a red tank suit, rested her hands on her sons' shoulders and laughed. Brian stood in front of the boat, one foot planted before him in the sand, his body angled slightly toward his family as if to say proudly, *This is what I've done.*

By the time they received the Sewalds' holiday card, the cancer had already moved into Helena's mother's liver. There had been talk for a while about a bone marrow transplant, but her doctors had ruled it out; her body was already too weak. Now Helena's mother took Taxol twice a month, a thin red chemo made from Pacific yew trees. Every other Wednesday she would come home pale and speechless from the hospital and make casseroles, riding out the last few hours before the drugs hit her full-force. Helena and her sister and father would eat the casseroles for the next three days while her mother lay in bed or on the bathroom floor, in alternate states of retching, fever, and cold. The medical conference in Orlando fell during one of her mother's chemo-free weeks, and they decided that a family trip—this normal thing, something other families did—would be good for all of them. But a family trip wasn't supposed to include seeing your high school boyfriend. That should have seemed obvious to everyone, Helena thought, particularly to her father. It frightened her that he hadn't objected, though she could not have explained why.

They could see the gray spires of Cinderella's Castle in the distance, a sight that had once filled Helena's chest with a glad ache. Now, as she watched her mother pull at the collar of her shirt and check her brown shoulder-length wig in a tiny compact mirror, the spires seemed like an obstacle, like mountains they'd have to cross.

"Does it look all right?" her mother asked, frowning into the mirror and pulling a few bangs toward the center of her forehead. "To me it doesn't look any better than the other ones."

"It looks natural," Helena said. "It's much better than the

other ones." It was the truth, but she hated the wig anyway. Her mother's hair had been curly and long, a dark red-brown. Her friend Maya Kearn, a painter, had once portrayed her wearing nothing but that hair. Maya was an old college roommate of her mother's, disabled in a car crash, and Helena stretched canvases and ran errands for her on the weekends. Six years earlier, Maya had painted Helena's mother nursing Margot in a red velvet chair. In the painting Helena's mother was nude, and her hair fell around her body in loose waves.

"Nine-fifteen," Helena's mother said, looking at her watch. She craned her neck to check the length of the line, the tendons pulling beneath her skin. Helena worried that her mother would get heat exhaustion or something worse, standing in that line. The last time they'd all gone out together— it was to a street art fair where Maya Kearn had displayed her Wheelchair Nudes, along with a couple of Helena's own collages—her mother had been walking along, holding Margot's hand, when she suddenly turned pale and pitched forward onto the sidewalk. She knelt there holding her belly, silent and gray-faced, while Helena's father pushed back onlookers with his long arms, his cool physician's voice edging into panic as he told Helena to call EMS. The ambulance moved tar-slow through the masses of people; that was how it seemed to Helena as she knelt next to her mother, holding the ends of her head kerchief away from her face as she coughed and dry-heaved. That time the CAT scans had revealed that the breast cancer had moved to her abdomen and into her ovaries, causing them to swell and finally burst, and the doctors performed emergency surgery. Helena's mother woke to learn that she'd had a hysterectomy. "Your father fainted to the floor when he saw the scans," she told Helena as she drifted back from anesthesia. Helena's father was an oncologist.

Later, as her mother slept, Helena asked her father if he had really fainted.

"The rumors are true," he said quietly, adjusting the blanket over Helena's mother's feet.

"How bad is it?" Helena asked.

"We'll see." He folded his arms across his chest and looked at his wife. Her chest rose and fell, and her skin looked paper-thin in the fluorescent hospital light.

Helena wanted her father to be powerful, to speak with conviction about new things they could try. She'd seen video-tapes of cancer cells multiplying and extruding into healthy tissues, and she imagined that taking place now, within her mother's body. She wanted her father to reach in and put a stop to it. But he sat down in a vinyl chair beside the bed, his hands limp at his sides, a thin man exhausted from worry. Helena looked at her mother asleep on the bed, her arms bruised from blood draws and injections, and felt as if her own chest were being crushed to a tiny knot.

When they reached the front of the line, Helena's mother had to root around in her straw shoulder bag for the special convention coupons. Helena heard the children behind them whispering, and she thought she heard one of them say *wig*. She turned around and met the eyes of a dough-faced redheaded boy. His mouth opened dumbly as Helena threw him her Killing Stare. Finally Helena's mother unloaded the contents of her bag onto the ticket counter. There was the suntan lotion, her checkbook, the makeup compact, a hair-brush, and a square black velvet box with a gold clasp, which Helena had never seen before. Helena picked up the box and turned it over in her hands.

"That's not for you," her mother said, and took it away.

"Is that a present?" Margot asked.

Helena's mother shook her head, continuing to pile things onto the counter until she found the vouchers in their crum-pled envelope. Then she paid the ticket man, swept every-thing back into her bag, and at last they entered the park.

Helena's mother walked ahead of her daughters, her back narrow beneath a white cotton shirt, her brown highlighted hair blowing in the hot breeze. Margot and Helena almost had to jog to keep with her as she wove through the mass of Hawaiian-shirted parents and sweaty sunburned kids. The air smelled of funnel cakes and French fries and Coppertone, and underneath it all was the green mildewy smell of Orlando, the thick tropical humidity you had to work hard to breathe. Helena's arms and legs, bare for the first time after three months of Michigan winter, felt naked and spindly.

"There they are," her mother said, turning back toward her daughters. She licked her thumb and wiped a tiny orange stain from Margot's cheek. To Helena she said, "Stand up straight." Helena pulled her shoulders back until her mother turned away.

The Sewalds were not hard to recognize—a tall bronzed family in colorful clothes, standing near the stone ledge in front of the landscaped Mickey Mouse head. They seemed comfortable there, a natural part of the music and bright paint of the park. Helena's mother raised her chin and touched her hair as she headed toward them. Brian Sewald looked just as he did in his Christmas photograph—like someone who played a lot of golf. He wore gold-rimmed glasses and a red-and-white-striped polo shirt, and his skin was so tan and smooth it looked polished. When he saw Helena's mother he opened his arms and walked toward her. He embraced her and kissed her forehead. Nora Sewald flashed a gummy smile, then came forward and kissed Margot, mashing her little glasses askew. To Helena she gave a cold fluttering pat on the back. The last time they'd seen the Sewalds, Helena, five years old, had spilled grape juice on Nora's linen tablecloth. Helena's mother had offered to clean it for her, but Nora had said sharply, "No. Just leave it for the maid."

Nora may have been Tropicana Queen two years in a row, but Helena's mother was a pediatrician and had tutored Nora's husband. Helena had gotten the sense, even at that disastrous lunch, that her mother made Nora feel uninteresting and slow.

"Well, now," Brian Sewald said, holding Helena's mother at arm's length. His eyes traveled slowly from her highlighted wig to her sharp collarbone to her thin chest. "How's Nancy-Nancy?" He waited for her to say something, but she just raised the corner of her mouth in an unhappy half smile. After a moment he blinked hard and turned away.

"You're tall," Margot said, looking up at Brian.

"That's what I'm told," he said. He scruffed Margot's bangs and tweaked the ear of her Mickey Mouse hat. Then he turned to Helena. "Look at you," he said, reaching forward to squeeze her arm. "You've become a real lady." She smiled to be polite, then stepped away, crossing her arms over her small new breasts.

"Your sons have grown too," Helena's mother said brightly.

Nora Sewald leaned close to Helena's mother. "Don't tell them they look big," she whispered. "They're trying to lose weight for wrestling." She held Helena's mother's shoulders in her hands and stood behind her. "This is Daddy's friend," she said slowly to the boys. "Louis, Jeremy, you remember her, don't you? They remember you, Nancy. They're shy."

The twins nodded to Helena's mother, then looked at Margot and Helena. Helena pulled her sister in front of her. "This is Margot," she said. "She wasn't born last time we saw you."

The twins muttered a greeting.

"Which one's who?" Margot said.

"Louis is the one with the faggy earring," one of them said. He pointed to a tiny silver hoop in his brother's left earlobe. Louis mock-punched Jeremy in the gut.

"Nice touch, huh?" Brian came over to lay a hand on Louis's shoulder. "I look away for one minute, and they're putting holes in themselves." Brian shook his head, and Louis glanced at Helena. She smiled a little and rolled her eyes.

A ponytailed Disney photographer approached them and asked if they would like to have their picture taken with the beautifully landscaped Mickey Mouse head behind them. The Mickey Mouse head, she told them, consisted of forty different kinds of vegetation from all over the world, including three varieties of fern that were now extinct in the rain forests but preserved here by the careful hands of Disney landscapers.

"We want a picture, don't we?" Brian Sewald said to Helena's mother.

"Maybe just the kids," Helena's mother said.

"Oh, nonsense," Nora said, and touched Nancy's hair. "Everything looks fine." Nora's own hair hung glossy and dark, chin length, and her skin shone pink with health. She linked arms with Helena's mother and faced the photographer.

The Sewald boys stood behind Nora, and Helena's mother held Margot's hand. Helena found herself standing between Brian Sewald and her mother.

"On three, now," the photographer said, stepping back with the camera ready.

Just then Helena's mother began to cough, wet and deep in her chest. She bent at the waist and held her hand in front of her mouth, her shoulders jerking. After a few moments she gasped for breath and wiped her eyes.

The photographer lowered her camera and waited. Helena's mother's eyes were still tearing, and her face had flushed red. She coughed again and shook the hair out of her face, one hand open on her chest. Shuddering a little, she began to breathe slowly and deeply. Helena fished a tissue from her pocket and wiped the circles of mascara from beneath her mother's eyes.

"Don't fuss with that," her mother said, straightening her shirt.

"Is she all right?" Nora asked. "Are you all right, hon?"

"I'm fine," Helena's mother said, but her eyes flicked nervously toward Brian before she looked at the photographer and smiled.

While the adults took Margot to see the Enchanted Tiki Birds, Jeremy and Louis and Helena went to buy ice cream. The twins walked ahead of Helena, their hands thrust deep into the pockets of their baggy shorts. Jeremy had a biker-style wallet, and Louis kept trying to pull its chain. When he caught the chain, his brother would slap him on the head. After one particularly hard slap, Louis dropped back to walk with Helena.

"We heard your mom's sick," he said.

Jeremy glared back at Louis. "Shut up, fuckhead."

"What?" Louis said.

"You have to ignore Louis," Jeremy told Helena. "He's completely stoned. Both of us, actually. We smoked up before we came here."

"That's why we need ice cream," Louis explained.

"It's okay," Helena said. It was better they talk about it. She got so tired of her school friends trying to act as if everything was normal when it clearly wasn't. People noticed wherever they went. At the grocery store, strangers helped Helena and her mother load bags into the car; on the monorail that morning, a healthy Swedish woman stood so Helena's mother could sit down.

"I hear people take pot pills for cancer," Louis said. "Pure lab cannabis."

"My mom doesn't take that," Helena said.

"How long has she been sick?" Louis asked.

"A long time. Five years."

"Five *years*? Shit, I couldn't stand it. I'd shoot myself."

"No you wouldn't," Jeremy said. "You wouldn't have the balls."

"I would too."

"No you wouldn't."

They paused at an ice-cream cart and bought chocolate-covered bananas. The vendor, a Hispanic girl with icy orange lipstick, smiled at Jeremy and Louis and gave them extra napkins. They took their bananas over to a wooden bench and peeled off the wrappers.

"Our parents went to prom together," Jeremy said.

Helena bit off the tip of her banana and crunched the chocolate. "I know," she said. "We have a picture of them. Your dad wore a stupid frilly tux."

Louis gave Helena a tilted smile, his teeth full of chocolate. "Hey, do you think he got any action?" he asked. "You think they did the old bing-bang?"

"Jesus, Louis," Jeremy said. "Can you shut the fuck up?"

Helena wanted to smack the chocolate-covered banana right out of Louis's hand and grind it into the asphalt with her heel. Not that she hadn't wondered whether her mother and Brian had ever done it. Most recently she'd thought of it when the Sewalds' holiday photo had arrived—there was something about the way her mother had stared at that picture, and at Brian in particular. She knew her mother and Brian had gone steady all summer after the prom. They'd probably had plenty of opportunities.

One night, not long before this vacation, Helena dug up her mother's pink high school album. Her mother had pasted various scraps onto the black pages: a pair of lace gloves, the gilt-edged prom invitation, and, nestled between sheets of green tissue, the three gardenias Brian had given her. In the prom photograph she and Brian stood in a gazebo, rain slanting through the palms behind them. Her mother wore an airy-looking bell of white chiffon, and the gardenias were nestled into her dark curls. She was pinning Brian's boutonniere onto his lapel. His eyes were upturned and his mouth was open, as if he were laughing, and he had one hand on her mother's waist. "He looks like he's going to bite her," Margot had said when Helena showed her the picture.

Helena imagined the two of them later that night in Brian's car, her mother's dress damp with rain, the gardenias wilted in her hair. Did he try to kiss her, to touch her legs, her breasts? Helena's friend Fisher, a tall thin boy who built remote-control airplanes, had French-kissed her in his garage once and touched her through her shirt. His fingers had looked clean but smelled like plane-engine oil, and they'd felt warm on her breasts. Afterward his eyes were wet, grateful.

Helena finished her banana and held the sticky wrapper between her thumb and forefinger. "I think we should get back," she said. "They'll be done soon."

Louis took the wrapper from Helena and flicked it into a bush. "You know we live in Dade County," he said. "That's where Jim Morrison whipped his dick out and got arrested for it." He cackled loudly.

Helena felt a surprising twinge of anger. "We live in Detroit, where Joe Louis is from," she said. "Joe Louis kicks Jim Morrison's skinny ass."

"Whoa," Jeremy said. "Watch out."

Louis weighed his half-eaten banana in his hand for a moment, then drew his arm back and lofted it far over the bushes. After a moment they heard a dull metallic thud.

"Goodbye to that," he said.

Margot emerged from the Tiki Room holding a souvenir plush parrot and singing the Tiki Room song: *All the birds sing words and the flowers bloom, in the Tiki-Tiki-Tiki-Tiki-Tiki Room.* She ran to Helena and the twins, who were waiting near the exit.

"There was a volcano out the window," she said, "but it was a fake." She sniffed loudly. "I'm allergic to this air. I need my nose spray."

Nora and Brian came out arm in arm, and Helena's mother followed.

"I thought it was fun," Nora Sewald said. "I liked those birds."

"They didn't seem as real as they have other times," Helena's mother said. "You could hear their beaks clicking." She brushed a few strands of hair out of her eyes and placed one hand against the side of her head, steadying her wig.

They all walked together toward a fountain near the center of the park. Parents and children sat all around it, resting from the heat. The fountain itself was an amazing thing. Pink stone fish spat water toward a plaster Cinderella, skirting her in a dome of spray. Nora held Brian's hand and looked up at Cinderella, and the twins grinned into the sun, wholesome-looking in their stoned daze. Helena's mother, eyes dark underneath, cheeks sharp-boned, rummaged in her bag for Margot's nasal inhaler. Margot sniffed miserably and rubbed a hand under her nose. Watching them, Brian dropped his wife's hand and sat down on the fountain's edge.

Nora sat next to her husband and unfolded a map of all the different "lands." Their thighs met and she rested a hand on his knee. Helena's mother moved closer to the Sewalds, leaning over Brian's shoulder to look at the map.

"Tomorrowland's closest," she said. As she pointed, her arm grazed Brian's shoulder.

"Sounds fine to me," Brian said. He kept his eyes down and his hands folded in his lap.

"We should do whatever you're up for, Nancy," Nora said.

Helena's mother looked at the map again. "We could start with the Carousel of Progress and move on to the Astro Orbiter, and then maybe have lunch."

Nora raised her eyebrows. "That's a lot of walking."

"Not really," Helena's mother said. "It's all close together."

"You and I could drink a lemonade while Brian takes the kids on the rides."

"If I want to rest, I'll rest," Helena's mother said. Helena could hear the strain in her voice. She was glad when Brian glanced sharply at Nora and said, "Nancy knows what she can and can't do."

Nora looked like she meant to say something more, but then she slapped her knees and stood. She went over to her sons, who were tossing an empty Coke can back and forth between them. "What are you doing?" she said. "That's trash."

Louis gave a thin cold laugh that made Helena wince.

When he set the can down on the fountain's edge, three dazed bees crawled from its mouth and danced in circles, their wings gummed with soda.

Nora's eyes grew wide. "Get away from that! God!"

"Hey," Brian said. "Who wants to go to Tomorrowland?"

"Me," said Margot.

"Well, let's not stand around all day here, then." He offered a hand to Helena's mother, and she got to her feet, lifting her yellow straw bag onto her shoulder. Nora didn't wait for them. She took her sons' arms and began to walk, her steps clipped and quick between the twins' loping strides.

Helena saw how difficult it was for her mother to keep up as they walked from ride to ride. The lines of her mouth were drawn tight, and one arm was folded against her chest as if to protect her scars. The things cancer had taken from her, it seemed, were beginning to compete in size and mass with what remained. Some time ago Helena had constructed a small collage of her mother as the invisible woman—the woman-becoming-more-and-more-invisible—one outline of her on the right side, filled with everything she had now, and another outline on the left side, with everything she'd lost: colored wool for hair, shellacked hazelnuts for breasts, millet lymph nodes, glass-bead ovaries, pumpkin-seed uterus. This was what dying meant, Helena thought—everything that had been you, leaving. Late that night, Maya had come into the studio to find Helena just finishing, gluing the last seeds to the blue paper. She wheeled over to the table to look at Helena's work. "What's happening there?" she asked.

It would be a series, Helena explained, the woman on the left finally claiming the one on the right, outline and all, until in place of her mother there was blank blue paper.

Maya held the collage for a few moments, frowning. "Hmm," she said. "This would seem to suggest that a woman's just a bunch of organs."

Helena was surprised, hurt. She'd wanted to please Maya, to show her she could say something new and complicated about illness, as Maya had with her Wheelchair Nudes— women sitting in their chairs in groups of two or three, wearing their scars without shame. "I thought you'd like it," she said.

Maya touched Helena's knee. "This is your *mother* we're talking about," she said, her voice patient and slow, and Helena had wanted to cry.

By the time they'd toured the Carousel of Progress and ridden the Astro Orbiter and eaten lunch, Helena's mother's shoulders were sagging and the circles beneath her eyes had darkened to violet gray. She sat at the restaurant table picking at the bun of her chicken sandwich, her wig drooping in the humidity.

"Are you all right?" Helena asked her. "Can I get you more lemonade or something?"

Helena's mother let out a sigh. "I'm fine, honey," she said.

Beside her, the twins sprawled in their chairs, drumming their sneakers against the tiled floor. Nora sipped her lemonade and looked out at the white peaks and antennae of Tomorrowland. But Brian sat watching Helena's mother, his own sandwich unfinished in its plastic basket.

"Maybe you and I should sit out awhile," he said. "Nora can go on ahead with the kids."

"That's right," Nora said. "You take a break, Nancy."

Helena's mother didn't seem to have the strength to argue. Instead she sat back in her chair and said, "I think it's the heat. I'm not used to it anymore."

"Why don't I take the kids to Space Mountain?" Nora said. "That'll give you two time to catch up." She stood and took Margot's hand. Margot looked anxiously at her mother, then at Nora, as if she wasn't sure what she was supposed to want to do. Helena wasn't sure herself. She didn't like the thought of leaving her mother alone with Brian.

"Go on," Helena's mother said. "We'll be right here."

"That's right," Brian said. "We're going to sit here in the shade. I think I may have gotten a little too much sun myself." He raked a few strands of hair across his bare scalp and then quickly pushed them aside, as if embarrassed by the act.

Space Mountain was housed in a complex structure of interconnected cones, white metal jutting like an iceberg into the Florida sky. Sunlight glinted from the high ridges, and shadows hung ghostly blue in the valleys. Nora steered Margot and the twins through a black arching doorway twenty feet high. Helena followed them into a long tunnel where they waited with other parents and children, watching projections of stars and planets and listening to synthesized space music.

"It's just like I remembered it," Helena said, to no one in particular.

"You should ride with me," Louis said. He reached over and pinched her waist, and she swatted his hand away, moving toward Margot and Nora.

"How're the allergies?" she asked Margot.

"Bad," Margot said, lifting her glasses to rub her eyes. "I'm all itchy."

"Don't rub," Helena said, holding Margot against her. "You'll make it worse."

Nora gave Helena and Margot her tight, gummy smile. "You must be a big help to your mom, Helena," she said. "It must be terrible for Margot. But you're so much older. You must be like a little mother to her yourself."

Helena felt words coming to her, a polite response. Then she looked at Margot, who was still rubbing her eyes, and something contracted in her chest, a kind of visceral fear. "Margot has a mother," she said, her voice hollow in the tunnel.

Nora stopped smiling. "I didn't mean otherwise," she said. She inspected her fingernails for a moment, then met Helena's gaze. "You must be proud of your mom," she said. "Both your parents. It's lucky they're doctors. They'll get her the best treatment possible."

Helena nodded, and said yes, that was lucky. But she wasn't sure how lucky it was. She'd seen her mother turn pale as she palpated some growth beneath her own skin or examined the tracery of veins in her arm. Other husbands wouldn't pass out when they saw their wives' CAT scans. Other women wouldn't understand how sick they were.

In a few minutes they reached the front of the line. The place was rigged up like a high-tech loading dock, with curved plastic tubes and machinery tangled across the far wall. Whooshing fluty music filled the boarding area, and a woman's voice instructed them that their mission would commence in three minutes. An orange light flared from a tunnel as a set of three cars rolled forward onto the loading platform. The cars were made of sparkly black plastic, with foam-covered safety bars and working headlights. Two people could ride in each car.

"Margot has to ride with an adult," Nora said. "That's me, I suppose."

Jeremy climbed into the car behind his mother's, and Louis took the one behind Jeremy's. Helena slid in next to Jeremy, who didn't look at her. She was glad they were finally getting on the ride. The thought that Brian Sewald and her mother had been alone together all this time made her uneasy.

The ride workers moved forward to secure the safety bars and to wish everyone a good journey. As the cars rolled into the dark tunnel, Helena felt Jeremy's hand brush against her leg. She shivered and moved closer to the edge of the car. Behind them she heard Louis whispering, "Do it, man, you have to do it."

"I'm trying," Jeremy said, under his breath.

Helena's back stiffened as they began to ascend on a clicking track. They clicked higher and higher, and it was dark all around them except for the pinpricks of electric stars glowing high above. Screams and mechanical rumbles echoed far off, and Helena could see the headlights of other cars looping and shooting in the distance. Jeremy touched her thigh again. Margot giggled in the car ahead of them, and Nora laughed with her.

"Stop it," Helena hissed. "Your mother's right there."

"So?" Jeremy said. His hand moved over her shorts, and she covered her lap with her own hands. He shoved his fingers beneath hers and squeezed her thigh. Helena wanted to scream. She pinched his hand, but he didn't move it. There was the caramel pull of the last moment up, when she knew they were already hanging over the drop, and then the air slicked her hair back and she became weightless. The padded metal harness pressed hard against her shoulders and legs. Margot and Nora shrieked. Jeremy's hand moved toward Helena's crotch, and her body went rigid. They fell into the back-crunching pit of the drop, the car snaking right and left, and Helena flushed hot with anger and shame as Jeremy rubbed the denim between her legs. She curled her fingers and scratched his wrist as hard as she could. He yelped and pulled away, whispering "Fuck!" under his breath. Now they were clicking up another track. Their car slid over the top again, down into the crush of gravity, and then they looped upside down, suspended for one clacking moment over a sea of formless black. There was another loop and a series of sickening dips and rises. Helena let her hands relax for a moment, and just then Jeremy reached inside her shorts and ground his knuckles against her. An orange light loomed ahead, and they shot into a screaming tunnel of tangerine strobe light. At last the car slowed as they rolled up to a red-lit unloading dock. "Please step off to your left," a disembodied female voice instructed. "Please step off to your left."

Margot was crying as she climbed out of the car, holding a broken plastic ear from her Mickey Mouse hat. The other was still attached. "My glasses fell off," she cried. "They're gone, Helena!" She held the broken ear and stood there watching the cars move back into the tunnel.

"Shh, shh," Nora said. "Your dad will buy you a new pair."

"But I can't see!" Margot wailed.

Nora took Margot's hand and led her along the corridor. The twins walked just ahead of Helena, laughing. Jeremy whispered something, jabbing his hand forward rhythmically, and Louis clapped him on the shoulder. Helena felt as if she were burning or bleeding, as if her body were marked; everyone would see what had happened as soon as she stepped into the light. She wanted to take Margot and crouch inside the blue-lit tunnel forever. She never wanted to see the twins' faces on the refrigerator again, or be told to stand up straight for their sake. She wanted to scratch their blue eyes out. The only thing that kept her feet moving and her arms still at her sides was the thought that she had to get back to her mother.

When Helena broke into the light, she had to squint and shield her eyes. Margot ran ahead of Nora and the twins, weaving a little, toward the restaurant. As Helena got closer, she could see Brian and her mother still sitting at the table. She went inside just behind Nora, ready to tell her mother what had happened, to show her who these people really were. But her mother's expression stopped her. She was pushing something toward Brian—the black velvet box—and saying something Helena couldn't make out. Her face was red and puffy, and a twisted Kleenex lay before her on the table. Brian shook his head, eyeing the box as if it frightened him, as if it contained something he wasn't supposed to touch. But when he looked up and saw his family coming, he took the box and put it in his pocket.

"Something terrible happened," Margot said, pulling the hat from her head.

Helena's mother dried her own eyes and then reached forward to dry Margot's. Her arm froze in the air. "Where are your glasses?" she asked.

Margot's voice rose in a wail, and she balled a fist against one eye.

Helena stepped forward and laid the plastic ear on the table. "They're in Space Mountain," she said.

"Oh, no," her mother said quietly. She looked from the disheveled Margot to Helena, who blushed as she tried to straighten her shorts.

"You're still a beautiful mouse in my book," Brian said to Margot, and set the hat back on her head. "We'll just look at you from the one side."

That made Helena's mother smile. She touched Margot's cheek. "Don't cry, now," she said.

As they moved through Fantasyland, Helena stayed close to her mother, taking in the faint ripe odor of her sweat. She still wanted to tell her what had happened in Space Mountain. But her mother seemed to be in another place now, untouchable. She wasn't adjusting her wig anymore or pulling at her shirt to disguise her small false breasts. Helena could see the pride she carried in her narrow shoulders as she watched Brian Sewald walk with his sons and wife. There was a silence in the way she moved, almost as if she were floating. Helena imagined that if she glanced behind her, she might see a trail of things her mother had let fall: bits of iridescent fabric and glass, white petals, locks of hair. She seemed truer to herself, finished with trying to make things appear different from the way they were.

Helena knew that was supposed to be better. She'd heard it a hundred times in school, seen it on banners in the halls: Be true to yourself! Celebrate yourself! But what if you were dying, losing yourself piece by piece? Were you supposed to be true to that? Helena had done everything she could think of to hold on to what her mother had lost. She'd imagined her mother's organs going through a kind of re-forging, a kind of mystical cleansing, after which they'd start their lives again in Helena's body—her mother's sick breasts becoming Helena's new healthy ones; her mother's ovaries, reborn, shooting estrogen into Helena's bloodstream. She'd seen herself as the woman on the right side of her collage, the outline into which her mother's organs were being transplaced. She'd saved strands of her mother's hair, fingernail parings, eyelashes, things she'd be able to touch six months or two years from now. She hadn't been able to say what it was she was dreading—not her mother's death, because that was beyond imagining. But as she watched her mother walk through the Magic Kingdom, eyes half focused, arms limp at her sides, past six-foot-tall mice and cotton-candy vendors and pink benches, in the shadow of Brian Sewald and his family, Helena knew that this was what she'd feared: her mother's decision to let go, to shrug off the things she'd saved. She wanted to throw herself down in front of her mother, hold on to her feet and scream. But her mother walked on, and Helena followed her.

After a while, Margot paused at a bench to tie her shoe. "Can you help me, Mom?" she asked. "I can't see the laces."

"I think we should go back to the hotel soon," her mother said, bending to tie Margot's shoe. "I'm getting tired." She finished the knot, then drew a hand across her forehead and closed her eyes.

"We can go back right now, if you want," Helena said, touching her mother's arm.

"No," Margot said. "I want to ride the teacups."

"Mom said she's getting tired. We can ride them tomorrow."

Brian and Nora turned around to see what was going on. But Jeremy and Louis were still headed for the teacup ride, and Margot pulled on her mother's hand. "One more ride," she said.

"Well," her mother said, "maybe just one more."

They went on toward the Mad Hatter's Tea Party, a huge pavilion beneath which pink and yellow teacups twirled on a rotating platform. It was late afternoon and the lines had thinned as people went to early dinners. By the time they reached the ride, the previous turn had ended and people were leaving through an exit on the other side of the pavilion. The ride supervisor opened the gate, and people ran to board the teacups. Jeremy and Louis scrambled into a yellow one with Nora, and Margot and her mother took a pink one.

"Look at us!" Margot yelled. "We're in a cup!" She waved to Helena and Brian, who stood near the rail.

Helena's mother took a kerchief from her yellow straw bag and tied it around her head, securing it under her chin so her wig wouldn't blow away. As the music started and the platform began to rotate, she took the metal disk at the center of her teacup and turned it, tentatively at first, then faster. Margot shrieked with pleasure as they whirled away.

"Those things make me sick," Brian said, leaning against the railing. "They make my head spin." He twirled a finger to demonstrate.

"Me too," Helena said.

The pink teacup came back toward them, close enough for Helena to see the thin muscles of her mother's arms straining as she turned the silver disk. She was laughing, her eyes closed against the wind as she spun herself away. Then Nora and the twins passed, hair whipping, mouths open with laughter.

"We're all tired," Brian said. "It's been a long day." He smiled at Helena, a weary, kind smile that made her feel the heaviness in her own arms and legs. She wanted to go back to the hotel and lie down.

"I'm going to sit in the shade," she said, motioning toward some benches.

He nodded. "Meet us when the ride's done."

She moved away from the railing and went toward the bank of benches, a little way behind Brian, next to a hot pretzel stand. The yeasty scent of the pretzels made her hungry, and as she squinted against the afternoon sun, a dull pain pressed at her temples. After a moment she saw Brian take the small velvet box out of his pocket, open it, and examine the contents. When his family whizzed by again, he closed the box and concealed it in his hand. Then, looking over his shoulder as if to make sure no one was watching, he knelt next to the railing and slid the box under a flattened paper cup.

The ride began to slow, and Brian looked up as Nora called his name. He went around to the far side of the pavilion to meet her. Helena moved forward to the railing, nudged the paper cup aside with her toe, and picked up the box. She felt its worn plush, the resistance of its hinges. Inside, on black velvet, lay three wrinkled and yellowed hulls, and Helena recognized them as the gardenias her mother had worn in her hair nineteen years before. There was an odd pain in her chest, a sharp constriction. She closed the box, feeling as if she'd seen something too personal, a kind of private leave-taking, and when she looked up she was almost surprised to see her mother coming toward her, blue eyes glazed with sun, laughing and tired and alive.

Stations of the Cross

  .
  .
  .
  .
  .
  .

Three weeks into our stay in Mexico, my mother sent the article from the *Times:* a photograph of Dale Fortunot and a brief note about his life. He'd been killed by a suicide bomber in Nablus, where he'd been working on a story for a political magazine. *Dear L,* my mother wrote. *Can this be the same Dale Fortunot? Don't want to upset you, but this caught my eye. Much lv always, Mother.* She'd written *P.S.* and then scratched it out, as if there were something more she'd meant to say but couldn't. I read the letter on the patio of the house we were renting, my husband and I, during the second trimester of my pregnancy. The trip was a kind of farewell to travel and to being alone together. I loved being pregnant and speaking Spanish all the time and waking up in the morning with nothing to do. The rest of the world and its coil of problems had come to seem like a dull, distant ache. The only newspaper we'd been reading was the local daily, *El Mensaje.*

The *Times* photo showed a fine-featured man in his late thirties, with small round glasses and light brown skin, smiling gravely, as if he already suspected his fate. The article described how he'd been interviewing Jewish settlers and Palestinian leaders for a feature that was to coincide with the fifty-fourth anniversary of Israel's independence. He'd been waiting at a checkpoint when a young Palestinian jumped out of a van and detonated a bomb strapped to his chest. Two Israeli soldiers had also been killed. According to the article, Dale had been writing about the Middle East for nearly a decade. He'd been married to an Israeli journalist, and they had a three-year-old son named Samuel.

Unmistakably, this was the same Dale Fortunot I'd known in south Louisiana. It must have been 1973 when we'd met, the year my mother and I had lived in Iberville Parish. Though my mother's note had made no mention of that time or of the incident that linked Dale Fortunot and me, I sensed in her scratched-out *P.S.* a kind of silent reproach. There I was, a grown woman, a professor of American Studies at Cornell, almost a mother, but suddenly I felt an old, fierce shame. I'd never forgotten Dale Fortunot or what had happened the day of his cousin's First Communion. My mother hadn't forgotten either. I wished she'd never seen the photograph, but there it was in my hand.

The first time I heard his name, Carney and I were sitting in her room rehearsing her saints. I remember some of them still—Saint Agnes, the patron saint of girls; Anthony the Abbot, saint of pets; Jude, the saint of hopeless cases—those mysterious holy men and women to whom you could turn with achingly specific needs, an opportunity Judaism did not afford me. I'd been taught to believe in a God who was everywhere and nowhere, a still small voice. That God seemed at once too grand and insubstantial to understand my problems. My parents had separated, and it looked like they weren't getting back together; soon afterward my mother had exiled us to Iberville Parish, where she had taken a job teaching high school drama. I was nine years old then, toward the end of third grade, and Carney was the same age. This must have been a few weeks before her Communion. We knelt on cushions in Carney's pink-wallpapered room, near her little shrine: prayer cards and images of the Virgin and rosary beads and a white Bible with Carney's name engraved in gold, set up on a carved footstool in the corner. Downstairs, her mother was making her a white tea-length organza dress with a satin sash. We could hear the thrum of the sewing machine and the groan of floorboards as Carney's mother moved from machine to cutting table. She was tall and queenly, probably the fattest woman I'd ever known. She smelled of lilac soap and wore tiny pastel house slippers and spoke with a deep Iberville Parish accent. Even when she wasn't home I could feel her presence in every room of the house.

"My godparents gave me a Saint Veronica prayer card," Carney said. "Look." She handed me a gilt-edged card that showed Jesus in rags, carrying the cross on his shoulder. A beautiful woman next to him held a cloth printed with a ghostly image of his face. Saint Veronica was Carney's saint. In a few days she'd take Veronica as her middle name.

"You should wear your hair like hers," I said. "Your mother could make two braids and join them in back."

"I'm not supposed to *look* like her," Carney said, "I'm supposed to *be* like her."

"How?"

"I'm supposed to be selfless and kind and full of compassion." She frowned, leaning the prayer card against a white candle. "She's an okay saint. I wish I'd gotten a martyr, though."

"I like the name Veronica," I said.

"I know, but still," Carney said. "A martyr would have been so perfect."

Carney was the kind of girl who craved drama—a girl, in other words, after my own heart. She made up games in which we got to be people like Marie Antoinette or Joan of Arc, people who died in flames or battle or terrible pain. In other games we were mistreated orphans who became suddenly, gloriously rich and exacted revenge upon our oppressors. Girls at school respected Carney and wanted to be chosen for her games.

People who'd angered her might come to school and find themselves shunned, invisible to everyone but the teacher. I considered myself lucky to be her best friend. She seemed a little awed by the fact that I'd come from New Orleans, a city she'd heard to be full of sinners and mansions and fancy restaurants. I pretended bored familiarity with all of the above, and faux-reluctantly devised games in which we went to Mardi Gras balls and dined at Galatoire's. Lately, though, Carney hadn't been interested in playing those kinds of games. She'd been sunk in the serious business of Communion preparation, a business that had required her to learn such things as the order of the Sacraments, the Stations of the Cross, the Holy Year and Fast Days, the Hail Mary and the Our Father.

Watching her, I was weak with jealousy. I wanted godparents and prayer cards and a shrine in my room. I wanted to carry a candle and wear a wreath. I wanted a white organza dress with a satin sash, and I wanted a new name, the name of an ancient and virtuous woman who'd protect me. I felt in need of protection. My mother and I didn't even go to synagogue anymore, because there was no synagogue in Iberville Parish. We must have been the only Jews within a fifty-mile radius.

I heard the sewing machine go silent downstairs, and the familiar creak and groan as Carney's mother crossed the living room. Her pink house slippers clicked as she made her way up the stairs. By the time she came through the doorway of Carney's room she was out of breath. The Communion dress was draped over one arm, and in her hand she held a box of pins.

"Time to pin your hem," she said to Carney. "Out of those clothes."

Turning her back to me, Carney shucked off her gingham shirt and jeans. Her mother lifted the Communion dress over her head and buttoned the ten pearlized buttons. When Carney's mother knelt to pin the hem, her hair fell forward to reveal the creamy sweep of her neck. I loved watching her work. Her nails were lacquered pink, and her hair was done in hot-rollered curls that hung over her shoulders like ripe plums. Her deep, rocking accent always lulled me into an admiring trance. My own mother spoke with a sharp accent from New York. I'd heard her students making fun of her in Pearson's Dairy, after school.

"Your Aunt Marian called this morning," Carney's mother said, pulling a length of hem between her fingers. "I never thought she'd come, but she says she will. She's bringing Dale, too, and you'd better be cordial."

"My *cousin* Dale?" Carney said. "The love child?"

"Your cousin Dale," Carney's mother said, her mouth going small and stern. "Your blood cousin, whom you will respect."

"I'll respect him, but I won't play with him," Carney said.

Carney's mother sat back on her heels. "I'll not tolerate that tone," she said.

"It's my Communion party," Carney said. "I shouldn't have to play with him if I don't want to."

Her mother took her by the shoulders and looked square into her eyes. "That is *quite enough*," she said, her voice low and full of warning. "Now, I can finish this dress, or you can take Communion in your underdrawers."

Carney dropped her chin, chastened, but I experienced a frisson of private pleasure. In the presence of Carney's mother, I was often rewarded with antique-sounding words like *underdrawers*.

"And I'll not tolerate talk about Aunt Marian either," she said. "I suppose she's not the best Catholic, but may the Lord strike me down before I judge her. I can't say what I would have done in her position." She released Carney's shoulders, her forehead creased, as if considering what she would have done. I glanced at Carney for a clue as to what this was all about, but she shook her head and gave me a look that suggested she'd explain later.

Carney's mother finished pinning the hem and stepped back to check her work. Stiff little organza sleeves rose from

Carney's shoulders like wings. The bell of her skirt floated around her legs, and the white satin sash trailed its streamers to below her knees. She looked ready to ascend to heaven. Her mother picked up a brush from the dresser and smoothed Carney's hair.

"You'll pass for a good child, anyway," she said. "I suppose that's the best we can do for now."

"She knows all her saints," I said, wanting her mother to believe I wasn't a bad influence. I'd gotten the sense that she didn't quite approve of the fact that I was Jewish. It was important to remain in her good graces, though. I'd been coming to Carney's every day after school, an arrangement that seemed precarious.

Carney's mother gave me a skeptical look. "*All* her saints?"

"All of them," I said. "Backwards and forwards."

"Well, that's something, at least," she said, but her tone was less than reassuring. She untied Carney's sash and unbuttoned the pearlized buttons. Carney stepped out of the dress and stood on the rug in her underdrawers. Her mother draped the dress over her arm and gathered her pins, but at the door frame she turned back and glanced around the room—at the dark rolltop desk, the carved bureau, the tall windows. She seemed to be remembering something. I knew this had been Aunt Marian's room, the room she'd had when she and Carney's mother lived here as little girls. Carney had shown me where she'd written her name in crayon on the wall behind the bureau: *Marian Beatrice Fortunot.* I wondered if Carney's mother would say something more about her sister, but she just turned and rustled out into the hall, muttering something to herself. We heard the click of her pink house slippers all the way down the stairs.

"So Dale's a love child," I said, once the thrum of the sewing machine had started up again. I tried to sound as if I knew what I was talking about, though I had only the vaguest idea of what a love child might be.

Carney finished buttoning her gingham blouse. She leaned close to me and whispered, "That's right. He's an actual dictionary-definition bastard. And half black. His daddy got my Aunt Marian in trouble and then went off to college up north."

"Your cousin's black?" I said. It hardly seemed possible.

"Black as night."

"Not if he's only half black."

"I don't know, actually," she admitted. "I've never met him. My grandfather didn't want him around. He didn't even want to see Aunt Marian. They hated each other, him and her. He tried to make her go to a Home, where she'd have her baby and then someone would adopt it. But she ran off to Biloxi and had it on her own. My grandfather just wanted to kill her. He wouldn't let her back in the house. He's dead now, though. He died in December. My mother said he had a drinking man's liver."

"Why didn't your mom ever take you to visit Dale?" I asked. "Wouldn't she want you to meet him?"

"I don't think she approves of him either. No one ever talks about it."

"Well, they'll talk about it now, with him coming and all."

Carney narrowed her eyes. "I don't see why he has to come," she said. "I don't want everyone looking at him and talking about him the whole time. It's my party."

"They'll still pay attention to you," I said, though I could see where they might be distracted. White people in Iberville Parish, particularly Carney's parents and their friends, had old-fashioned ideas about black people, ideas that seemed ignorant and provincial to me. My own parents had black professor friends from Manhattan, men with names like Ishaq and Lumumba, women who wore African head wraps and wrote poetry. Some of these people had come from New York to give guest lectures in my father's history classes at the university. But here in Iberville Parish, I'd heard white men call grown-up black men "boy." The black kids at our school didn't play with the white kids, and there were no black teachers at all. Close by, there were actual plantations that slaves had built with their own hands. And in town there was a restaurant with two separate entrance doors, one on either side of its brick façade. The words WHITE and COLORED were painted over now, but you could still see the red letters like ghosts beneath the paint. That restaurant was much closer to our house than Pearson's, but we never went there for dinner. When I walked by and saw people eating there I couldn't help feeling as if they must hate my mother and me as well. We were Jewish, not black, but we were outsiders all the same. They found little ways to remind us. At school last week we'd had to go around and tell how our families were celebrating Easter, and when we got to me the teacher had said, "Oh, y'all don't even celebrate Easter, do you?" The other kids stared. I was relieved to be able to say I was celebrating it at Carney's house, an answer that seemed to satisfy everyone.

The rest of that afternoon, as Carney and I finished up the saints and then played out back with her little brother and sisters, I kept thinking about Dale. For Carney's sake I wanted to be indignant about his daring to show up at her Communion, but for Dale's sake I was worried about how the guests would act. What I felt most, though, was a thrilling sense of dread. It was the way I used to feel in New Orleans when a hurricane warning had been issued. After we'd taped the windows and brought the garden furniture inside, I'd sit in my room and look out at the darkening street, willing the storm to come.

> *Lamb of God,*
> *You take away the sins of the world.*
> *Have mercy, have mercy on us.*

That was the song I was singing that evening as my mother and I walked from the high school to Pearson's for dinner. I didn't realize I was singing until my mother stopped on a street corner and looked at me as if goldfish were dropping from my mouth.

"What's that song?" she said.

"What song?"

"The one you were just singing."

" 'Lamb of God,' " I said, and my face went hot. I'd been singing a song about Christ. Carney had taught me the song because it was what everyone would sing while she and the other kids received Communion. It had seemed all right to learn it, because it didn't actually contain the word *Jesus* or *Christ,* but I'd never meant to sing it in front of my mother. She was giving me a hard look, her arms crossed over her chest.

"You're not turning Catholic on me now, are you?" she said.

"No," I said, indignant.

But she seemed thoughtful as we walked on toward Pearson's, and I worried again that I'd somehow jeopardized my afternoons with Carney. I didn't want to go back to doing my homework in the auditorium while my mother directed drama practice. Though the high school girls fascinated me, with their eye shadow and their bone-straight hair and their whispered bathroom gossip, I hated to see them snickering at my mother. It wasn't just the way she spoke. She wore crocheted berets and batik dresses and talked with her hands too much. When we'd lived in New Orleans it had never occurred to me to be embarrassed of her, but here in Iberville Parish I saw how people looked at her, and it made me want us both to disappear. What made it worse was that she seemed not to notice or care. Years would pass before I could admire her for that.

At Pearson's neither of us felt much like eating. It was Passover, so we couldn't even order the things we'd usually have. My mother had cottage cheese on a lettuce leaf, and I had a baked potato. I was thinking about the Communion and about Dale. I suppose my mother was thinking about my father. I still got to visit him twice a month, at his small brick house on Park Street in Old Metairie. Sometimes we cooked and sometimes we went to the Audubon Zoo and other times we just sat by the river, watching the barges haul their cargo toward the delta. My mother never saw him at all now, though. On the first night of Passover we'd always had a family seder, just the three of us at home, even when my mother and father could hardly bear to be in the same room together. This year my mother and I had a tiny seder together in the room we called the breakfast nook. We had both pretended to have a good time, but afterward I went to my room and lay in the dark and my mother took a long bath, the only thing that made her feel better when she was depressed. Now she ate tiny bites of cottage cheese and talked about *Twelfth Night,* the play she was directing. She'd wanted to do *Who's Afraid of Virginia Woolf?,* but the superintendent of schools had asked her if she was crazy.

"They keep doing their lines with English accents," she said, shaking pepper onto her cottage cheese. " '*Foh*-tune fohbid my outside have not *chahm'd* her.' I've told them fifty times it sounds absurd, but they won't stop doing it."

"It *is* an English play," I said.

"Whose side are you on, anyway?" my mother said. She twisted in the booth, looking for the waitress. The waitress was standing by the jukebox, talking to a tall boy in a red cap. They both laughed. My mother sighed and turned back to the table. She pushed at her cottage cheese with a fork. I watched her, trying to think of something I could say to distract her.

"Carney has a cousin who's a love child," I said.

"Oh?" My mother raised an eyebrow. "A love child, eh?"

"His dad was black," I said. "I don't think his parents ever got married."

"Oh," my mother said. "And what do you make of that?"

"I don't know. I feel bad for him, I guess. Carney's supposed to meet him for the first time this weekend. He and his mom are coming to the Communion."

"You feel bad for him?" my mother said. "Do you think he needs your pity?"

"I don't feel bad for him because he's black," I said.

"Is he black?" she said. "Why not white, if he has one parent of each color?"

I knew my mother didn't expect an answer. I looked at the salt shaker with its tiny holes, the napkin dispenser with its waxy napkins.

"It's his mother you should feel bad for," my mother said. "Imagine what she must have gone through, raising a child all by herself."

I heard the accusation in her tone, the reminder that she too was now raising a child by herself. I couldn't understand what had happened, why she'd gotten mad at me. I'd just been trying to make conversation. There was more I'd wanted to say, too, questions I wanted to ask, but now we weren't talking. It made me angry at all three of them, my mother and Aunt Marian and Dale.

We finished our dinner in silence, and my mother paid the bill. As we walked home I was thinking how strange it was that some people were Catholics and others were Jews, that some were prejudiced and others not. I wondered how it could be that people could love God and hate one another. I thought myself highly original for recognizing that paradox, and I felt proud of my own indignation. I knew the word *hypocrisy*, could almost feel it, salty and crackling, on my tongue. When we got home my mother took a bath. I lay in my room with the light off, feeling like a traveler in a strange and unforgiving land.

That Easter Sunday, for the first and only time in my life, I went to church with my mother. The church was St.

John the Evangelist, and it was Carney's First Communion day. Outside, my mother explained that we were there as guests, that we should act just as if we were at synagogue. If I had questions, she said, I should make a mental list and ask her later. We should be quiet and respect the prayers of others. I nodded, half listening, anxious to get inside that mysterious building and see what would happen at the Communion. I was so excited I'd almost forgotten about Dale.

The church was high and white and packed with lilies. Families in Easter clothes crowded the pews. My mother and I slid into a pew near the back, near a stained-glass window that showed Jesus bending over a sick girl. He looked like a worried father, his hand on her forehead as if he were checking for fever. At the front of the church there were racks of tall white candles, and a gold crucifix high on the wall. The Jesus there wore nothing but a gold cloth around his private parts. He looked sad and dead, his chest bleeding, his forehead crowned with thorns. There was a long white cloth draped over the arms of the cross behind him. The church smelled like wax and spice and the mingled scents of all the women's perfume. I hadn't expected to feel holy there, but I did.

Just before the service began, a woman and a boy slid in beside us. At once I knew that this was Dale and his mother. The boy, dark-haired and dark-eyed, wore a crisp dress shirt and navy pants. His skin was a pale walnut-shell brown. His small silver-framed glasses gave him the look of an older boy, though I could see he was about my age. His mother's hair hung lank and blond against her shoulders, and her arms were white against the blue of her dress. There was a fierce, open look in her eyes, a kind of challenge. She held Dale's hand tight and whispered something to him. He seemed embarrassed by what she'd said. When he glanced at me I took a hymnal and opened it, not wanting him to know I'd been watching him.

A priest and some boys in white robes entered from the

back. They walked up the aisle slowly as a great red swell of music rolled out into the church. I knew it was a pipe organ—I'd heard music like that on Sunday TV—but nothing had prepared me for the deep layered resonance I felt in my breastbone. I turned around to look up at the balcony, and there was a choir in white robes, and racks of silver organ pipes, some reaching to the ceiling, others so small they looked like little flutes standing on end. Behind the priest and the boys came the Communion children, each with a pair of adults whom I'd learned were their godparents. They all walked slowly and wore somber expressions. The children carried their white candles, the light falling gold on their chests. Carney came out last of all. Her hair was dressed in ringlets and she smiled with her mouth closed, her eyes lowered, as if she knew a holy secret she would never tell. I wanted her to see me but she wouldn't look up from her candle. Her godparents, high school friends of her mother's, smiled down at her as if she were their own child. Carney's mother and father stood beaming in a pew near the front of the church. Her little sisters Patty and Eleanor crowded forward to see her, and her three-year-old brother Jonah reached out to touch her skirt as she passed. Carney didn't look at any of them. She walked all the way to the front of the church, her face composed into that private sacred expression, and lined up with the other children on the altar steps. Dale's mother bent to him and whispered, loud enough so I could hear, "That little girl all the way on the right is your cousin."

The congregation sang hymns and said prayers, and the priest spoke about Jesus. He talked about how Jesus and his disciples took the Paschal meal together, and what Jesus said at dinner. After a while, I came to understand he was talking about Passover. The last supper had been a seder. Jesus and his disciples had eaten matzah, and that was why the Communion wafer was unleavened. I'd known Christ was a Jew, but I'd never pictured him having an actual seder. I imagined him singing "Dayenu." It almost made me laugh. I nudged my mother to tell her what I'd discovered, but she put a finger to her lips. Instead I stared at Carney, trying to make her look up from her candle. After a few moments she did look up, her eyes moving over the congregation. When she saw the boy standing next to me, beside a woman who looked like a sadder, slimmer version of her own mother, her holiness seemed to drop away. Suddenly she looked like the Carney I knew from the playground at school, someone who liked to stir things up.

At the altar, the Communion began. The priest made his way down the row of children, starting at the left. He said their saints' names and made each one of them eat a wafer. He drew an invisible cross on their foreheads with his thumb. Carney was still looking at Dale when the priest got to her, but when he said her new name, Caroline Veronica, she became holy and serious again. She opened her mouth and took the wafer. A shiver went through me as I imagined what was supposed to be happening at that moment: The wafer was supposed to change to Christ's body, there in Carney's mouth. The organ sent its blast of sound out into the church and all the congregants began to sing about the Lamb of God. Dale, too, knew the song. He moved his mouth, but I couldn't hear his voice among the other voices. My mother took my hand and pressed it.

"You can sing if you want to," she said.

At Carney's house we all got Easter baskets. Mine was wrapped in pink cellophane and had three chocolate eggs with the real-looking white and yolk, a net bag of tiny pastel-coated malt balls, two boxes of marshmallow Peeps, and a rabbit in gold foil—all the things I'd seen in the grocery store, things that were not supposed to be for me. My basket was as big as Carney's, bigger than the ones that belonged to

Carney's little sisters and brother. Dale got one too, just like ours. He took his basket out into the backyard while Carney and I opened ours on the porch, our mothers watching us. I began to unwrap one of the chocolate eggs, but my mother stopped me with a glance.

"What's wrong, Lila?" Carney's mother said.

"She can't have that chocolate yet," my mother said. "It's still Passover."

Carney's mother gave my mother a quizzical look. "I thought y'all just gave up bread."

"It's not that we give things up," my mother said. "It's that certain things are forbidden." She started to explain how most chocolates contained corn sweeteners, and why corn sweeteners weren't considered kosher for Passover according to Ashkenazic tradition. I wished she didn't have to make it all sound so foreign.

"Well," Carney's mother broke in, laughing. "I thought I had it bad, giving up ice cream for Lent."

"We don't feel like we have it bad," my mother said. "Do we, Lila?"

I sat there looking at the chocolate egg in my hand. I wondered what would happen if I said, *Yes we do!* But my mother wasn't going to give me the chance. She gave me a sharp look, as if to remind me I'd better not sneak any chocolates behind her back, and then she and Carney's mother went into the house to set up the drinks. I stayed on the porch and watched Carney eat her Easter candy. She unwrapped two chocolate eggs and ate them quickly, not looking at me. I could hardly bear the smell of chocolate coming from her wrappers. She tore open her package of Peeps and bit into one of them, the marshmallow pure white inside its coating of yellow sugar crystals.

"You're lucky, actually," she said, chewing. "You'll still have all of yours to eat when I'm done with mine."

It was the kind of thing Carney said sometimes, the kind

of thing that sounded like it was supposed to make you feel
better but actually made you feel worse. I pushed my basket
under one of the porch chairs and stood up as if to leave.
Carney dusted the yellow sugar from her hands and folded
the cellophane over what remained in her basket.

"All right," she said. "Let's go out back." She told me her
mother had said she was supposed to mingle with the guests,
but I suspected she was looking for Dale.

On the patio, the ladies drank cold drinks and the men
smoked cigars. Carney's father stood beside an outdoor pro-
pane burner and stirred gumbo in a tall pot. Her mother
arranged trays of corn bread and miniature shrimp quiche.
Aunt Marian sat at a picnic table alone and smoked a cigarette, looking out across the backyard as if she wished she
were somewhere else. My mother was drinking lemonade
and talking about *Twelfth Night* with Carney's godparents,
describing some elaborate problem she'd been having with
the set design. Carney's godparents nodded politely and
sipped their drinks. It was clear they were only pretending to
be interested, but that didn't stop my mother.

Carney and I drifted from one group of adults to another.
They smiled down at us and stirred their ice with Easter-
colored swizzle sticks, but they went quiet when we approached, the way adults did when they were talking about
something they didn't want you to hear. Some of them kept
glancing over at Dale, who was crouched by the toolshed,
examining a pile of dirt on the ground. I knew Carney was
paying attention to everything. She saw the adults looking at
Dale. She saw them growing impatient when she drifted into
their circles. Her forehead began to flush and she scratched at
her silk-flower wreath. She took my hand and pulled me over
to where her father was stirring the gumbo.

"We're hot," she announced. "We want Cokes."

"Run get some in the kitchen, then," her father said. He
was a sturdy, beefy man, maybe six inches taller than my own
father. He had an aluminum boat in which he'd once taken us

fishing. Now he wore an apron emblazoned with the words CHEF DE CUISINE.

"You get them for us," Carney said, fanning herself. "We're too hot."

"Well, I have to be the chef, honey," he said. "You can go get them, can't you?"

"We don't want to."

"Go play, then. It's cooler in the yard."

Carney shuffled to the edge of the brick patio. In the yard, her sisters Eleanor and Patty swung on the swing set and her brother Jonah pushed his dump truck around in the sandbox. Dale was still playing all alone by the toolshed. He'd abandoned his Easter basket on the patio, untouched, and had rolled up the sleeves of his white dress shirt. His silver glasses glinted in the sun. In his cupped hand he held some potato-chip crumbs, which he was dropping one by one onto an anthill. If he knew the adults were watching him, he didn't show it. Carney gave me a look and motioned for me to follow her. She crept up behind Dale, leaned close to his ear, and whispered, "Yah."

He gave a little jump as if she'd poked him in the ribs.

"That's just an old anthill," she said, kicking its edge with her white shoe. "My daddy keeps pouring poison on it, but they just keep building it again in a different place."

"You shouldn't pour poison on them," Dale said, squatting down to look. "Ants like these don't even bite. They all have jobs to do. These worker ants here are bringing food to the queen."

"You like ants or something?" Carney said.

He turned his head to look at her.

"You got an ant farm at home or something?"

Dale wiped his hands on his pants and squinted warily. "I have a book about ants," he said. "I've read about them."

"We all know about worker ants and queens," I said. "It's not like you have to do research. I learned about them in second grade."

211

Dale shrugged. "Worker ants are just the beginning," he said. "There can be five different classes of ant in a single hill. I just finished a ten-page report."

"Well, whoop-dee-doo for you," Carney said. She picked up a long stick from beside the toolshed and gave the anthill a good stir. The hill became a glittering confusion of ants.

"What'd you go and do that for?" Dale said, getting to his feet.

"Because I wanted to," Carney said, and skipped over to the swing set. She twisted the chains of Eleanor's swing until they wouldn't twist anymore, and then she let go. Eleanor shrieked as she whirled around and around, her blond curls flying, her dress a yellow blur. Dale and I stood beside the toolshed and looked down at what remained of the anthill. I could see the white shapes of larvae amid the glinting brown of worker ants.

"I'm Lila Solomon," I said. "I'm originally from New Orleans."

"It could take them weeks to build another one," Dale said, squatting to look closer at the ants. "That's more than three years in the life of an ant."

"I said my name's Lila," I repeated, but Dale didn't seem interested in making my acquaintance. I wasn't going to press the issue. Instead, I went inside the house to get the present I'd brought for Carney. I could tell she was working herself into a bad mood, but I knew the present would make her feel better. It was a china carousel-horse music box from Tinker-bell, our favorite store downtown. I'd left the package on the bureau in Carney's bedroom. As I went upstairs to get it, I heard Carney's mother and Aunt Marian come into the kitchen, arguing. I paused on the stairs to listen.

"Well, that's just a lie," Carney's mother said. "I never said any such thing."

Aunt Marian answered. I couldn't hear what she was saying, but I could tell she was almost crying.

"You're overreacting, as usual," Carney's mother said. "You never did have any sense of proportion."

"I know what I heard," Aunt Marian said, louder now.

"You only hear what you want to hear," Carney's mother said.

"Don't try to twist it around," Aunt Marian said. "Don't you try to blame *me*."

Now Carney's mother said something under her breath. Whatever it was, it must have been terrible. Aunt Marian came down the hall, a handkerchief pressed to her face. My heart pounded. I didn't want her to know I'd been listening, so I ran upstairs and slipped into Carney's room. From the hall came the sound of footsteps, and then Aunt Marian opened Carney's door. Her face was wet, her eyes red, the handkerchief a crumpled ball in her hand.

"Oh," she said. "I'm sorry. I didn't think anyone was here."

"It's okay," I said, and picked up the present from the bureau. "I was just going. It's your room, anyway."

She tilted her head at me.

"You're Carney's Aunt Marian," I said. "I saw your name on the wall." I planted my feet and pushed the bureau away from the wall with my shoulder. There was her name, in red crayoned letters against the pale wallpaper: *Marian Beatrice Fortunot. I live here.*

"Well, look at that," she said, bending down to touch the letters. "Marian Beatrice Fortunot. I hardly remember writing that." She ran a hand over the side of the bureau. "This was my furniture, too." She glanced around the room, her eyes coming to rest on Carney's shrine. She went over and knelt on the cushions where Carney and I had rehearsed the saints. For a moment I thought she might start praying, but then she gave a small, hard laugh, so full of bitterness it frightened me. I went downstairs as quick as I could, being careful not to drop Carney's present.

When I came out, I found my mother sitting with a younger

woman at the picnic table, dandling a baby on her knee. The baby kept grabbing handfuls of my mother's hair. The younger woman kept saying, "No, sweet pea, no," but my mother was laughing.

I touched her sleeve. "Can I give Carney her present?" I asked.

"Say hi to Lila," my mother said, making the baby wave its pink hand at me.

"Can I?" I said, not waving back.

"*May* I," my mother said. "I guess you may."

I knew she might have wanted me to wait until we could give Carney the present together, but I went ahead anyway, leaving her with the baby. Carney was still playing with her sisters on the swing set. Eleanor and Patty were sitting on the swing-glider, and Carney was pushing them as hard as she could. Her face was flushed, her silk-flower wreath askew. She pushed the glider with such force that her sisters screamed as it soared up into the air. I ran across the lawn and held the gift out to her.

"Happy Communion," I said.

"I'll bet I know where that's from," Carney said. She took the present and gave it a little shake. Just then, the glider swung back and struck her on the shoulder, and she stumbled back and dropped the box. There was a tinkling sound, the sound of a delicate thing breaking. Carney stood there, one hand on her hurt shoulder, looking as if she might cry. She picked up the present and ran to the shade beneath the chinaberry tree at the edge of the yard. There she sat with her head in her arms, the present beside her on the grass. Dale had been watching all this from the toolshed. He took a few steps toward her, but when she heard him coming she raised her head and said, "Leave me alone."

"Hey," I said, going over to kneel beside her. "Are you okay?" Carney shook her head.

"Open the present. Maybe it's fine."

She tore off the wrapping paper and broke the gold seal on

the box. Inside was the carousel-horse music box I'd chosen, the one she and I had admired in the window. The china horse had broken off at the base of its pole.

"Maybe your dad can fix it," I said.

She sighed and stuffed the horse back into its tissue paper.

"Let me see it," Dale said, coming closer.

"No." Carney held the box against her chest.

"I fixed a cuckoo clock for my mother once," Dale said.

Carney got to her feet and stared at him. "This is not a cuckoo clock."

"You could fix it with epoxy," he said.

"Why don't you go away?" she said. "No one invited you here in the first place."

Dale stood there with his arms crossed over his chest. "Yes they did," he said.

"Fine," Carney said, and turned her back on him. "Stand there if you want. My friend and I are going to do a play, and you can't be in it." She turned to me and said, "What play should we do, Lila?"

"Well," I said, trying not to look at Dale. "We could do an Easter play."

"*I* know," Carney said. "We can do Stations of the Cross. I get to be Veronica, and you can be the Virgin Mary."

I didn't think my mother would approve, but when I looked at her again she was still cooing at that baby. And anyway I was angry at her for not letting me eat my Easter candy, for talking about things people here didn't care about, for reminding them that we didn't belong. She wasn't about to stop me from playing Stations of the Cross. Carney was offering me the best role, the role of Mary, tragic mother of God.

"Okay," I said. "I'll be the Virgin Mary."

Carney called to her brother and sisters, and they came running. Eleanor always wanted to play whatever we were playing. Patty was quieter, but she didn't like to be left out. Jonah, the youngest, was only three. He would do what you told him to do.

"Who wants to do a play with us?" Carney said.

"Me," Eleanor said. Patty shrugged, sucking her thumb. Jonah nodded mutely.

"It's an Easter play," Carney said. "It's called Stations of the Cross. I'm Veronica, of course. Lila's going to be the Virgin Mary. Eleanor and Patty, you two are the Women."

"What about him?" Eleanor said, pointing at Dale.

"Dale's not playing," Carney said.

"Yes, I am," Dale said, stepping into our circle. "I've been in plays at school."

"Well, you probably didn't have any lines," Carney said.

"I did too. I've even been the lead."

"I don't care," Carney said. "You still can't play."

"Who's going to be Jesus?" Dale asked her. "It's Stations of the Cross, but you never said who was Jesus."

"Oh," Carney said. "Well, I guess it has to be Jonah, because he's the boy."

"He can't be Jesus," Dale said.

"Why not?"

"He's just a baby."

"Well, *you* can't be it either," Eleanor said. "You're black."

Everyone looked at Dale. Dale filled his chest and put his hands on his hips, narrowing his eyes at Eleanor. "I can too be Jesus," he said. "Jesus was closer to black than any of *you*. The Jews were a desert people, and he was a Jew."

"He was *not* a Jew," Eleanor said. "That's such a lie."

"He was too a Jew," I said. "He ate matzah. The priest said so."

Carney gave me a look, as if to ask what I was doing taking Dale's side. I hadn't meant to; I'd just wanted to tell what I'd figured out in church. But Carney didn't protest like I thought she would. Instead, a cold, mean light came into her eyes, and she gave Dale a slow smile.

"Okay," she said. "If you want to be Jesus, you can."

Dale tried not to look surprised, but I could see he was caught off guard. All at once I wanted to warn him about

Carney, about what she might do. At the same time I knew I couldn't go against Carney. Without her, I was just as much of an outsider as Dale. Maybe even more so. At least he was related to Carney by birth. I wasn't even a Catholic, much less a cousin. I was a Jew, less common in Iberville Parish than children of mixed race. I turned away from him and said nothing.

"Okay," Carney said, "if you're going to be Jesus, you need to carry a real cross."

"We could make one," Dale said. "I saw some wood behind the toolshed."

He led us there as if he were the one in charge, and stopped beside a pile of weathered two-by-fours. Carney picked up a long one and a shorter one and examined them. I could see her coming up with a plan, something beyond my own imagining. She handed the two-by-fours to Dale and disappeared into the toolshed. When she came out she was carrying a length of brown rope, a spade, a hammer, and a box of nails. I looked at that box of nails and thought of the Jesus in church. Carney saw me looking.

"Don't be stupid, Lila," Carney said. "We're not going to hurt anyone."

Carney gave the rope to Eleanor and the hammer to Patty, and she let Jonah carry the spade, just so he wouldn't complain. Then she led us all through a break in the hedge and out into the back pasture.

The back pasture was a rolling sprawl of land, maybe three acres of tall grass shot with spiny pigweed and thistles and black-eyed Susans. Sometimes we played Capture the Flag there with other kids from school. Earlier in the year we'd had a cardboard fort, but it had collapsed after a rainstorm. I could still see one corner of it near the hedge. Fat bees hovered above the grass, buzzing loud in the sun, and a few blackbirds tussled in a holly bush. At the far end of the pasture stood a line of creek willows. Beyond the trees ran Cottrell Creek, where we were forbidden to play. A little girl had died there once, playing where she shouldn't have, too soon after a rain.

"I've got my good shoes on," Eleanor said. "They're going to get all ruined."

"You're not even wearing those shoes anymore," Carney said. "You're wearing a long blue homespun cloak. You're wearing sandals. Try to feel holy. Try to feel sad for Jesus, because he's been condemned to die. Now, let's have those two-by-fours, Dale."

Dale set them down on the grass.

Carney took some long nails from the box and nailed the two-by-fours together in the shape of a cross. The two-by-fours were grayed and weatherstained from lying out behind the shed, and the cross they made looked to me like the real thing. It seemed heavy, too, when Carney lifted it. She set it against Dale's shoulder and let the tail drag in the grass. Dale gave us a grave and tragic look, and then he turned his eyes upward.

"Okay," she said. "Now, Dale, you've just been condemned to die. You have to drag this cross to the middle of the field, toward that little hill. But you're not going to get there right away. You're just going to take ten steps and then fall. That's the first Station."

Dale took ten steps, dragging the cross through the grass. He rounded his shoulders and shuffled his feet. When he fell it seemed like he was exhausted already.

"Now go stand by him," Carney whispered to me. "Try to cry."

I knew I was a better actor than Dale. I was the one who'd been raised on Shakespeare and Chekhov and Ionesco, after all. I tried to envision the Virgin Mary on Carney's prayer cards and devotional candles, her folded white hands and her sad, forbearing look. I took slow steps and fell onto my knees beside Dale, hunching and hunching my shoulders. I knew crying seemed more real when you didn't make any sound at all.

"Now, Jonah, this is where you come in," Carney said. "You're going to be Simon. Simon helps carry the cross."

Jonah ran through the grass and put one fat hand on the cross. Dale gave a sigh of relief, as if to let Jonah think he was really helping. Together the three of us took twenty more steps toward the hill.

"Great," Carney said. "Now Veronica wipes the face of Jesus." She made her way across the pasture and stood beside Dale. "Look at me," she said. He looked at her. I could tell the cross was getting heavy for him now, for real; his shoulder was trembling, and sweat had begun to bead on his forehead. Beside him, Carney wore an expression of anguish. In her Communion dress she might have been an angel of mercy. She lifted the top layer of her dress and brought it toward Dale's face. At first he pulled away, but then he closed his eyes and let her wipe his forehead. Something seemed to change in Carney's features as she did it. The hardness around her mouth softened, and she glanced back toward the house as if she'd just thought about her parents, or about Dale's mother. But the softness vanished as quickly as it had come. She shook her skirt straight and gave Dale a little push.

"Now you fall again," she said. "Come on. We're waiting."

Dale dropped to his knees. The cross tumbled off his shoulder and lay half hidden in the grass. He took off his glasses and tucked them into his shirt pocket.

"It's time for you to say your line to the women," Carney said. "Eleanor and Patty, come on over here. Both of you, you have to cry." She got them into place, and then she bent to Dale's ear. "Now, Dale, say, 'Cry not for me but for your sins and those of your children, for they are the cause of my suffering.' "

Dale stretched out his hand toward Patty and Eleanor's heads. He didn't say anything, but the gesture seemed like enough.

"Fine," Carney said. "Now pick up the cross and take it

over to that little hill. Go on. You have to fall down one more time. It's the last time you fall, so make it good."

Dale squared his shoulders. He lifted the cross and dragged it to the hill, and then he sprawled in the grass, arms splayed at his sides. I knew this was my cue to lament, and so I ran to him and made a low moaning sound. It came out more dramatic than I'd intended. Dale got up and took the spade from Jonah, then dug a hole in the soft earth, upturning clumps of grass and stones until he could reach in almost to his elbow. He dragged the cross up the little rise, stood it in the hole, and packed dirt around its base. All at once I understood that this was where Carney had meant to bring us: to the crucifixion, where we would tie Dale up and leave him out here all alone in the field. Carney smiled her cold mean smile at Dale. I would rather have died than have her look at me that way, but Dale didn't notice. He kept packing dirt around the cross until it stood upright and stable.

"There," he said, getting to his feet. He stepped back against the cross and raised his arms. His eyes turned upward in dramatic imitation of martyrdom.

"Okay," Carney said, leaning close to me. "Tie him up."

"Me?" I said.

"Go on," she said. I stood there looking at the rope in Eleanor's hands. I thought of lynchings, of the photographs I'd seen in the textbooks for my father's classes—black men hanging from bridges, white men in cone hats standing around and cheering. I thought of my mother pointing out the WHITE and COLORED signs beneath the paint, and of how much more humane I'd felt than all the people eating at that restaurant. I thought of the words my mother and I had read at our own seder: *You shall not oppress a stranger, for you know the feelings of the stranger, having yourselves been strangers in the land of Egypt.* Then I thought of what it would be like to live in Iberville Parish if Carney were no longer my friend. I thought of what things would be like at school, and after school, and how there would be nothing to protect me from being up against a cross myself, waiting to be tied.

I was the one who took the rope from Eleanor. I tied it around Dale's ankles so he couldn't move, then wrapped it around his body, all the way up to his arms, and knotted it tight against the tendons of his wrists. We didn't have a crown of thorns, so I took the wreath from Carney's head and set it on Dale's.

"There," Carney said. "Done."

We all stood and looked at him. It would have been the perfect time to run away and leave him there. The afternoon sun came down hot on the backs of our necks, and the bees shot past, humming. Dale moved his wrists a little. I'd tied them so tight his hands must have been going numb.

"Okay," he said. "Now get me down."

"No," Carney said. "That's not how the game goes."

"Come on, Carney," I said. "You just said we were done."

"No, we're not," she said. "You know what comes next. You helped me learn it."

I might have argued with her then. I might have untied Dale myself. If I had, the whole thing might have remained a secret. We might have all gone back to the house and eaten lunch. In all likelihood I would have forgotten about Dale Fortunot, and my mother would have forgotten about him too. She never would have sent the article from the *Times*. I wouldn't have found myself wondering what Dale might have been trying to find in Israel, the place where the real crucifixion had happened. I would never have known about Dale's wife, or about their son, Samuel, who would now grow up without a father. And I wouldn't have been looking at that P.S., wondering what my mother had meant to write. *Maybe you'll teach your own child better than I taught you,* she might have written, in her dramatic way.

But I did not argue, and I did not untie Dale. "Jesus dies on the cross," I said. "That's the next Station."

Carney took Dale's glasses from his shirt pocket and threw

them far away into the weeds. Then she picked up a stick from the ground and poked him in the ribs, hard enough to make him cry out.

"Stop it!" he said. "Get me down now!"

"No," Carney said. "Jesus dies on the cross. He *dies*."

The heat and the smell of grass and the distant sounds of the party seemed to fall away as I watched Dale wrestle against the ropes. Carney jabbed him in the belly and legs with that stick, and when he started to cry she told him to shut up. Patty and Jonah and Eleanor just stared. The sun beat down. Bees swung around Dale, darting toward his face and hands. Carney raised the stick and whipped his bare forearms. He began to shriek, a harsh, high-pitched sound that hurt my ears.

I grabbed Carney's arm, certain that someone would hear us. Carney looked back toward the house. I thought she might be ready to stop, ready to untie Dale and go eat lunch beneath the chinaberry tree. But there was a noise behind us, and I turned. Aunt Marian stood at the break in the hedge. Her face was white above the blue of her dress, her hands pressed to her mouth. She was shouting something I couldn't understand, shouting so the men and women came running, and then they were all coming across the grass.

Acknowledgments

Heartfelt thanks to the Iowa Writers' Workshop, the Wallace Stegner/ Truman Capote Fellowship at Stanford, the Marsh McCall Lectureship, and the San Francisco Foundation, without whose generosity this collection would never have come to be.

I am grateful for the patience, time, and insight of my mentors: Edgar Rosenberg, Dan McCall, and Lamar Herrin at Cornell; Frank Conroy, James Alan McPherson, Marilynne Robinson, and Thom Jones at Iowa; and John L'Heureux, Elizabeth Tallent, and Tobias Wolff at Stanford.

Infinite thanks to Aaron Cohen, David Meeker, Peter Rudy, Doug Powell, and Nathan Englander, who were there from the beginning; to Adam Johnson, Stephanie Harrell, ZZ Packer, Angela Pneuman, Ed Schwarzchild, Malinda McCollum, Doug Dorst, Katharine Noel, Lysley Tenorio, and Gabrielle Calvocoressi, incredible readers and friends; and to Matthew Brown, Nancy Laist, Jonathan Flinker, and Jennifer White Doom, who helped me through the worst times and celebrated with me at the best.

Thanks to the editors who took a chance on me: J. D. McClatchy, George Plimpton, Don Lee, Tamara Straus, and Michael Ray. And to Dana Goodyear, who quietly got my stories into the right hands.

Great volumes of thanks to Kim Witherspoon, Maria Massie, and Alexis Hurley at Witherspoon Associates, whose unfailing belief and expertise helped me bring this collection into reality.

Acknowledgments

I am endlessly grateful to have found in Jordan Pavlin a wise, insightful editor and friend. Thanks also to Emily Owens and Sophie Fels at Knopf for their tireless help and good humor.

Love and thanks to my family, the Orringers, Tibors, and Hartys. Thanks to my father, who taught me how to write; to Linda, for her support and strength; to my brother and sister, Daniel and Amy Orringer, king and queen of my heart.

And finally to Ryan Harty, best reader and best friend, whose care is in every page of this collection, and whose love is my breath and life.

In memory of my mother, Agnes Tibor Orringer.